BETTING ZOO.

Cory Hope.

CiCAC Press
Centre for innovation in Culture and the Arts in Canada
Thompson Rivers University
Kamloops, British Columbia
Canada V6C 1N4

Betting Zoo is set in 11 pt Caslon typeface
Cover illustration by Cory Hope

ISBN: 978-0-9812329-6-6

For my father,
who sparked my interest in writing,
and my wife,
for throwing gas on the flames.

The Wrong Room.

Frank Heatley slipped off of the sofa with as much grace as he could muster, which was not very graceful at all and reminded some who had witnessed the event previously of a worm attempting to remove itself from a manhole cover on a hot summer day. As with most of his movements and gestures, and much of his conversation lately, it appeared over-caffeinated, and as he clumsily put on his slippers he looked as if he were a marionette being fought over by a trio of drunken invalids. Eventually, his movements ground to a good pause, after which he sat back down and pressed his palm to his forehead, rocking back and forth in a futile effort to shake himself loose of the haze that had overcome him.

The hangover was overwhelming and unexpected, as he had no recollection of having any more to drink the previous night than he normally had in the course of an evening. This wasn't to say that he shouldn't be feeling some ill-effect, but he felt he didn't deserve to feel as bad as he did. He looked at his watch, noting that it was almost a full fifteen minutes later than he normally woke up, and wobbled himself into action.

Heading lopsided towards the kitchen, Frank began his morning ritual by making coffee. The beans, grinder, and coffee maker were laid out on the counter as they were left for him every night, and his favourite mug, an item too important to spend time in line at the dishwasher, stood upside-down on a dishtowel by the sink. He dumped what he deemed an appropriate amount of beans into the grinder, which was as much as it could possibly hold at one time, but his trembling hands failed to close the bag before it overflowed. Several beans spilled out of the grinder, dropped to the counter and spun their way across the floor. He ground up the beans in the grinder, dumped the grinds into the filter, slapped the basket closed and turned the machine on. A red light on the coffee maker conveyed to

Frank that it would be just a few minutes brewing, and then he could wake up.

He turned his attention to the beans that had escaped the fate of their comrades in the grinder. There weren't enough of them to bother grabbing the broom, so he stooped to pick them up by hand. They made a trail that led under the refrigerator. Frank picked them up one at a time, inching his way over to the fridge, where he grabbed an ancient flashlight attached to its side by a magnetic bar. He got down on his knees and pressed a cheek against the floor to see if any beans were taking refuge underneath the fridge. The flashlight's beam captured a brown oval in stark contrast with the white tile and white walls of the kitchen. Frank spent a moment contemplating the best tool for the job of reaching under the fridge and getting the bean, when he was startled by something he didn't see.

What he didn't see was anything else. Not a rubber band, another bean, a pea, a bottle cap, a mouse dropping, a dust bunny, or anything else that said that the room saw any use. He recoiled from the fridge and scrambled backwards on the floor until his back hit the cupboard under the sink. He dropped the flashlight, expecting it to roll around on the floor dramatically shining its light in circles like they always did in the movies. The magnetic bar on the side of the flashlight prevented it from rolling, however, and the impact from being dropped from little more than a foot had broken the bulb. The kitchen was also brightly lit, which would have cut down on the dramatic effect anyhow. A bubbling noise began to fill the otherwise quiet room, telling Frank that his coffee was ready. He had no idea why he was so on edge about the cleanliness of the kitchen floor. Maybe Susan was simply the best cleaning woman ever, or perhaps he might just be overreacting because he didn't feel well in general. He had almost calmed himself down when a knock at the front door sent him into a panic.

After a moment of silence, the knock came again. This time a muffled female voice followed the it into the room. "Mr. Heatley?" it asked. "Are you okay in there? It's Joan."

Frank's blood pressure peaked and then came down to a level befitting a man of his age, hangover, and mental state, which was still unhealthy, but nothing a prescription couldn't manage. He reached into the pocket of his housecoat, and grabbed the little orange bottle he kept there. Both the bottle and the pills it contained were unlabelled. He popped one of the pills into his mouth and started to choke, then began looking for something to wash the pill down. Clutching his throat with one hand and the kitchen counter with the other, he struggled to his feet, then coughed his way to the sink where he fumbled with the taps until water started pouring. He was still cupping water into his mouth when Joan burst into the room.

"Oh my god! Mr. Heatley! Are you okay?" she called out as she rushed to his side.

Heatley took one final handful of water before turning to face her. "I'll be fine once you get me some new pills," he spat at her. "Who the hell makes a pill you're supposed to take when you feel panicked that makes you goddamn choke to death?"

"Dr. Edmunds told me that-"

"Dr. Edmunds is a damn quack! I want something that's easier to swallow. Some gel caps or something like that, and I want them here tomorrow."

"Yes, Mr. Heatley, I-"

"And why the hell do I never get a label on these things?"

"Dr. Edmunds said that he-"

"Oh, screw Edmunds," Heatley said, throwing the bottle of pills at the sink. The rounded bottom of the sink threw the bottle back into the air, where gravity grabbed it and brought it back down onto the corner of the counter, popping the top off of it. Pills scattered across the counter, then down to the floor, an homage to their bean predecessors who had made the same remarkable journey only minutes earlier. Heatley watched them disperse, then turned back to Joan. "And give Susan a raise."

Joan pulled out a notepad she kept on hand and wrote 'Screw Edmunds / Give Susan a raise' at the end of her list of largely crossed out items, most of which were things she hadn't actually done. Lately, she had just been assuring Heatley that she had done what he had asked of her, when the truth was she had simply crossed them out while she had been waiting for her car to warm up or her coffee to brew. Heatley grabbed his coffee and shuffled his way past her, motioning for her to follow him into the living room, where they would conduct their morning meeting. Joan circled 'Give Susan a raise' on her notepad to remind herself that this was one thing the old man had told her to do that would actually get done. "What the hell, he's cute," she said as she circled 'Screw Edmunds' as well, then grabbed herself a coffee and followed after Heatley.

Joan had become much more relaxed towards her employer and his current situation than she had believed possible. She took notes during their meetings, sometimes throwing in a doodle or two to amuse herself, but generally just taking enough down so she could answer him with some accuracy when he would trail off and ask her what he had been talking about. She made sure that instructions she approved of, such as Give Susan a raise, or ones that Heatley would notice not being done, like Get an electrician/plumber/exterminator in here, got done. Tedious tasks like picking up dry cleaning or groceries, or other errands of the personal assistant calibre that she used to do herself, she would get someone else to do and take credit for it. This wasn't done maliciously, but out of necessity, as Heatley hadn't paid her enough to have her own personal assistant, and if he found out that she suddenly had one, he may have become suspicious.

Joan sat down and placed her coffee on the table beside her chair, making sure that it was on a coaster to avoid the fury of Susan, who claimed that her job was hard enough cleaning up during Heatley (as he never left the apartment anymore, it was never cleaning up after him) without having to clean up after anyone else as well. She turned her attention back to Heatley, who appeared to be experimenting with greater and greater states of dishevelment, and was about to ask him about his morning when he dropped a bomb on her. "I want to go for a walk, Joan," he said, as if this were a normal, everyday occurrence.

Joan barely concealed the massive convulsion that her brain had requested from the rest of her body. She dropped her pen and notepad, forced her mouth to close and clenched her skirt as tight as she could with both hands for just long enough to get her composure close enough to pleasant surprise. "Why, th-that's wonderful, Mr. Heatley," she said. "It's been almost ten mon-"

"Nine months, three weeks, three days, and-" he glanced at his watch "four hours since I closed the doors," he waved his hand around in a grand gesture to Joan, as if to present to her the deadbolts on the doors leaving the living room, as if she hadn't been the one that he had called and told to hire somebody to bolt the doors closed, as if she hadn't been the one he called and asked to bring him some toilet paper because he had decided on a whim that he was never, ever leaving the house again and hadn't done any shopping to prepare for it. A thoughtful look crossed his face. "You don't happen to have the keys for any of these doors on you, do you, Joan?"

"No, Mr. Heatley. I stopped carrying them around after the first few weeks. They were taking up a lot of room and were quite heavy," she offered in apology. "I'll get them right away." Joan picked up her pen, clicked it closed, and tried to stand up. Her mind was racing her body and winning, leaving her feeling light-headed when she tried to move.

"Are you okay, Joan?" Heatley asked. He had been feeling the slightest bit better since he had made his decision to get out of the house, but even as self-absorbed as he was by nature, he could tell that Joan had seemed put off by their discussion. He couldn't put his finger on why, though. "Joan?"

"Yes, Mr. Heatley."

"Is everything okay with the company?"

"Why, of course, Mr. Heatley," she said with no trace of a lie in her voice, because she wasn't lying. The company had been performing fabulously since Frank Heatley had stepped down as President and turned all of the decision-making, as well as the title of President, over to David Meyers. The only problem was that Heatley had no idea that he had stepped down. The reports he was given each morning looked the same as they always had. They just weren't the real reports.

Frank relaxed, placed his right arm over Joan's shoulder, and began walking her to the door. "Good then. I'll be expecting you back shortly so we can get my running shoes out of the closet. I'll walk you to the elevator."

"That's really not necessary, Mr. Heatley," Joan began, and made an attempt to walk faster so Frank could not keep up. The anchor that he had made of his arm prevented her from moving faster than him, though. Joan removed his arm from her shoulder using just enough force to tell him that she did not want it there. Frank didn't fight with her, and he opened the front door, holding it open for her. They began the short walk from Heatley's penthouse to the elevator. There was only one other door along the way, marked with a sign depicting a flight of stairs. They arrived at the elevator, Frank's gesture of chivalry requiring him to only travel thirty feet from his front door. He thought about escorting Joan all the way down to the lobby, or perhaps all the way out to her car, but decided against it because he was still in pyjamas, a housecoat, and slippers, and would probably want to keep on moving after all this time spent indoors. No, a few more hours won't kill me, he told himself. Joan pressed the call button for the elevator, and the doors opened immediately. She stepped in, turned around, and pressed the lobby button, and fell into the awkward silence that accompanies an elevator ride, regardless of how many people were in the car. The doors began closing and Heatley stuck his hand in to stop them.

They opened again, and Joan reached out and held the Door Open button. "Joan, one more thing,"

"Yes, Mr. Heatley?"

"Make sure you bring over some tools to remove the boards and such from the windows, and the keys to remove all the padlocks. I'm done with being shut in up here."

"Yes, Mr. Heatley," She was ready to cry.

"Oh, and maybe a few workers to use the tools. See you in an hour or so?"

"Yes, Mr. Heatley," She attempted to shatter the Door Close button with her finger.

Once the elevator doors had closed, Joan turned around and pushed in one of the decorative panels on its back wall until she heard a click. The panel popped back out on one side and revealed a keypad. She punched in an eight-digit code, and the panel closed itself. The entire back of the elevator slid to the left, revealing an office bustling with twenty or so people, one of whom approached her with a clipboard in hand, writing furiously and talking to someone through a headset. Joan handed over her notes from her meeting with Heatley, and grabbed a quick drink from the water cooler.

"How's the old man today, Joan?"

She crumpled up her cup and threw it into a garbage can that was filled with other crumpled white paper cups and a few brightly coloured pieces of gum. "We're in trouble, Mr. Meyers," she said bluntly.

The man with the clipboard appeared at her side and returned her notes. "And I think Joan here is gonna screw Edmunds!" he said as he walked away.

David Meyers raised an eyebrow at her. "What kind of trouble are we talking about here?" he asked.

Joan took a deep breath, and she told him.

The Path Of Judgement.

Edna was having her morning tea on the balcony, her favourite part of the apartment. An incomplete pyramid of sugar cubes, the top of which had been dissolved into the dark brown tea in her gold-trimmed cup, sat on a gold-trimmed plate. A gold-trimmed creamer was tipped to make the tea both lighter in colour and thicker in texture. Eighteen percent cream because it was the richest and most decadent. Edna had an appreciation for all things decadent that most people viewed as tacky. Thrift stores were lined with the stuff, with price stickers written in coloured pencil, offering the set of eight pieces for $6.99, although Edna would never have known it as such places were beneath her. The list of things that were beneath her was quite extensive and grew virtually every day.

Most of the people who passed by Heatley Tower at almost any respectable time of day were unknowingly subjected to Old Blue's critical gaze. The only safe time to pass by was during Oprah. She never missed an episode, and didn't know how to record it. Outside of that one-hour block of time, five days a week, it was impossible to tell when one might fall victim to her condemnations. The Path Of Judgement was the territory of Edna Sheldon, or Old Blue, as she was called by some of the locals with whom she dealt. Never to her face, though, and usually not without a nervous glance over a shoulder first. Old and frail were words that might be used to describe her by those who didn't know her, but there was something fierce behind those eyes, a fire-and-brimstone glare for those who dared to not agree with her, or to disrespect her, or happened to glance into a window of any of the adult stores along the street facing her building. Neon lights were a symbol of the blasphemer, so far as Edna was concerned. Her pinky finger was pointing straight out at the sinners while the rest of her hand went about its business lifting her teacup to her lips and back down, when she heard the sound of a skateboard clacking down the sidewalk, sending her blood pressure into an unnecessary spike.

The skateboard, and presumably the skateboarder, screeched to a halt just below her window. How on earth do they control those things? she thought to herself. By her own rationale, if she could not feasibly control something, then there was no way that somebody else could. She heard William, the doorman, talking to the offending skateboarder.

"Hey there Sherman," he said without any of the formality he used when he greeted Edna. "How's it hanging?" She almost spat her tea out in mid-sip at this, instead choking it back and convulsing slightly. Her tea found this series of commands to be needlessly complicated, and tried to purge itself through the path of least resistance, which, to Edna's dismay, happened to be her nostrils. Through her choking she continued to miss most of the conversation, but she managed to pick up on a word here and there, sending her spiralling into further levels of discomfort. "...tits on that..." cough hack "...so drunk last night..." hack cough choke "laughed my balls off..." choke choke cough "...old bat up on the third floor..." cough hack cough choke hack hack cough.

Edna got up and emptied her teapot over top of the railing, then listened for the scream she hoped would come back up in reply. It came up sounding like this: "What the hell was that?" and "Crazy old bitch!" They went on, and became more offensive as they did so, but Edna tried not to let the potty-mouthed kids down below get to her any more than the other blasphemers. She was just going to have to go to church and pray for the salvation of everyone on her list. It was Wednesday, and although she didn't normally go to church on Wednesdays, there would probably be a prayer group available for her to pray for the souls of those who had made her list so far that day.

It was a long list for a Wednesday, especially considering she hadn't left the apartment yet, Edna thought as she pulled it out from behind a refrigerator magnet, a large white square with purple dots all over it that read in large-print "No kidding! I'm a cat person too!" She grabbed a pencil that dangled from the fridge by a thick white string, and added "Skateboarding ruffian" and "William the doorman" to it. She quickly gave the tea set a rinse, then placed everything beside the sink to be properly washed later on and got herself ready to go out for the day. After a quick trip to the bathroom to touch up her makeup, she changed from her slippers into some proper shoes, put on her fur coat, then grabbed hers purse and an umbrella. She unlocked all six of the deadbolts on her door, only two of which were visible from the outside, then dipped her crystal Holy Water bottle into the bowl she kept by the door, waiting until the air bubbles ceased to rise to the surface. She placed the cap back on the bottle and sprinkled the remaining droplets about her clothes with a flick of her fingers, a spiritual disinfectant routine she would repeat when she came back home.

Edna stepped out, locked the two deadbolts that were visible from the outside, each of which required a different key, then made her way down the hall towards the elevator. She pressed the call button and waited impatiently for the doors to open, as she did every time she pressed the button and the doors failed to open immediately. She wondered what was so important that somebody else needed to hoard the entire elevator for. Finally, after what she decided was ultimately an unacceptable amount of time, a soft-pitched bell announced the arrival of the elevator. As the doors opened, Edna stepped forward, and almost collided with Joan as she stepped out.

"Oh!" Joan yelped. "Mrs. Sheldon. You startled me." She tried to leave the elevator again, but the entirety of the doorway was being blocked by Edna, whose fur coat seemed to have raised its hair in alarm, making her appear bigger than she was. Edna kept this posture in silent dominance over Joan. The doors started closing, but Edna raised her umbrella in time to get it in between them, and they opened again obediently. This time Edna forced her way in, and Joan meekly stepped out afterwards. The hair on the fur coat appeared to go down now that the conflict was over. Joan slunk down the hallway towards her apartment, feeling chastised, as she always did after running into Mrs. Sheldon. That they lived next door to each other didn't make things easier for either of them, but in recent months Joan found other things occupying her mind, like conspiracy and kidnapping and paranoia about getting caught, and as such she had hardly thought about the old lady next door.

Edna pressed the lobby button, then pulled out her list and added THE HUSSY THAT LIVES NEXT DOOR to it. As the doors closed, Edna seemed to get bigger as she inhaled all of the moral superiority that was in the air, and Joan, already in a panic from her morning meeting with Heatley, seemed to shrink into herself as she walked towards her apartment as if she were attempting some form of turtle-inspired self-defence.

When the elevator doors opened into the lobby, Edna stepped out in her customary manner of royalty in full swing. She watched as the employees of the building scampered around, keeping themselves busy and making sure that everything was in the process of being put just right. She didn't know that the girl behind the counter was talking to a dial tone to avoid talking to the crazy lady from the third floor any more than she knew that her next-door-neighbour was standing back by the elevator doors counting to one hundred before pushing the call button just to avoid facing her twice in one day. In her mind they were making sure that everything was being made to her liking. The reality was that they just didn't want to talk to her. Intercoms and cell phones were abuzz between people who had agreements with their peers to warn them if they saw Old Blue. Men in crisp suits with fresh haircuts suddenly decided that they needed haircuts and ducked into the barber shop. People who had just come out of the bathroom suddenly realized they forgot to wash their hands and turned back around. The entire lobby area of Heatley Tower, from the restaurant to the souvenir shop, gave the widest possible berth to the blue-haired lady as she passed through. They felt, as a rule, if you were close enough to smell her perfume (which was powerful enough to fight its way upwind against a stiff breeze for seven or eight metres before losing ground) you were close enough to run the risk of direct confrontation. Not everyone had the good fortune of being able to find an excuse to avoid contact with her, though.

An hour earlier, during the changing of the guard for the doormen, two of whom were working at any point during the day, a quick round of Rock, Paper, Scissors was played. Best two out of three, loser greets Old Blue. Today Karl had suffered the loss. Bill drew paper, covering Karl's rock on the first draw. Karl had then shaken his hand out, making it nice and limber to avoid any jerky movements or muscle twitches that would give away what his next draw would be, but somehow Bill had seen through his ruse, because when Karl's hand once again came down as rock, Bill simply smiled at him. "Paper covers rock, Karl," he said , slapping his flat open hand over top of Karl's closed fist. "Thought you would have learned that the first time."

Karl had muttered "Shit," under his breath and accepted his fate. His only hope now was to have a perfectly-timed need to use the bathroom, the only method of legitimately getting out of greeting Old Blue under the rules set out by the union.

Bill noticed the commotion in the lobby. "Looks like you're up, old boy," he said with a hint of better-you-than-me in his voice.

Karl didn't look back right away, as one of the most important aspects of greeting Old Blue was not to look as if you had to muster up the fortitude to deal with her. "Think of her as a wild animal," he was told at his job orientation. There was an entire section of a PowerPoint presentation dedicated to her. "If you show fear, she may attack. If you try to establish dominance over her, she may attack. If there are any awkward moments involving eye contact, she may attack." The supervisor had gone on for some time about many of the different reasons Edna Sheldon had been set off in the past, about how many of their employees had quit because of her, and what resources the company to assist the employees in dealing with her. After the orientation, when the group had been addressed and asked if they had any questions, Karl had asked why it was that they didn't just kick the old lady out if she was such a problem.

The supervisor, whose name Karl had since forgotten, and who had quit his job two weeks later after helping Blue bring her groceries up to her apartment, had shown visible strain in his attempt to sugar-coat his answer. "We had tried to evict her at one point, at which time we were informed through an email sent from Mr. Heatley that under no circumstances was Mrs. Sheldon - we never refer to her as Old Blue to Mr. Heatley - to be evicted. In fact," the supervisor must have clenched his teeth on an exposed nerve in his cheek at this point, "we were informed that Mrs. Sheldon, Old Blue, the mistress of a dozen other names that are unmistakably her, even though we would never admit it, was to be treated as if she were Mr. Heatley's sister." Edna, in fact, was Heatley's sister, but even he tried to distance himself from her as the years had gone by. He still took care of her, provided her with an apartment and an allowance he didn't know she didn't need, but it was out of a sense of obligation as opposed to any real affection for her.

Karl reflected on the warnings, the meetings, and the rest of the insanity involved in dealing with Mrs. Sheldon when he should have been trying to get himself in a state of meditative calm as she approached. He held his head high and smirked unconsciously. Bill, who had been working at Heatley Tower for years, recognized the look in Karl's eyes immediately, and knew Karl was done. He couldn't hack dealing with the old lady any more, and was going to swear and storm off. Bill stepped forward to get the door, but Karl held his hand up and told him "No, Bill. You won fair and square. I've got this one."

Bill's first reaction was confusion, which was quickly replaced by revulsion and horror as he imagined Karl pulling out a shotgun he had somehow managed to conceal in his uniform, the crowd running away screaming until it came time for Karl to say something witty before pulling the trigger, making Edna explode in a gooey haze.

Instead, to Bill's surprise, Karl stepped forward and grabbed the door for her. However, he placed his foot in front of the door and pretended it was stuck. Bill was mortified: he was sure Mrs. Sheldon was going to complain about this indignity and as the senior employee on that shift, the blame would probably fall on his shoulders. Old Blue got to the door, and waited impatiently. Karl pulled on the door, keeping his foot pressed against it to prevent it from opening. Old Blue stood with her hands on her hips. Bill tried to look away, but couldn't. He wanted to preserve his job and prevent Karl, whose company he found enjoyable, from losing his. He also wanted to prevent Mrs. Sheldon, whose very existence he feared, from losing her mind and causing such a scene the building had not seen since - he wasn't sure that anything had happened in the building which could compare to what he believed Mrs. Sheldon was capable of doing. Bill's body, receiving too many impulses from his brain, paced back and forth for a few moments. Distracted by what was happening at the door, he was paying little attention to anything else. His pacing brought him onto the sidewalk, where he was run down by a bike courier.

A crowd had begun gathering to watch the events play out. Old Blue was waving her arms at Karl, giving the impression of a dragon showing off its mighty wingspan before reducing the villagers to smouldering ash. Somewhere in the crowd, a child hid behind his mother. A totem pole of clean-shaven business faces peered out of the bathroom. But Karl was ready to face the dragon; he was no longer afraid. An ambulance could be heard in the distance. It had been called by a passer-by who had seen Bill get hit by the courier, but the hostages in the Heatley building believed it had been called in anticipation of the carnage that was about to ensue.

"Young man, you will open this door right this instant," Edna said with a voice that was accustomed to being obeyed.

Karl could see she wasn't fooled by his this door seems to be stuck routine, so he tried something he had thought up once upon a few to many drinks. "Five bucks, Blue," he said, and smiled at her through the glass door. The crowd cowered back in order to avoid being burned.

Edna leaned forward, her heavy breaths condensed her words on the glass as her words penetrated through it. The low reverberation of her voice reached back to the businessman totem. "What. Did. You. Say?" There appeared to be fire in her eyes.

Karl held his ground. "I said 'Five bucks, Blue,' meaning if you give me five dollars, I'll open the door for you. If not, the door at the back of the building is free to use, provided you don't mind the smell of garbage and urine." He could see the scorn rising in her eyes, but he continued unabated "And the last bit was 'Blue,' as in 'Old-Blue-Haired-Bag' which is what we call you whenever your back is turned. In fact-"

Edna became fury as she pushed her way through the door, and Karl stepped backwards, momentarily forgetting he was at the top of a flight of stairs. He never found out what she was yelling at him, as he fell back and struck his head. The siren from the ambulance drowned all other noise as it came down the street. The last thing he remembered was the self-satisfied look on Old Blue's face. The power of the dragon had struck down the valiant hero who had stood up to it, quelling potential insurrection.

She stopped to read his name tag, pulled out her list and added Karl the doorman to it, then stepped over him. A police cruiser pulled up moments later, and an officer started asking questions and taking notes. The paramedics loaded both of the injured doormen into the ambulance and took them away. It occurred to the remaining staff at the Heatley building they would be needing another doorman or two before Old Blue came home.

Officer Bratton flipped his notebook closed after interviewing the last of the cute girls he could find at the scene. They had all told him pretty much the same thing. "Yes, I'm sure I'm okay. No, I don't need to talk to anyone about it. Yes, I have a boyfriend." His previous line of questioning, the one that had involved the other witnesses, had yielded a few potential leads, all of which involved the old lady who was making her way down the street, and how he could easily catch up to her if he would just leave. He had asked the girls to stay, though, and he had lined them up in order of how attractive he thought they were. After the second round of questioning, he headed back to his car without having collected a single phone number. He looked down the street in the direction the witnesses said the old lady had headed.

"She'll be back, Officer. She lives there."

Bratton turned around to face a scruffy looking kid with a skateboard under one foot and a cigarette in his mouth. "I know that!" he snapped. "What do you think this is for?" he said, waving his notebook at Sherman.

"I think it's for looking official while trying to pick up girls at crime scenes," Sherman said through a puff of smoke and a mischievous smile.

Bratton flipped the book open, and started to walk towards Sherman, pulling his pen out and clicked it open, trying to make the gesture threatening.

"Is this going to take long, Officer?" Sherman asked, with a quick glance at his watch. "Or do I just have to tell you I have a boyfriend? I have to get to wor-"

Sherman found himself pinned down to the ground, hands bound behind his back and a boot between his shoulder blades. He spit out his cigarette, and watched the world go by sideways. Even from this vantage point he could still make out Old Blue, as she hobbled her way along The Path Of Judgement.

Post-Cognition.

Prior to shutting himself into his apartment, Heatley had begun shutting himself out of many of the rooms within it. He began by having the windows boarded up. As his assistant, Joan had become accustomed to the eccentricities of her employer, but being asked to bring in a carpenter to cover up the windows had made one of her eyebrows creep its way up her forehead. The carpenter had done such a spectacular job of covering up the windows that by the time a painter had gone over the rooms, they could only be located by memory, or by accident during a brick fight, which was not an activity that Heatley regularly participated in.

After a period of adjustment to his windowless quarters, Heatley decided to have his storage room locked, permanently. A deadbolt was put on the door, and he gave the key to Joan to take away from the apartment. He was elated. Patricia, his cleaning lady at the time, no longer had to worry about the extra room, so she was happy about it too. Next came the spare bedroom, followed by the dining room. With every door that was locked, Heatley felt himself more content. The apartment had been an immense series of doors and rooms, with the front foyer serving as a large hallway which connected most of them. Or at least is used to be. Throughout Heatley's bout with what some of his employees had written off as senility, he had taken what he used on a regular basis from the different rooms in the apartment and converted the foyer into his new bedroom/study/living room/dining room. The only rooms he didn't lock himself out from were the kitchen and the bathroom. Even the front closet had been made off-limits, but he had purchased a coat rack for any potential guests to use. This endeavour created a large, crowded room filled with expensive furniture and doors that didn't open. A skylight provided the only natural illumination in the room. Several large bookshelves, filled with an eclectic array of volumes, many of them first-edition hardcovers, were used to break the monotony of looking at all the doors in the new room. The books were largely unread, at least by Heatley, who merely kept them on the shelves as trophies, always claiming "Oh, I haven't got around to reading that one quite yet," whenever a guest would ask him about one of them. A pair of couches faced each other across a coffee table that was perpetually covered with several ashtrays that were never empty despite the best efforts of his cleaning lady, and a chess set that was never played. There was also an indeterminate amount of coasters which would frequently be occupied with empty tumblers or beer bottles, depending on the vice of preference from the previous night.

With Joan running reports back and forth to the Heatley Company, and doing virtually everything else he could need for him, Heatley had created for himself a working and living space that he would never have to leave. Anything he wanted from the outside world he would have brought to him, and he wouldn't have to deal with lousy service, weather, or traffic. Most importantly, he wouldn't have to deal with people any more. That had been the deciding factor for Heatley to finally shut the rest of the world out. Once upon a seventh or eighth tumbler, each three fingers deep with scotch, he had come to the conclusion that there must be more clairvoyants than the world knew about, and the reason he didn't run into them more often was because they had the gift of foresight. They knew how many stupid people they would have to deal with in the course of an afternnon running errands so they got other people to do everything for them. Heatley knew that he did not possess The Gift, but he enjoyed the idea of belonging to such an elite group. After he had poured himself another scotch he pressed a speed dial button on his phone. It didn't matter which button he pressed, because they had all been programmed to dial Joan.

"Urrrrm." She began the conversation this way because it had been 2:30 in the morning when he called.

"Joan, I am a post-cognitive psychic," he had said with triumph in his voice, which was totally lost on Joan, who had been trying to process why she was awake and was only dimly aware she was on the phone.

"Yes, Mr. Heatley," was a standard response that could get her through most of their conversations, so she said it. She had always told herself she was physiologically ill-equipped to be an errand-boy or a yes-man, and had therefore been caught off guard when she had become one. It was point of contention in her life.

Feeling that Joan may have missed the significance of what he had just said, Heatley pressed on. "I have the gift of hindsight."

Joan was now awake enough to know that she was awake, and able to make out the two on her alarm clock through bleary eyes. She was not impressed with being woken up for this. "Is that the power of observation you have, then, Mr. Heatley?" she managed to speak clearly enough that he should be able to spot the contempt in her voice.

Heatley became excited. "Yes!" he said. "The power of observation. I have the power of observation!"

"Then you may observe that it is past two o'clock in the morning, Mr. Heatley, and I have to be at the office to have your reports ready and make your coffee for whenever it is you choose to roll in tomorrow."

"That's not my office anymore, Joan. I'm working out of my home now," he sounded like he was pacing and unable to keep up with his own brilliance. "No! I'm working in my home! In fact, I'm not leaving here until I'm dead," another revelation tried to fly by him, but he slapped it to his forehead with his palm. "Wait, find out if I can have my ashes spread in the apartment."

"Yes, Mr. Heatley. Can I go back to slee-"

"Wait! No." A conspiratorial tone took hold of Heatley. "The cleaning lady."

"You mean Patricia?"

"Is that her name? The pretty one with the short uniform and the vacuum cleaner?"

"That short uniform, Mr. Heatley, was picked out of a catalogue-"

"Yes, I know-"

"A fetish catalogue."

"It was-"

"By you."

"Joan, I-"

"Despite the best efforts of your legal team."

"Well, they-"

"And your mother."

"She didn't want-"

"She didn't want her cleaning lady to show up at her door looking like she had just stepped out for a smoke break in between shots in a porno, Mr. Heatley." Joan had become more irritable with each syllable. "Now what about her?"

"We just have to make sure that she doesn't vacuum my ashes." There was genuine concern in Heatley's voice. Joan shrugged it off.

"We'll just have to have you buried then, Mr. Heatley," she offered as what was, by her estimation, a fair alternative. "I'll make the arrangements, and I'll bring the paperwork to your house this morning."

"Thank you, Joan, I-"

"Good night, Mr. Heatley," Joan said as she clumsily hung up the phone. It was a cordless phone, so clumsily hanging it up involved pressing the wrong button three times before finally hitting the End button. Three different digital notes made their way from Joan's irritation to Heatley's ear, making him jerk the phone away from his head four times before he realized that she really had hung up on him.

"Good night then, Joan," he said to the empty room. Placing the phone back down in its cradle, Heatley picked up his tumbler, swirling the glass around to hear the ice cubes clink against the sides of the glass, then downed the rest of the scotch and went to sleep without brushing his teeth.

With the rationale of becoming a revered post-cognitive psychic Frank Heatley decided to shut himself into his apartment, vowing never to leave it again. Joan had reported the incident to David Meyers when she got to work that morning. He presented her with a non-disclosure agreement he pulled out of a locked drawer in his desk, and handed her the pen out of his jacket pocket. Joan signed the paper with little more than a cursory glance, as these types of documents were commonplace in her line of work. Non-Disclosure Agreement. Yadda-Yadda-Yadda. Don't talk about your boring-ass day at work or we can sue you.

"Oh, by the way, Joan, how did you expect him to be buried in his apartment?" he asked with a smile as he slipped his pen back into his breast pocket. "Were we going to make a chandelier out of him for his neighbours downstairs?"

Joan looked out his office window, suddenly wishing that the fine print of legal documents was written in a larger font, or that she had actually read the contract she just signed before she signed it. She watched with a sense of something bad she couldn't put her finger on as Meyers slipped the papers back into his desk, and locked the drawer, putting the key in his wallet. "I just wanted to get him off the phone," she told him. "It was two o'clock in the morning. I suppose if he can't figure out the logistics of being buried in his apartment, we can just offer to have him mummified or enclosed in a Perspex case."

"Yes," Meyers seemed to be mulling over the brilliance of this. "Or, perhaps" he offered, "perhaps we could just have him taken to a taxidermist. Pose him at his desk, or on his couch with a coffee mug in his hand. I believe he'd like that." He leaned back in his leather chair, turned towards the window, and put his hands behind his head. "Joan, we need to have that discussion about the future of the Heatley Company and your role in it."

Joan's eyes darted around the room, coming back to the drawer containing the contract several times and bouncing right back off of it, as if it had a gravitational pull on her mind. "Yes, Mr. Meyers." She was feeling the gift of post-cognition herself.

Abducted.

'Anxious' was not a word Frank Heatley would normally have used to describe himself, but then again, he was not normally anxious. He wouldn't have used the word 'old' to describe himself either though, and he was old all the time now. It was the anxious bit that was causing him trouble at this point. He had been pacing the single room he had left for himself, looking up at the sunlight and cursing himself for his decision to lock everything away. Perhaps, he thought, I was a little overzealous. It wouldn't matter soon, though. Soon he would be going for a walk. Soon he would be back in the fresh air. For the moment, however, he was feeling anxious.

Heatley decided he couldn't wait for Joan any longer. He just wanted to go outside, and maybe go to that cafe down the street to get something fancy he couldn't pronounce. Something that ended in "uccino" sounded pretty good. He grabbed his mug from the coffee table and his housecoat off of the back of his chair, thinking that it would be inappropriate to be outside wearing just his pyjamas and slippers, and headed out the door.

Frank had no idea what a sight he was at that moment. His slippers were a brown plaid, his pyjamas a green plaid, and his housecoat a red plaid. His beard, thick and unrestrained from its natural tendencies, had a single line of nicotine stain running through it, leading to a small circle on the right-side of his mouth where his cigarettes had burned through. His hair was a mess of equal standards, minus the stain and burn. It did, however, contain the remains of two or three cigarettes which he had placed in there for safe keeping during the previous few months while making coffee or pouring drinks. His matted hair prevented them from being completely washed out, but they had been reduced to greasy filters and tattered bits of paper. A freshly lit cigarette dangled from hidden lips, and his coffee mug was sloshing warm brown liquid over its rim, leaving an easy trail for him to follow home, should he require one. He wouldn't get far this time, though. The fire alarm went off moments after he pressed the call button for the elevator.

Heatley had a brief spasm when the alarm went off, and he shuffled back off to his room to call for help. His phone was already ringing, call display informing him it was the front desk. He answered in a panic.

"Hello?"

The voice on the other end of the line was calm. "Mr. Heatley, sir?"

"Yes. It's me! Is there a fire?" Heatley had never imagined that this could happen to him in one of his own buildings, and wondered why it was that he insisted on having the penthouse built for him on the top floor. He owned the place. He had the damned thing built for him. He could have had the penthouse put on the ground floor if he wanted, couldn't he? Of course, he would have missed his skylight.

"I'm afraid so, Mr. Heatley, but don't worry. It's under control." The voice on the other end was soothing, and Heatley's fears about the building burning down relaxed a little bit.

"I want to get out of here," he told the voice. "I want to go for a walk and order a coffee I can't pronounce."

"I'm afraid the elevator is out of commission right now, Mr. Heatley. The fire has done some damage, but we'll have it fixed as soon as possible, sir." The voice was reassuring. "There's a lot of stairs in between the penthouse and the nearest cafe, sir. Would you like me to have somebody run something up there for you?"

Heatley thought briefly about this before replying. "No. No, thank you. Just call me when the elevator is running, please."

"Yes, sir. Anything else I can do for you?"

"No, that's all," Frank hung up the phone without saying goodbye, then immediately dialled Joan. She picked up on the second ring.

"Mr. Heatley. How are you?" Heatley believed there was something off in her voice, but was still feeling frazzled himself, and unable to tell what was just his own mind racing and what his post-cognition was telling him he could hear in her voice.

"There's a fire in the building, Joan, and I-"

"Are you okay, Mr. Heatley?"

"Yes, but the elevator is out of commission."

"Maybe it's a sign you're not supposed to leave. What's your post-cognition telling you about this?" she asked, suppressing a laugh.

"It's a sign I need to move to the first or second floor, knock out some walls, and make a new penthouse closer to the ground. Do you have those keys with you?"

"Ye-yes, Mr. Heatley. I'll be there, soon. Uh, ish. Soon-ish." She sounded like she may have been on edge before. Now she sounded like that edge was cutting her deep.

"How long do you think it will take you to get here?" he asked, even his voice was pacing the room now.

Joan's brains were back-pedalling, looking for an escape. She hoped that Meyers would have a plan formed by the time she got there. "Do you really want me to take the stairs the whole way up, Mr. Heatley? You're on the twenty-fourth floor."

"Yes, and I'm trapped here alone!" Heatley snapped at her. "Now, please get up here with those keys!" He was claustrophobic, now stuck involuntarily in what was supposed to be his sanctuary.

"Yes, Mr Heatley," Joan tried to sound reassuring, but she couldn't hide the nervousness in her voice. Her concern wasn't for him, though. If the Heatley Situation got any more out of control, she might be the one who needed help. "I'm almost there." She hung up.

As she walked around the last corner on her way to Heatley Tower, she noticed an immaculate black-panelled van. It was a little too plain, too stripped-down. It was that particular style of nondescript that stands out like a sore thumb. The scenarios that ran through Joan's head almost all involved riot squads or SWAT-types of police action, bringing to an end carefully laid out plans, and not just the company's plans. Joan had not thought out what she wanted to do for the rest of her life, but she was certain that a monotonous orange wardrobe and a cellmate weren't a part of it. When she had just about reached the building, a serious looking man in a serious looking suit stepped out into the sunlight. A shaved head and square jaw surrounded a pair of mirrored sunglasses. She tried not to look at him as she was passing by, certain that he was with the Bureau Of Something Important, or the Gonna Put You In Jail Agency, or something that had an ominous-sounding acronym.

The suit stepped directly in front of Joan, forcing her to stop without touching her. The mirrored lenses each cast a fisheye reflection of Joan that made her look as small as she felt at that moment. "Ms. Miller?" The voice fit the suit much better than the rest of him. The rest of him looked ready to burst out of it.

There was no point in attempting escape. She had about the same chance of getting away from this goliath as he would have fitting into a pair of her heels. Her reflections looked meek as she replied. "Yes?"

"You'll need to come with me, ma'am," he said, and he turned to lead the way, positive that she would follow. She did.

"Is there something wrong, officer?" Joan was sure there was no way she had sounded innocent, but it had been worth a try.

Joan flinched as the suit rounded back on her. He had not meant it to be a threatening gesture, but his girth made it difficult for people to relax when he moved. He often felt like a wrecking ball trying to navigate his way around a world built of sandcastles. "I'm not with the police," he said.

Joan took two steps for every one that the suit took, and still barely kept up. "Then who are you?" she asked as they turned off the sidewalk and disappeared through a door marked 'Underground Parking Lot, Section 2.'

The suit turned to face her while they were still descending the stairs. Being two stairs behind him, Joan could just about look him in the eye while he was talking. He had not taken off his sunglasses when he entered the building, which irritated Joan more than it should have. He reached into his suit pocket, and pulled out a an ID wallet. "We're with the Company," he said as he flashed the ID at her. Joan recognized the style of the ID card; she had helped design it, after all. It was a Heatley Company ID card, and it said his name was Rupert Pinkson. It also had a picture of him, and below it was an alphanumeric code where there would normally be a job description. Although she couldn't remember seeing a code like that on a Heatley Company ID before, she couldn't honestly say she paid attention to every single one she saw during the course of the day.

"And what do you do for the company, Mr. Pinkson?" Joan asked him. She pulled out her own card and showed it to him, pointing at the job title. "See here? Where it says 'Personal Assistant?' That's what I do. But I must say I've never heard of being a CB-1 001. Is it fun? Does it pay well? Are you going to kill me?"

Rupert recoiled at the last question. His eyes were obscured by the sunglasses, but the rest of his face looked offended as he turned his head away. Is he going to cry? Joan wondered. "No, I'm not going to kill you," he managed after he regained his composure. "Why does everyone I talk to think I'm going to kill them?" he asked the air between them.

Joan didn't want this behemoth to need her shoulder to cry on, as she would likely be crushed under the weight. She reached up and patted him on the shoulder. It was a solid piece of shoulder, and Joan briefly thought that perhaps she was supposed to keep one hand on him at all times so that he would not accidentally kill her with a stray kick. "Well, I can't speak for anyone else, but for me it was the way you abducted me off the street and forced me to follow you into a dimly lit stairwell. One, I might add, that smells as if someone has been using it as a bathroom for the last year or so."

Rupert deflated so much that his suit momentarily developed a pocket of air large enough to comfortably slip his wallet back in to. He took advantage of the moment and tucked the wallet away. "They only pay me to do this because I'm so big," he said, shifting his weight from foot to foot. "In the eight months I've been doing this, I've never even had to hit anybody. They just sort of do what I say." His voice dropped to a whisper. "I don't even know how to fight."

"So what is it that you do for the company, Mr. Pinkson? What does CB-1 001 mean?"

He smiled at her. "Call me Rupert. It means that I'm the first employee in the company with the designation of Choir Boy. CB-1 001."

"Choir Boy?" Joan said, the left side of her face wrinkling itself briefly as her brain tried to contort his reply into something that made sense to her.

"Yeah, the old man thought that it would seem less threatening that way."

"So Mr. Heatley thinks that Choir Boys is a-"

"Oh, no ma'am," Rupert interrupted. "I don't think that Heatley knows we exist. It's kind of a secret thing. See, we're the ones that keep tabs on Mr. Heatley. Make sure he's happy where he is."

Joan took offence to this. "You must be confused. I'm the one that keeps Mr. Heatley happy where he is."

Rupert shook his head at her. "No ma'am. You misunderstood me. You keep him happy where he is. We make sure he's happy where he is. Because if he's not, then-"

It was Joan's turn to recoil now. "Then what?" Her hand flew to her mouth.

Rupert raised both of his hands at her. "No ma'am. No. It's not like that. You see, if he's not happy then we have to fix things."

Joan rolled this about in her mind for a moment. "So, the problem of him wanting to go for a walk is going to be placed in your lap, then?

Rupert inhaled deeply, removing any wrinkles that may have been forming in his suit, and tried to not look as guilty as he felt. He forced his right hand into the pocket of his pants, and fished around for something. It took a while because of the lack of space in his pocket for a hand that large, and Joan began to feel awkward as the large man continued to dig around his crotch. Finally, he pulled out a small, padded, zippered pouch, which he handed to her. "Mr. Meyers asked me to give this to you. His instructions are in there."

She opened it, revealing a small, unlabelled vial, a dropper, and a folded piece of paper. As she took out the paper, Rupert looked around the stairwell and out the door to the parking garage. Presumably, he was looking for anyone who might be lurking about, perhaps paying attention to business that wasn't their own, and reminding them where their business ended and his began. Joan unfolded the paper, finding it difficult to keep her focus anywhere but on Rupert and his attempt at skulking. He wasn't very good at it, and reminded Joan of a cartoon she had seen as a child, in which the giant and a small boy were playing hide-and-seek. The giant kept trying to hide behind trees and such, but was much too large and could be seen right away. She turned her attention back to the note.

> It has become necessary to alter our plans for the future of the company. A few drops will assist in relocating. Contact the Choir afterwards.

That was it. No signature, no details. Joan was surprised when the note failed to burst into flames after she was done reading it. As she began to re-fold it, Rupert snatched it from her hands, and set it on fire before dropping it to the ground. The paper only burned for a few moments, after which Rupert stamped the blackened ash beyond recognition with an enormous shoe. "Do they expect me to poison Mr. Heatley?" she asked, feeling the meek creep back up in her.

"It's not poison," Rupert told her. "It's going make him sick, and then we're gonna move him to a hospital." He kicked at the spot where the paper had landed, and sounded like he was trying to convince himself as well as Joan that their actions were still within the realm of not evil. "The plan is to make him sick so he doesn't want to leave the apartment anymore. Once he's happy there again, we're back to normal."

"And by normal you mean you continue to be a part of a secret security organization within the company, and I continue making sure that my boss thinks that staying in his apartment for the rest of his life is the best decision he's ever made?"

"Yeah. That sounds about right."

"But I wouldn't go so far as to call it 'normal', Rupert." Joan shivered. It wasn't cold in the stairwell. She thought it was probably the result of her conscience stabbing her in the heart, and she told it to go away. "Let's get this over with," she said, and headed up to the office.

She took out her ID card, and waved it over a sensor that was mounted on the wall outside the office door. It beeped at her, the red light on the sensor turned to green. She opened the door to find the office bustling as usual. Her clipboard hung by a nail on the wall underneath a label that said her name in a 48-point font that she wasn't crazy about, though no one ever asked her how she felt about it.

Joan went over the notes, and almost told Rupert how she thought it was funny how she got over so many of the immoral and illegal things that her job had been requesting of her over the the better part of the last year, but she couldn't get over that damned font. It bothered her every day, and yet she had never told anyone about it. She felt that if she could just tell someone about it, someone who wouldn't think that she was crazy, she would feel better. "You know, Rupert," she began, but cut her sentence short because there was no one there to hear it. Rupert had disappeared. More likely, she thought, as she looked around the room, he had walked her up to the office and then left. He certainly hadn't come in. None of the cubicles had the capacity to conceal a man of his size. Joan continued reading the reports that had been prepared for Mr. Heatley, the falsehoods about the effects of the decisions that he had made regarding the company, and the results of his orders that were never carried out.

She made her way to the back of the office, where she would enter the back door of the false elevator. Her coffee mug was waiting for her on the table by the water cooler, but it was filled with the same coffee she had left on the counter when she had left it there that morning, so she put it back down. As she stepped into the elevator, her nerves shot back into high gear, threatening to make her vomit should Heatley ask her so much as how she was doing. She closed her eyes tight and forced herself to stop shaking, muttering something to herself about prison and corporate-logos on cement shoes. The front door of the elevator opened up, and Joan stepped forward, the determination she had to stay out of prison swelled inside her, steeling herself. It wasn't to last.

As she opened the front door to Heatley's apartment, she tuned into the sounds coming out of it. There was a lot of thrashing about, far more than the usual noise of the old man stomping around his apartment. This sounded more like fighting. The grunting and the hollow sound of drywall being smashed brought Joan running into the room. She expected to see Heatley being beaten to a pulp, possibly by a teary-eyed Rupert, who would be apologizing to the old man as he beat him to death, but more likely by another one of the Choir Boys, who would no doubt have a better stomach for this type of work.

What she did not expect to find was Frank Heatley alone in the room, attempting to dislodge a chair he had smashed through a wall. The heavy wooden antique had lost a leg in the battle with the drywall, and Heatley let the rest of it drop to the ground. Joan could see the cement behind the drywall, where Heatley would have been expecting to find a window.

"Joan, where am I?" he asked, his voice cracking with fear. "What's happening to me? Joan?" he called out, but she was already gone, running back down the hallway towards the elevator.

The Master Beta.

Officer Bratton let Sherman go without without any charges being pressed, but without an apology, either. Not that Bratton wasn't sorry, because he was: He was sorry he wasn't allowed to beat people up for being insolent anymore, like he used to do when he was in high school, before he knew what insolent meant. He had just referred to them different, and justified hitting people based on that. He also missed the days when beating people didn't require paperwork to be filed afterward. The police academy had taught him that although being different may have been wrong enough to justify a beating during high school, it wasn't something he could arrest anyone for. He watched Sherman walk away, ready to pounce on him again and give him a ticket should he decide to be a wise-ass. His radio belched out what sounded like incomprehensible squelches of static. It was a bulletin telling him an old blue-haired lady was seen heading north on Church Street, lashing out at people with her cane. He hopped back into his car and sped away, a theme tune he was writing for himself running through his head.

Sherman walked across the street to work, rubbing his neck on the spots where it was sore, which was pretty much all of it. He glanced at his phone to check the time, and found he was now late despite having left his apartment early to grab a coffee before his shift. He opened the door to Gary's Empornium and found Gary, his boss, standing at the counter tapping his watch. Before Sherman could begin to explain why he was late, Gary chuckled and said "Don't worry, Sherman. I saw the whole thing."

Sherman took off his sweatshirt, which was covered in dirt from his altercation, and hung it up behind the counter. "Man, that cop's really got it out for me."

"And I'm sure you didn't do anything to piss him off," he replied, the sarcasm oozing from him.

"I didn't! I was just-"

"Just talking to him?" Gary chided him. "Sherman, I've know you long enough to know that your conversation can be - antagonistic, at times."

Sherman wanted to hold his ground, but the smirk he tried to subdue overtook him. "I don't even know what you're talking about."

"Sherman, I'm watching your face lie to me. I don't care what your voice says about it."

"Damn," Sherman said, looking down at the counter. A manilla envelope with his name on it sat there quietly waiting for him to notice it. He picked it up and looked at it more closely. It continued to just say his name and not divulge any more information, so he asked Gary what it was.

"It's a new 'Terms of Employment' contract from the Heatley Company." Gary looked around the room. "I sold the place."

"Ah, crap," Sherman muttered, and threw the envelope at the garbage can. He threw it too low, however, and it hit the side of the can before it fell to the ground. "Do you have any idea how hard it's getting to find a job in this town where you're not working for those idiots?"

"Those idiots are going to give you a raise, Sherman," Gary cut in. "The Heatley Company has a lot more money than I do."

"It's not about the money," Sherman said through clenched teeth. "It's the principal of the thing. It's about not wanting to work for the big nameless corporate dickheads who shut down the little mom-and-pop operations that people spent their lives developing." He turned back to Gary. "What's going to happen to you?" he asked.

"Well, I'm staying on here for now. I'm going to manage the place for six months to ease the transition, and then I'm probably going to head down south somewhere. Beaches, bikinis, relax for a while and then maybe start up a new place." Although Gary had often spoken of this, Sherman had thought it nothing more than a pipe dream, never believing that Gary might actually make it happen while simultaneously encouraging him to do it. "Look, at least think about signing it. It's not like you'll be working for them forever. I mean, you can just quit whenever you want, right? It will be a few changes, and then you won't even notice the difference, at least until I leave, and that won't be for a while." Gary picked the envelope off the ground and put it back down on the counter.

Sherman silently debated which he hated more; job hunting or the idea of his new job, which he couldn't see as the same as his old job. Not with The Heatley Company at the helm. He tore the envelope open and took out the contract, which had been marked in several places for him to sign. He read enough of the contract to know where he was supposed to sign or initial, and he signed and initialed accordingly, then passed it back over to Gary. "Thanks, Sherman. I like having you here."

"I just can't stand the thought of job hunting right now," Sherman grumbled at him. "Hey, why does the Heatley Company even want to own a porn shop anyway?" He looked around at the decor, as if somewhere amongst the shaded windows and neon lights lay some insight into the company's decision to buy something so out of character for them.

Gary shrugged. "I would think it's just their new strategy: buy everything in town. Why not this place, too?" He picked a newspaper out from inside a beaten and disheveled leather briefcase, and tossed it on the counter. "There's an article in there about how they bought a church earlier this week. Can you imagine? A church." Gary shook his head as he said this, as if he was hearing it for the first time.

"And you want me to work for them?"

"Not for them. For me," Gary took the staples out of the contract and ran it through the fax machine. "And you can leave after I'm done here, no problem, but I've already told the corporate boys that I think you'd be a good candidate to manage this place when I'm gone."

The door swung open and the silhouette of a tall man in a trench coat sleazed its way into the store. The silhouette faded, revealing a pale-faced man with dark, greasy hair and sunglasses tinted almost to opaqueness. He looked at the two men behind the counter, and they all nodded a quick acknowledgment of each other's existence before going back about their own business.

Gary checked his watch again. He knew that he was late getting out, as Sherman had been late coming in. He handed Sherman a copy of the contract, placing the original back into the envelope, and the envelope into his briefcase. "Well, I gotta run, Sherman. Got a meeting with the new owners and some lawyers."

"Sounds fun," Sherman said with a chipper tone in his voice to counteract the sarcasm it held underneath.

"I get a fun cheque at the end of it," Gary said as he headed for the door. "Oh, and somebody will be coming by later this morning to measure up the front of the store for the new sign." He smiled at the question in Sherman's eyes. "Did you think they'd just call it Gary's Empornium, a Division of The Heatley Company? You didn't read much while you were signing, did you, Sherman?" The door swung shut behind him, taking the daylight with it, leaving Sherman in the fluorescent light with the man in the trench coat.

Sherman thought about reading the book he had brought with him, a collection of short stories that were edited by or chosen by another author whose name he often couldn't recall. Holding the contract in one hand and the paperback volume in the other, Sherman compared the two. The contract seemed to weigh much more, but he dismissed this as if it were his brain spewing metaphors at him. He opened the envelope again and scanned the front page of the contract, skipping over most of the legal jargon and complications that struck him as gratuitous, until he saw a sequence of words that didn't look like they fit in to the rest of the document. "The Master Beta," he read aloud, unsure of whether he had needed to say it out loud to confirm to what he had read, or if he had said it out of sheer disbelief. He tried it again. "The Master Beta." Yes, there it was. Just like he thought it had been. The words on the paper begged to be spoken out loud.

"Job getting to you?" The voice came from behind the papers Sherman was holding in front of his face. When he lowered them, the voice revealed itself as belonging to the customer in the trench coat, who had still not removed his sunglasses, and looked even more shifty up close than when he first slunk into the store.

Sherman felt he had already spoken to enough people that day. It wasn't even noon, and he had been assaulted by a stray cup's worth of tea and a police officer, his boss had broken the news to him that the dynamics of his job would now have him answering the phone saying 'Master Beta' who knew how many times per day, and now he had a pseudo-goth trying to make small talk with him while renting a German bondage film. "Not really," he said. He took the video off the counter to ring it through. The goth had covered part of the box with his membership card and exact change for the rental, and the second Sherman took the card and money off it, the goth shifted self-consciously, as if part of his psyche had just been exposed as much as the girl on the cover. Sherman finished the transaction by placing the video into a black plastic bag. "Hey, it's between you and me," was unspoken between Sherman and virtually every customer he had. He wasn't their realtor. They didn't do lunch. He didn't ask how things went with their purchase when he saw them outside of the store.

The goth pushed the door open slowly and poked his head out, possibly to see if the coast was clear, possibly testing the strength of the sun. Had he been out all night and miscalculated the time of sunrise? Sherman knew that he should probably not be so callous with the people around him the same way he knew that he should quit smoking and call his mother more often. He dropped the contract on the counter and opened his book to where he had left off. His spot was marked by a playing card, a Jack of Diamonds he found on the street a few years back and had picked up for no reason he could think of at the time.

The door opened again and three men wearing suits and dark glasses walked in. Their demeanour didn't leave much guesswork as to who they were. These men were not shopping together. They had to be the men from the Heatley Company Gary had told him about. "The basement should be over this way," one of them said. Sherman assumed he was the alpha of the bunch, judging by how he stood more or less in the middle while the other two hovered around him, appearing ready to do whatever he might ask of them. They left his sides in the direction he was pointing, obedient as well-trained dogs. They opened the door to the basement and went down the stairs without a word, leaving the alpha upstairs with Sherman. A badge was flashed from the alpha's wallet, a display of some authority that Sherman wasn't sure if he or anyone else would have any obligation to respect. The alpha flipped his wallet closed, and was putting it back in his pocket when Sherman asked if he could see the identification again.

"What for?" asked the alpha. He hadn't prepared for this in his nightly sessions in front of the mirror at home, and wondered why his wife hadn't asked what he would do in this situation to prepare him.

Sherman held his hand out across the counter. "I'd just like to know who it is I'm dealing with here."

The wallet was pulled back out and passed over to Sherman, who opened it to examine the ID. The badge and the ID card were set opposite each other, both claiming that the man in front him belonged to an organization that referred to itself as The Choir Boys, if the alpha's decryption of the acronym could be believed, but there was no mention anywhere what that meant or what authority they might hold. The photo ID of the alpha looked official enough, complete with layers of barely-visible security features that would make it extremely difficult to counterfeit. It also introduced the alpha as one Bill Griffin, CB-002. "I'll tell you what, Bill," Sherman started at him, folding the wallet back over and passing it back to him. "I don't believe I have any obligation to do what you say, or to do anything more than direct you to the appropriate shelf for whatever your particular fetish might be. So," he smirked, "men or women?"

Bill was losing his cool on the inside, but kept relatively calm in appearance. "I don't suppose you have a copy of your contract with The Heatley Company handy, do you, Mr. Klein?" he said with a smile.

Sherman was caught off guard by this, and grabbed the envelope off the counter, took out his contract, and stared at the cover page, wondering what the hell he had signed. Bill leaned over the counter. "Page 16, fourth paragraph," he said. Sherman turned to that page and started reading. "I'll paraphrase it for you, Mr Klein. It says that The Choir Boys are in charge of security for The Heatley Company, and as such, having signed this document, you are now legally obligated to do as we say." He leaned back before mumbling "Provided that we are not asking you to do anything… illegal."

Sherman tried to decipher the jargonese document, and concluded that Griffin wasn't lying to him. He actually had authority within The Heatley Company over anyone who had agreed to the terms set out by the contract. It also, he realized with a grimace, gave them authority over anyone who had been foolish enough to sign without reading it. "How was I supposed to know that this was in here?" Sherman said. "I couldn't go through this whole thing this morning!"

Bill smiled like a crocodile watching a no-legged cow roll itself towards the muddy banks to get a drink. "Well, Sherman. May I call you Sherman? Of course I can. Your generation detests being called Mr, doesn't it? So, Sherman, on the front page of your contract, just underneath the basic introduction where it welcomes you to The Heatley Company, you will find an offer from The Heatley Company to visit a company lawyer to go over the terms of the contract, page by page and item by item with you." Sherman flipped the contract back over and read the first page again. The font was tiny, and decreased in size as it got to the section Bill had mentioned, but sure enough, it was there. Griffin opened his mouth as if he was about to go on, but snapped it shut without making a noise when the other Choir Boys came back up the stairs without the subtlety of a three-car pileup.

"Sir," one of them began. "Everything checks out down there. Looks like it won't take too much work to get it ready."

Bill took out a notepad and jotted something down, then put it back in his pocket. "You went over the whole list?"

"Yes, sir." He produced a paper from his pocket and handed it to his superior, who looked it over with an unreadable face. He pulled his notepad back out and placed the list inside it, then slipped it away again. "Call in the crew," he told the younger men. He turned to Sherman. "You're closed."

"But what about my-"

"A day off with pay," Bill interrupted. "Is that going to be a problem for you?"

"I'll just count out now," said Sherman. "I'll be out of your way in less than ten minutes."

"Very good, Sherman. Very good."

Sherman pretended to count his till accurately, but as he had only made one transaction, he simply deducted that amount from the till and threw it in the safe below the counter, then shoved the register closed again. He grabbed his skateboard and headed for the door. "I take it you guys have keys and alarm codes and that sort of thing?" he said to one of the agents, who tried to look like he wasn't checking out penis enlargers while he was waiting for 'The Crew' to show up.

"Of course we do," he said in his best 'I wasn't checking out the penis enlargers' voice. "We have them for all of the buildings belonging to The Heatley Company. Part of the job." He shifted his weight from one foot to the other, then leaned in and dropped his voice to a whisper. "Do any of these things actually work?"

Sherman smiled. He always got a kick out of how uncomfortable his customers got about this sort of thing. "Just the expensive ones," he said with a grin. "But don't worry. You probably get the staff discount." He flipped the sign on the door from 'Open' to 'Closed', and said "Lock up behind me, kids," as he left for the day.

Miss Interpretation.

Edna Sheldon moved about town in a bubble of self-righteousness so thick it was tangible. She appeared to have control over it, able to transform it to serve her needs. It formed a cowcatcher that tossed pedestrians aside, put up walls of "It's my right of way" with a nod of her head that stopped drivers who came within twenty feet of her, and lashed out as tentacles that slapped unwary men across the face for looking lustily at members of the opposite sex. Occasionally, some unfortunate soul who had not been aware of the legacy of Old Blue would treat her with disrespect. Those who frequently traversed The Path Of Judgement would look away when this happened, shielding the eyes and ears of their children. The events of the morning had taken their toll on Edna's demeanour, however, so even those who had never seen or heard of Old Blue could sense she was to be left alone.

She came to a rickety halt as she rounded the corner onto Church Street. Something was different. Something was wrong. She stood on the corner, holding her cane with both hands, looking like a sorceress channelling her energy. As she squinted down the street, she could make out her church at the end of the block. There was something wrong down that way, but she couldn't put her finger on what it was. She plodded on towards the church with fire in her eyes. Perhaps it had something to do with the work crew in front of the building, with their Heatley Company uniforms and vehicles, or the flashing lights and the construction barriers that told passers-by they would need to use the other sidewalk. More than likely, she realized as she got closer to her place of worship, it was the Heatley Company logo on the sign that was being put in place where the sign for her church stood until yesterday. "The Church Of Blessed Interpretation?" she exclaimed. She was close enough to be face to face with a group of construction workers who were drinking coffee, had she been tall enough to look them in the eye. She observed them for just long enough to figure out which of them would likely have the most seniority, then cracked him in the shins with her cane to get his attention.

"Ow! God dammit, lady. What the hell?" he shouted at her. Edna's only reply was another shot to his shins. "Ow!"

"That one was for blasphemy," she said. "Now, young man, what is the meaning of this?" She pointed at the sign.

Another worker in an orange Heatley Company vest walked up to him and whispered something into his ear, stabbing at his clipboard with his index finger several times before they both looked from the clipboard to the old lady in front of them. The glance went back and forth once more before they turned their attention back to her. It was too late, however, as she was already in mid-swing and she struck his shin again with her cane. "Ow! Bitch!" And again. "Ow!" He stepped back and bent over to rub his shins with his hands, and swore at her under his breath. As it turned out, it was not quite quietly enough, and the next blow from the cane hit him across the face, knocking him over. He howled in pain. Old Blue stepped forward and pointed the rubber end of her cane at him, poking him repeatedly in the nose with what she thought was enough restraint to earn her some respect. To the injured man's relief, the rest of his crew took advantage of this opportunity to overpower the crazed woman who was assaulting him. Three of them grabbed at her at once, being somewhat gentle at first, but then readjusting the effort they put into it when it became obvious she had more fight in her than they thought. Despite her best efforts, she was immobilized by the men, who were at the moment oblivious to the attention the scene had brought upon them.

Edna strained against the grip of the men to no avail. "What have you done to my church?" she demanded.

"We haven't done anything to your church, Mrs. Sheldon," the man with the clipboard told her, his hands half-raised in a gesture of 'I'm unarmed' in an attempt to put her at ease.

Old Blue did not get put at ease, however. Instead, she was put on edge. "How do you know my name?" she said with a fresh struggle at the grip on the construction workers.

"Ma'am," the man with the clipboard began, in the most comforting voice he could muster up. "Your name was given to us as one of the most valued members of this church, along with your picture. We've done our best to put a file on you together so that we could identify you so we could assure you-" he took a deep breath, "assure you, because you are a valuable member of this congregation, that there was nothing wrong, and that the church is open for business as usual."

"Business?" Edna's rage could be felt by the hands attempting to restrain her.

"De bidness ub zalvation ad vorgibness, I'b sure," the man on the ground managed as he slowly stood up. He was digging around his pockets for something to stem the flow of blood that had been caned out of his nose. "Uh'll be ride beck," he said, and limped his way over to one of the company vehicles in search of a cooler and a first-aid kit.

"He said 'The business of salvation and forgiveness', Mrs. Sheldon. My name is Tony, and I'm not actually with the construction team here." He tucked the clipboard under his arm and took a cautious step towards her. "May I call you Edna?"

"Certainly not!" she growled at him. "Have these men release me, at once." Tony waved at the men to let go of her, which they did then simultaneously jumped back as if someone had punched a rattlesnake in its face and dropped it at their feet.

"Now, Mrs. Sheldon-"

"Give me the clipboard," she demanded, holding out one hand while the other one held her cane at a threatening angle.

Tony pursed his lips and looked for a way out of the situation that did not involve handing over the clipboard, while still doing the job of containing the Old Blue situation. He knew her cane was set to do him some damage and he didn't have much time. He glanced over his shoulder at Stewart, the man Old Blue had first attacked, who had strapped cans of beer from the cooler to his shins using tourniquets from the first-aid kit, and was alternating a third can between his cheek, his nose, and his lips. Large balls of cotton had been placed hurriedly up his nose. "May I just talk to the foreman, Mrs. Sheldon?"

"Young man, you will hand me that clipboard right this minute!" He slowly handed the clipboard over to her and then backed up, maintaining eye contact as he did so. When he was about ten feet away, he turned and sped towards Stewart, who was sitting on the rear bumper of a van, his head tilted up with the beer can soothing his nose.

"Uhnnnn," Stewart said, but Tony was unsure if it was by way of greeting, an acknowledgement of his presence, or just at random.

"I gave it to her. I'm sorry."

Stewart didn't look at him, just nodded awkwardly while keeping his head angled upwards, and reached out blindly for the cooler. He sloshed his hand around in the ice until it came up with another can and held it out for Tony, who took it without a word. They both knew it wasn't over, that the worst was probably yet to come. The scream they heard was not a surprise, but it chilled them to the bone anyhow.

Edna looked at the clipboard, holding it alternately closer to and farther from her face in an effort to read it without her glasses. She tucked her cane under her arm and reached into her pocket for her glasses, holding them in front of her face without putting them on. She saw the picture of herself, and she could make out her name in a large font below the photo. Below her name, however, in a smaller font, were the words 'A.K.A. Old Blue'. The scream they had prepared themselves for came in right about here. She read on, and found there was far more information about her than the church would have access to. Besides the nickname there was nothing offensive in any way. It was cold, factual information, detailing her bank accounts and spending habits, credit history, drivers license status (revoked), and various other pieces of information that would not have been acquired through the church. She was just about to crumple up the page when her eyes quickly scanned to the bottom lines. It read:

> Based on the withdrawal history on Mrs. Sheldon's bank account, when compared to her observed spending habits and fixed monthly spending for her lifestyle, it is estimated that her monthly donations to The Church Of Blessed Interpretation could be in excess of $3,500.

As she finished this sentence a police car pulled up, lights flashing red and blue. Edna was heading towards Stewart again, oblivious to the arrival of the squad car, focussed entirely on finding out why a construction worker would have so much personal information about her. She was a predator, closing in on its prey. Granted, she was an aged predator, like a shark with only three teeth left that hurt when its cartilage made the motions required to turn left, but a shark is a shark and Stewart was nervous as she approached. She raised her cane off the ground, transforming it from walking aid to beating stick again, and pointed it at his chest.

"Where did you get-"

Just then, one of the officers stepped in front of her, taking the cane in his solar plexus, which was protected by a bullet-proof vest. "What seems to be the problem here, ma'am?" he asked. His partner was just a few paces behind him, one eye on the situation with the old lady, the other scanning the area for any other signs of trouble; another old lady wielding a cane, perhaps. There appeared to be nothing more than a construction worker with beer cans strapped to his shins, and a skateboarder off in the distance.

"The problem, officer, is this!" Edna screeched at him, holding up the wrinkled paper with her picture on it.

"Now, ma'am, I'm going to have to ask you to put down the cane before someone gets hurt," he said with a smile. "Besides, I can't reach your paper until you let me in a little closer."

Edna lowered her cane and leaned forward on it to hand him the document, which he thanked her for as he began to read over it. His partner, a younger officer with a look of "To Serve And To Protect And To Be Really, Really Eager To Please" about him, began to read the notice over his partner's shoulder. Edna thought the older officer was annoyed by this, and it didn't surprise her when the younger man caught an elbow in his gut, causing him to choke on something, quite possibly his pride. What Edna didn't notice about the exchange was the lightning-fast reflexes of the older officer, who had read enough of the paper to realize that the creature in front of him was "Old Blue", and could very likely cause an exchange that would result in him being battered in public by an old lady. The younger officer had begun to snicker when he read her alias, and had been struck for it. It may not have saved his life, but his dignity had certainly been spared a bruising. Another squad car pulled up, and Officer Bratton stepped from the vehicle. He kept his sunglasses on while he surveilled the scene, looking for cute girls who might know something about what was going on. He would have to settle for the officers already on the scene for his information, he decided, and began a cocky swagger over to where the old woman appeared to be in custody.

"Well, well, well," he began in a condescending-lecture tone of voice he had developed while in the shower on Wednesday evenings after watching police reality-TV shows. "We meet again. Bet you thought you gave me the slip for good this morning when you got away." The other officers looked at each other, then over at Bratton, who realized that he had just admitted he let an elderly woman escape him only a few hours ago. "There was an incident this- um, that is… Listen, it's complicated," he said to the other officers, who were only moments away from bursting out in a fit of laughter at him. He decided that his only course of action was to renew his condescending tone at the old lady and make sure she was brought in this time, preferably by one of the other officers, and preferably after he left the scene and wouldn't have to do any paperwork for the bust. He grinned at the thought of this, and was just about to attempt to get her riled up enough to cause some serious damage when he was interrupted by a voice that had been professionally conditioned into a state of perpetual kindness.

"Good Heavens! Edna Sheldon! Is that you? Officers, what is the meaning of this?" All three officers looked around to identify the source of the voice that would dare question them. Their eyes landed on a man carrying a weather-beaten Bible and wearing a uniform that could only be that of a member of the clergy. It was clean, ironed, and streamlined, and it also lacked any sense of flare. There were no logos on any of his clothing, save for a monogrammed "H.C." on a rather long scarf that looked like it would drape itself as far as he would allow it to. He had the bearing of a man who believed he had righteousness on his side, the kind that could only be achieved by a firm belief in something that did not allow for any leeway, no matter how rational the argument brought against it was.

Bratton spun on his heel to face this new element. The other officers could feel the conflicting opinions regarding the absolute rightness of things grating as the two faced each other. Bratton pulled out his heavily worn copy of the Criminal Code to counteract the Bible that had been brought by the cleric. The leather-bound editions were both clenched by sweaty palms. A metaphorical tumbleweed kicked up some dust as it rolled itself out of harms way when the church bells rang out. It was high noon. Bratton pulled a toothpick out of his breast pocket and put it in his mouth so he could roll it dramatically from side to side. "And just who might you be?" he asked through clenched teeth.

"Officer... Bratton," the cleric began, reading his name tag through squinting eyes. "I am Father Francis Anthony, and this woman is a member of my congregation. A valued member of my congregation."

"Shouldn't they all be considered valuable members, Father?" Bratton said as he spit out the toothpick. It had begun to splinter from being chewed, and he spit it out too late to prevent pieces from embedding themselves in his gums. He had been working on not chewing them so much before spitting them out, but hadn't mastered it yet. For a while, he had tried using plastic toothpicks, because they wouldn't splinter at all, giving him enough leeway to spit them out whenever the proper dramatic effect would be achieved, but the only plastic ones he could find were sold in packs of blue, green, red, and yellow, and sounded feeble when they hit the ground. He felt like people didn't take him seriously when he spat them out.

Father Anthony smiled. "Of course. You're right, Officer Bratton. I felt that by emphasizing her value to us, I could persuade you to let this - issue - go." He kept smiling, and tried to increase its level of disarming to 'Stubborn Angry Officer'. He forced the smile to extend beyond his mouth, trying to hide the strain in his eyes. Exorcism was strenuous work.

Bratton backed down, putting his copy of the criminal code back into his pocket. "I'll talk to the gentlemen over here, and see if they're willing to not press charges."

The other officers began talking to each other in the background. The older one made a Jedi gesture with his hand and mumbled "You do not need to arrest this woman." They took a quick look around, and decided Bratton should be able to handle the situation. They snuck away to grab a coffee before Bratton got a chance to do the same to them.

Bratton turned to instruct the other officers to do something he was going to make up on the spot after he had their attention, but they were already gone. He grabbed another toothpick out of his pocket, but he could still feel some splinters working their way around his mouth. There was no point in trying to intimidate anyone here, anyhow. He flicked the toothpick to the ground rather than put it back into the pack.

"Just get her the hell away from us, and make sure she leaves us alone while we're working from now on," Stewart called out to Bratton. Stewart, who had evidently overheard the exchange between the other men, was still rubbing his shins, and had opened one of the beers he had strapped to his legs to help console himself a little more. "You got that, you crazy old bag? Stay the hell away from us!" he yelled at Edna, who was in the middle of a conversation with Father Anthony, but turned away from him long enough to throw a bony glare full of malice and spite in their direction. Anthony grabbed her by the arm and ushered her up the stairs and into the church, the heavy oak doors gliding gently closed behind them. Bratton watched them disappear, then snapped his notebook shut with a flick of the wrist. He thought briefly about how perfect a time it would be to be able to spit a toothpick out in contempt, and made a mental note to not second guess himself. It was probably some form of cop's intuition that made him think a good toothpick spitting was going to be appropriate, he figured, and there was no reason for him to go against his instincts. The academy had taught him to trust his gut, after all. He could hear the dispatcher on the radio, calling all cars for something or other that was lost in the static and squelching that was characteristic of the device. He took off his sunglasses, mimicking a television detective who used the manoeuvre for dramatic effect, then put them back on as he headed back to his car. He tried to show enough urgency to look like he was in a hurry, while being careful not to appear as if he had lost his cool. Sirens could be heard in the distance, a sound that always started Bratton humming his theme tune as he made his way to the action.

As they made their way to the front pew, where Edna habitually sat, Father Anthony found himself being interrogated rather than thanked by the old woman. No, he didn't think she needed help. Yes, the church had a new name. No, that wasn't going to be the only change. Yes, it had been purchased by the Heatley Company. No, that wasn't as significant a change as she thought. As Edna was not terribly quick on her feet when she wasn't in a rage, she managed to badger him like this for quite some time before they got to the front pew, where Anthony made his excuses and left her there to pray. Pray, he thought with disdain towards her. It was his opinion that Edna didn't pray so much as gossip with the rest of the self-righteous circle of old ladies that congregated there on an almost daily basis. There were at least a half-dozen of them, and they drove him nuts. He unlocked a door behind the altar, and passed into the hallway that lay behind it. He closed the door, then put his eye up the the peephole and watched the old ladies gather from the corners of the church. The bits of gossip that Edna brought them would draw them to her like pigeons to an old man brandishing a loaf of bread at a park bench. He turned away, shaking his head in disgust at what the "truly devout" of his congregation had turned become. Any qualms he may have had about allowing the Heatley Company to absorb the church into its ranks had been settled months ago. The financial state of the church had been stagnant for long enough, and the company had all but guaranteed him that things would change within just a few months. The charts were impressive. Lots of colours, high percentages where percentages should be high, and low percentages where they should be low. There were even some animations showing how the people had gone from being sad to happy now that they were all part of the same big company that had promised to take care of them. Some big hits had been taken in the faith and tradition aspects of running a church, but the charts had shown where these differences could be made up and according to the questionnaire he had filled out, his faith was slipping yearly, and might slip from the yellow into the red within the next five years. By signing on as the Salvation Manager for the new Church Of Blessed Interpretation, he was virtually guaranteeing himself that his faith level would be back in the green in just a few short years, possibly less. There would be a substantial pay raise in it for him, too, if that would help persuade him at all. The Heatley Company had faith that it would.

The opulence in the back of the church was impressive by any standards, and was kept behind a locked door to dissuade anyone who might have had questions about how collection plate funds were spent from asking those questions. The antiquated hardwood did not end with the floors. There was no pressboard panelling to be found back here, nor was there anything that was an imitation of what it looked to be. The crystal was fine crystal, the paintings were all original works, and not one piece of furniture had been brought there in a box or put together with an allen key. A heavy oak door on the left led into a wine cellar where expensive vintages were kept stored for the communion of wealthy congregants who might choose to congregate elsewhere if they found the taste of the blood was more to their liking. A wealthy congregant had a tendency to feel guilty for something, and by use of a skillfully crafted sermon could be made to think that a cheque with an extra zero or two on it could serve as penance enough to bribe their way through the gates of pearl when their time came. At the end of the hallway was a set of large double doors that opened up into an office of such a size that it attempted to defy the actual capacity of the building, and its grandeur would have made even the wealthiest congregants think twice about the size of their donations. At the far end of the office, past the Persian carpet, there was a desk that looked as if it must have been there before the church and was too big to move, forcing them to build around it. The chair at the desk was impressive as well, although it could not be seen due to the size of the man that was currently sitting in it, drinking a scotch that cost sixty dollars an ounce and smoking a cigar that cost a hundred dollars an inch. Father Anthony thought the man looked to be having an eight hundred dollar afternoon at the church's expense, but he didn't blink. The fat man, after all, gave more than that to the church every day, now.

"Good afternoon, Father," he said, standing up and extending his hand across the desk. Anthony shook the proffered limb, despite how disgusted he was by it, and the man it was attached to. That fat man's grip was so intense that Anthony felt it could crush every bone in his hand if it wanted to, or if it was just really excited to see him.

"And a good afternoon to you, Roger," Anthony replied, anxious to have his hand back so that he might discreetly wipe it clean. No matter the time of day, Roger Clemens' hand always felt as if it had just been between pieces of fried chicken. "To what do I owe the visit?" He omitted the words 'pleasure of your', as he wasn't sure how convincing his poker face was.

"Business, my dear cleric. Always business." He sat back down and held his glass up, looking through it at the stained glass window, admiring the way the liquid and crystal caught the light and danced with it. "We have something here to be installed for you at three, so make sure you've got the place cleared out by then."

Anthony didn't like the idea of decisions involving the church being made without his consent, or even his opinion, being sought, but such were the terms of his contract with the company, and the benefits so far still seemed to outweigh the costs. "And what do you have for me today, Roger?"

The big man smiled. Even his teeth were immense. They looked as if they could make their way through bone like a series of mallets colliding to mash into dust whatever lay in their path. In front of him was a laptop computer, which he turned around so it was facing Anthony. "I present to you, the future. This is the Konfessional 3000."

Anthony tilted the screen back a touch so he could see it better in the light. On the screen was a largish booth with ornate wood carving along its exterior, and what looked to be an ATM interface at its door. "It looks like a large confessional booth, with-"

"It is a confessional booth!" Roger said excitedly. "It's a pay-per-use confessional booth!"

Anthony looked up from the screen and accepted the drink that Roger was bringing towards him. He was fairly certain that if he hadn't accepted it, the glass would have kept coming until it struck him in the face. "But Roger," he began, and took a sip of the scotch, "we don't do confessional. That's for the Catholics."

"And that, my good man, is why we spell it with a 'K' instead of a 'C'" Roger told him with a confidence in his voice that said he had answers for any argument.

"And we want to give the impression that we can't spell, then?" Anthony asked.

"Anthony, misspelling is hip and edgy. It will give the kids the impression that they can come to us, and-"

"And their parents that know better than to think that misspelling something intentionally to try and make it cool? Will we not lose them? They have more money than the kids you're targeting with this thing. And their sins can be much more... costly to them, if that's what you're after, here."

Roger sat back in the chair, and moved his jaw in smug circles. "Their parents will accept it the way they accept everything else, with some griping and some 'Back in my day' speeches, followed by a desire to be with the times. We just have to sell them on the idea of us trying to help their children, and they'll let us do whatever we want. You must think outside of the box, Cleric."

"The words 'think outside the box' are cliche, Roger. It should be an indication about the originality of your thoughts. If you want to do me a favour and never, ever use that phrase again it would be appreciated." Anthony took a meagre sip of his drink and put the glass on his desk, making sure to use a coaster. "Okay," he said. "How does this thing work?" Roger opened a video program on the computer and pushed the Play button.

The video began with an attempt at a dramatic circling of the booth against an all-white background, gradually coming in closer and closer until it came to a halt in front of the door. A credit card appeared out of nowhere and swiped itself down the card slot, and then a few numbers hi-lighted themselves. The door opened up to reveal a comfortable-looking chair which faced a large screen. The camera angle took the viewer to a sitting position in the chair and the screen lit up to show a silhouetted character, presumably the person who would be presiding over the confessions.

"Is there supposed to be any audio to go with this?"

Roger grabbed the computer and spun it so he had a view of the screen. "Yes, it's supposed to be on already," he said, and began to fidget with it for a few moments until the screen flickered and then froze. A squelching noise, followed by a dinging sound that was supposed to tell the user off that there was a problem, assuming that they couldn't figure that much out for themselves, preceded the screen going completely blank. The computer made a final gasp of a noise, sounding like a fuse somewhere had blown, and then the room was silent save for the crackling of a log on the fire. Roger slapped the computer on its side, the caveman in him thinking that hitting things could yield results. He looked at the screen for another few seconds before closing the laptop. "Well, I can just tell you the rest," Roger said, though it was apparent that he had been quite proud of the video presentation that had been put together. "The booth will offer various services, and different models will be made available for different locations. The model from the screen will be the one available in your church, and there will be similar ones available in office buildings around the city, for starters. We're targeting the law offices, of course. Other places, like the adult video store recently acquired by the company, will have a more stripped down version to avoid undue vandalism or theft, and allow for easy cleaning. Incidentally, the adult store location will be kept in the basement. This will give the patrons of different places an opportunity to feel a sense of forgiveness or redemption, in some cases, just for being in a place, even if they choose not to purchase anything. Clever, yes?"

Anthony's mind was reeling. He had too many questions begging to be asked. The biggest ones came first. "Who is going to man these things? I mean, I can't be everywhere around the city just because somebody somewhere feels bad about something. You don't really expect me to go into an adult video store, do you?"

"Not for anything more than your usual renting habits, Your Grace." Anthony recoiled at this, and Roger was smiling again. "Yes, Anthony, we did do a search on you through the company database, and your name turns up in the most surprising of places."

"I… I just…"

"Save it for someone who cares, Cleric." Roger placed his glass on the computer, demoting it to a coaster almost as expensive as the other ones found in the office. "As for the personnel required to operate the booths, are you familiar with messenger programs on the computer?"

"Um, no, I've… heard of them, of course, but-"

"How about video phone? Or video voice mail?"

"Once again, I've heard of them, but I-"

"We will have someone a little more tech-savvy come down and act as your assistant on these matters to get you started, but the booths themselves won't have to be manned at all. You will be able to coordinate the entire operation from your office, and during the hours you are not in your office, messages, both audio and video, will be deposited for you to peruse at your leisure. Your responses can be sent back via e-mail, or pre-recorded audio or video messages. If the price is right, an arrangement for a real-time Konfession can be made, but we have set the bar pretty high for that, so you won't be bothered very often, and when you do your cut will be - substantial."

"So we're starting a pay-per-sin confessional booth where we'll just take a message and get back to you during business hours?" Anthony was caught between disgust and awe, as if he were watching nuclear testing.

"And I haven't even told you the best part yet."

"The best part?" Anthony wasn't sure how much more of this type of good news he could take.

"We will be recording your responses for the first few months, and generating a series of generic reproductions that we feel could accurately represent the appropriate penance. When enough data is collected, you will only be required to respond to the barest of minimum of the clients."

"So you've automated confession? And you feel that the people will respond well to this?"

"My dear preacher, do you know how many sins go unpaid for because people don't want to admit to another person what they've done? They tell their little machines at home what they wish to see and do because they feel guilt about their own desires. To tell another machine to forgive them instead of admitting it to an actual human will be a great relief to them, and they will pay for it." Roger looked at his watch, and his eyebrows leaped half an inch up his forehead. "I must go. There is an important meeting I must attend. To the sinners!" he announced, and tossed back half of his drink.

"To the sinners, then," Anthony picked up his glass, took a small sip, and watched in revulsion as Roger put his cigar out by dropping it into what remained of his own drink. Just as he thought Roger had no concept of how much these things actually cost, the fat man grabbed his glass and hurled it into the fireplace, where it smashed into hundreds of pieces, the remaining alcohol briefly flaring up as it came in contact with the fire.

Anthony put his glass down gently on the coaster again, and began to walk Roger to the door. "You'll send me an assistant soon, then, if these things are already being set up?"

"Not to worry, my dear preacher, we'll have you set up in no time."

They passed through the door leading back into the nave, where it became necessary to make their conversation more cryptic. Roger noted with admiration the change in Anthony's demeanour. He had removed any trace of doubt he had been displaying, and was once again evoking the movements and tone of a spiritual leader. "We shall be seeing you again soon, then, my friend," he said as they passed by Edna, who had stayed to thank Anthony by sharing her gossip with him. He didn't want her to do this, but he understood it as her way of being friendly.

Roger had not realized that by passing by Edna in the company of Anthony, he had piqued her curiosity, nor that she had a tendency of turning her hearing aids up as high as they could go when she was in a quiet room so she could gather as much gossip as possible. Had he known that she were listening to him so intently, he may have chosen his words more carefully, for even though she had heard him correctly, she hadn't understood him properly when he said "Take care, Anthony. And don't you worry about a thing. We'll be seeing a profit within the next two months." Edna's eyes bulged. The ladies were going to have a fit.

The Wrong Building.

Heatley was too stunned to run after Joan right away, plus she had youth and terror on her side, allowing her a higher octane run than she would normally be capable. Plus, Frank was not a psychopath so the horror-movie rule of young females tripping and falling, allowing him to catch up to her, did not apply. The combination of these circumstances led to Joan having a big head start. She disappeared into the elevator before he had a chance to yell after her to stop.

He walked to the elevator after her using one hand to brace himself on the wall. His surroundings felt sinister when they should have held a sense of familiarity and comfort. He reached the elevator and pressed the call button. After a few moments something dawned on him. A feeling of terrible foreboding overcame him, and he pressed his ear to the elevator door. There was no noise coming from it. There were no echoes, no cables-hitting-other-cables noises, no elevator in motion noise, no other people in the elevator car getting it on as if there wasn't a security camera in there noise. There was nothing at all. Then, without any warning, such as a noise would have provided, the doors opened. He stuck his head in and looked around before risking a step into the car. The complete absence of logic in the decision to stick ones only head into an unknown situation rather than, for example, a left hand (or a right hand, for a left-handed person), suddenly struck him as odd. He pressed the Lobby button, then repeatedly pressed the Close Door button, as the instant-gratification nature of the push-button age had taught him if you pushed a button and nothing happened, pushing it again and again and again would yield results. The door would close 'instantly', just as soon as the elevator realized that the button had been pushed. The door closed. And then nothing else happened.

The elevator sat stagnant, and Heatley decided that the elevator looked as new as, as — it hit him. He had lived in that penthouse for several years now, and the elevator looked as new as the kitchen floor under the refrigerator had. Heatley's desire to be brought to the lobby increased, yet continued to go unfulfilled, so he picked up the emergency phone. A voice on the other end answered immediately. "Mr. Heatley, sir? Are you okay?" it asked.

The elevator seemed too small to Heatley, especially after he decided to get outside rather than continue his shut-in existence. He needed a window. He needed air. "No," he said. "I am really not okay. You could say that I am about as far from okay as possible, and perhaps that might entice you to get me the hell out of here!"

A moment of static belched its way out of the earpiece. "Mr. Heatley, sir. The elevator is still out of commission."

"That's bullshit!" He yelled at the phone. "I just watched my assistant disappear in the damned thing, and I want out of this place!"

An awkward silence was the first reply he got, followed by "I'm sorry Mr. Heatley, but nobody has come through the elevator since the alarm. They've been locked down."

Heatley began to panic. He clenched his hand on his chest, thinking perhaps he was having a heart attack, and fell into the fetal position in the corner of the elevator, dropping the phone. It stretched the cord and bungeed itself, hitting the floor three times before bobbing to a halt a few inches above it. Heatley could hear the voice over the phone repeating his name as he reached into the pocket of his housecoat to get his pills. "Mr. Heatley? Mr. Heatley, sir. Are you there?"

He uncoiled himself and grabbed the phone, then pulled it until the cord snapped and dropped it to the ground. He crawled back over to the other side of the elevator, just a few feet, but dreaded every inch of it. He reached up and pressed the Door Open button, just once, and waited. A moment later the doors opened, and as Heatley picked himself up to get out of the elevator, he noticed there was no gap in between the elevator and the hallway in which he could lose his house key, a thought that had him pat down his pocket for his keys after almost every time he had crossed the threshold of an elevator. He stepped over the non-gap, his keys the least of his concerns. Keeping one hand on the wall for balance, the other still clutching his chest, he leaned his way into motion. He staggered forward, the door to his apartment seeming farther away than it ever had, and tried to clear his head. Was he having a heart attack? He knew if he was going to have any chance of escape, he had damn well better not be having a heart attack, so for his own sake he was just going to have to be having a panic attack. A bad one, no doubt. The panic attack to end all panic attacks. The realization-that-they-really-were-all-out-to-get-him of panic attacks. A paralyzing, monstrously, horribly bad panic attack.

But a panic attack nonetheless. He slid his hand down the wall in front of himself to keep from falling over, when he remembered there was an alternative to heading back to his apartment: there was the stairs! He was flooded with a rush of adrenaline that was so foreign to his system after many months of not leaving his apartment it almost knocked him out. He stood up and looked through the small window that led into the stairwell, fearing that it might end in an inky black void instead of a brightly lit escape route. He could see the stairs through the window, so he pushed the door open to make a run for it. It wasn't much of a run, looking on the surveillance cameras like an old horror-movie zombie on the prowl after smelling some brains nearby. He grabbed the handrail to steady himself, and headed down the stairs. He rounded the corner at the bottom of the first flight, already breathing heavy. He lowered his head to catch his breath. He attributed his lack of breath to the endless cigarette bender he had been on in his apartment. After he caught his breath he raised his head and continued his descent, but he fell to his knees when he discovered his way was blocked by a brick wall. He was sure it had not been there before, despite having never taken the stairs down, and he let out a low moan. Heatley picked himself up, turned around, and ran up the stairs with the same lack of coordination that had assisted him in his descent, passed the landing that went to his apartment, and headed for the roof. This time, much to his relief, he was faced with a door in front instead of a brick wall. He had previously, on occasion, had the company helicopter pick him up or drop him off at the roof of the building, so he had expected the door. What he hadn't expected was for the door to be chained shut. He hit the bar to try and open it anyway, but the chain prevented the door from opening more than a few inches. It was enough for Frank to see his helicopter sitting on its landing pad. The trouble was that it was sitting on top of the building across the street, which looked suspiciously like the one he was living in the last time he checked.

Heatley moved back down the stairs knowing he was trapped in what, despite all appearances to the contrary, could not possibly be his apartment. He tried to be silent, tried to control his trembling, and tried to think of another way out. He thought about calling Joan to ask her for help, but he knew she must be in on whatever was going on and couldn't be trusted. There must be another way out, he thought. There must be somebody he could call, or some way to get the attention of somebody who wasn't in on whatever he was pitted against. He went grudgingly back into the hallway that led to the apartment that wasn't his regardless of how many of his possessions were there, laid out exactly as they were at his place. He stared at the door to the apartment for a moment, fishing in his robe for the key, which he clasped tightly in a shaking palm. Each step he took towards the door he wished he was taking in the opposite direction, but he had exhausted all the possibilities that way and was going to have to find another way out. Maybe there was a way out behind one of the other doors that he had locked shut all those months ago, even though they couldn't be the same doors. He was breathing heavier as he took the final steps up to the door and then held out the key with a shaking, sweaty hand, repeatedly missing the keyhole. He tried to hold the key with both hands, but as luck would have it his left hand was as shaky as his right, and at the best of times wasn't half as coordinated. It took almost two minutes before he was able to calm himself down enough to get the key in.

He let himself into the apartment, grabbed a cigarette, then sat down and had a good fret while attempting to light it. After he had decided that he was too shaky to use his lighter, he dragged himself to the kitchen to light it off the toaster. He found himself dreading the kitchen more than he thought he would. It was the first room in which he had discovered something was amiss in the perfect world he had constructed for himself. His bubble of solitude had been burst there earlier that morning and he hadn't even realized it. He pressed the lever on the toaster down, and waited for the elements to heat up, leaning backwards against the counter and looking around the room. "How long?" he asked the toaster as he leaned over it to light his cigarette. "How long have I been held here?" The toaster didn't respond, of course, but it did singe his beard when some stray hairs found their way over to the elements. The kitchen was simultaneously filled with the smell of cigarette smoke and burned hair, and Heatley pulled his face away from the toaster, hoping to get away from the odours. One of the smells he brought with himself intentionally, and the other was constantly connected to his face. The smell of the singed hair was really getting to him, and he decided that before he did anything else, he was going to have to trim them from his beard. He opened a drawer filled with kitchen utensils, grabbed out a large pair of scissors, and headed for the bathroom.

The bathroom was an immense affair, not when compared to the rest of the original apartment, but grossly out of proportion to the remnants that Heatley left for himself to live in. The bathtub could seat two comfortably, and three if they were all very friendly. Heatley had spent a lot of time in that tub, but always alone. He grabbed a handful of singed beard, and as he was cutting it off, he noticed that his custom made, tub-mounted dinner tray still held a martini glass from last night, and a plate half-full of browned apple slices. Susan hadn't been in today, he realized, and as he was throwing the bits of toasted beard into the garbage can beside the toilet that he realized just how far the conspiracy against him must be running. Joan had been with him for five years now, and Susan had worked for him at least a month before he had shut himself in, which meant that both of them had to be in on it. He wondered if there was anyone that he could trust. He looked at the scrag of uneven beard he had left on his face, and decided that the rest of it could wait. For the time being, his biggest priority had to be getting out of the apartment. As he put the scissors down beside the sink, he heard the elevator bell go off, and some commotion in the hallway. He fought to stop himself from calling out for help, covering his mouth and running out of the bathroom instead. He realized he didn't have anywhere else to go and ran back into the bathroom, where he tried futilely to conceal himself behind the door.

"Mr. Heatley?" a voice called out to him. It sounded convincingly like a concerned voice. "Frank Heatley, it's the police! Are you in here?" Heatley didn't know whether or not he could trust the voice, but not knowing was maddening. Was it really the police? The only way to find out was to go to them, he thought. Besides, it wasn't like they weren't going to find him in the bathroom, whoever they were.

"I'm here!" he called out as he stepped out of the bathroom. He saw two policemen and two paramedics in the front hall. He ran towards them as if he were trying to outrun the flood of relief that was overcoming him.

One of the officers stepped forward and grabbed him gently by the arm. "Are you okay, Mr. Heatley?" He shook his head in an emphatic 'No', and the paramedics ushered him back to his couch, where they started making him uncomfortable in various ways to determine if he was okay.

A needle was brought out, and the paramedic squirted some liquid out the end of it, just as Heatley had seen it done in the movies and on television a thousand times before. His sleeve was pushed back up his arm, and he heard a voice say "This is just something to help you relax." Heatley tried to pull his arm away, but it was held in place by the other paramedic. He quickly became so relaxed he was unable to remain conscious.

The Hospital Room.

Heatley awoke in a blurry room with an intrusive light which prevented him from being able to make much sense of anything. Parts of him didn't feel right. After a few moments he realized it was his vision that was blurry, and not the room itself, and as things came into focus after his drug-induced nap, he found he was lying in a hospital bed. The parts of him that didn't feel right were connected to hospital machinery, most of which was beyond his comprehension. Some of the machines displayed numbers, others made beeping noises, and some displayed lines that certainly had some medical significance, but meant nothing to him. The intrusive light, it turned out, was sunlight coming in through four large windows which covered much of two of the walls in the room, and met in the corner. He looked around the rest of the room to find a nurse changing a clear bag filled with clear fluid that was being fed to him through a clear tube.

"Ergh abbed oo ee?" he asked, hoping he sounded more coherent to her than he did to himself. She turned her attention from the bag she had just hung up to him, and smiled as she leaned over and removed something from his mouth. He tried to cough his voice back to normality, and was about to ask a series of pressing questions when his eyes completed their journey back into focus, and began to have a roam around his nurse. She looked as if her uniform had been purchased somewhere disreputable and had been unavailable in her size. There was a large red "H" on each breast pocket, and she excused herself as she leaned over him, apparently having carelessly placed something important directly behind him which she now needed. She stood back up and handed him the remote control to a large television set that hung on one of the walls that wasn't built out of glass.

"Welcome back, Mr. Heatley. How are you feeling?" She smiled a bright-red lipsticked smile at him, pulled a thermometer out from her cleavage, and pressed it into his mouth without waiting for his response. "I'll tell Dr. Edmunds you're awake. He'll be relieved." She waited a few moments and pulled the thermometer out, looked at it briefly, and stuck it back in her bosom without wiping it off. "You've had quite an ordeal, Mr. Heatley, but it looks like you'll be fine." Heatley turned his head and watched her as she spun around and walked away. He couldn't help but notice, among other things, that she was wearing stiletto heels, and thought it to be an unconventional choice of footwear for a nurse. *Then again*, he thought, *the rest of that outfit isn't fit for nursing much more than my imagination.*

He heard the door click quietly shut behind her, and he sat up to look out the window. Was it all a dream? More likely I'm dreaming now he thought, judging by the outfit his nurse was wearing. He tried to get a decent look out the window, but the array of wires, suction cups, and various other things attached to him prevented him from doing much more than a feeble half-sit-up. He found a control panel for the bed built into the armrest at his right-hand side, and pressed the button that had the diagram he voted most likely to have him sitting up in a comfortable position. Some gentle whirring noises accompanied the transition of the bed, and he found himself looking out at the city. He had some difficulty orienting himself as to where in the city he was, as the only window he had looked through in the better part of the last year had been his skylight. He was relieved and a little surprised when he determined his view from the hospital bed was approximately what he thought it should be from a window in the hospital.

The door opened briefly, the sound of telephones ringing and some shuffling around broke the relative tranquility of the room. "Good morning, Mr. Heatley," Dr. Edmunds said as he entered the room. He looked over a clipboard as he approached the bed. "You're looking better today."

Heatley stared out the window, and the events of the - what was it? An hour? A day? A week since he had been conscious last? - began to come back to him, and he began to panic. He remembered the deception used against him, the conspiracy he suspected, and the terror he had felt at not being able to leave his apartment. "I need a cigarette and a stiff drink."

Edmunds smiled at him. "Of course, Mr. Heatley. There's a balcony right there," he said, gesturing at one of the windows, which turned out to be a set of sliding doors, "and I'll have Dora - your nurse - come in and unhook you from the machines. We can talk about what happened when you feel up to it, Mr. Heatley."

"That floozy? She didn't look like much of a nurse to me," Heatley said as he began to pull some of the wires away himself.

"On the contrary, Mr. Heatley. I believe that you'll find yourself in very capable hands with her," Edmunds' voice trailed off a little, appearing to be lost in some happy memory. "Very, very capable." He began to help Heatley remove the wires, absentmindedly.

Heatley was uncomfortable with what appeared to be the aroused reminiscing of his doctor, but he allowed Edmunds to remove the tube in his arm that was actually held in by a needle. He helped himself out of the bed. He felt the air on his backside, and looked back to find it exposed by the gown. "Doc," he said, "I'm sure you know where my smokes are?"

Edmunds pulled himself out of his daydreaming. "Oh, yes. Of course, Mr. Heatley. You'll find your cigarettes and lighter at the table on the balcony, just as you requested." He crossed the room and opened the sliding glass doors for Heatley, then stepped out onto the balcony himself, mulling over the ethical nature of encouraging his patients' bad habits like this. Although he was against smoking himself, the Heatley Company had provided him with very specific instructions about the care that was to be provided to their benefactor, and he was informed that the company's donations to the hospital could feasibly dry up if their demands were not met. Right down to the the location of the hospital room. Right down to the uniform, body type, and demeanour of the nurse attending to him.

Heatley stepped out the door to the balcony, and Edmunds closed it behind him, then stepped away from the old man who picked up his vice. "Smoke, Doc?" Heatley said, proffering the pack to the young doctor.

"Thank you, Mr. Heatley, but no," and then, out of a sense of duty to his patient, added, "They're very bad for you, and that's putting it mildly."

"Ballsy, Doc. Ballsy. I'm remembering things a bit better, now," Heatley said, tapping the side of his head with his index finger. "This place is exactly like I said I wanted a hospital room to be like, should I ever need one again, and the nurse. I mean, she's... wow. I even forgot why I was here for a minute. Nice job."

Edmunds leaned against the wall, feeling the suspicion coming off of Heatley and unsure of how he should deal with it. "Yes, Mr. Heatley. Everything is as close to your exact specifications as we could possibly manage." He was uncomfortable, and hoping for a segue into a conversation he could manipulate more easily. "I do apologize for breaking protocol by mentioning the ill-effects of smoking, but I am a doctor, and-" he wasn't sure if he was convincing, "and I only have your best interest in mind, Mr. Heatley. Speaking of which," the words stumbled out, and Edmunds hoped they didn't seem forced, "we do need to talk to you about what has happened to you."

Heatley blew a cloud of smoke which got caught in the wind before it had a chance to intimidate the young doctor. "You mean about how they abducted me and kept me prisoner?"

Edmunds shifted uncomfortably. "Yes, Mr. Heatley. We need to talk about that. You say you were taken prisoner in your own house?"

Heatley's eyes began darting around, looking to catch the paranoia before it could hit him. His voice dropped to a whisper. "They took me. They changed the outside."

"And when was the last time you had been outside, Mr. Heatley?" Edmunds asked, grabbing a pen and taking notes on a clipboard.

"It's been-" he reached back to grab a notebook from his back pocket, but grabbed his bare ass instead. "I don't know how long I've been here. Where's my pants? My notebook is in my pants."

"They're just inside, Mr. Heatley. I can get them for you if you like." Edmunds wanted to get away from Heatley as quickly as possible. "Or, you can just estimate for me. Was it winter out the last time you left your apartment?"

Heatley thought about this for a few moments. "Fall," he said, stubbing his cigarette out clumsily in the ashtray. The leaves were all yellow and red."

"And you shut your doors?"

"Yes."

"Boarded up your windows?"

"Yes."

"And it says here you even had deadbolts put on the other doors within your apartment so you only had a few rooms left that you were dwelling in, and your only natural light came from a skylight in the apartment?"

"Well, yes, but–"

"And you now believe that your own company kidnapped you and changed the outside?"

Heatley didn't like the way that the doctor sounded as if he had already reached a conclusion. "It's not like that!" he protested.

"But Mr. Heatley, you say that this mysterious group of conspirators, including your–" he consulted some papers on the clipboard, "personal assistant, the man who answered for room service, the operator of your building and your cleaning lady, kept you confined to your room for an undetermined amount of time, possibly as long as nine months, and you didn't realize it because you were a shut-in who was–" he looked back at the papers, "not afraid to, but just unwilling to deal with the outside world anymore."

"It's–"

"It's not like that. Yes, I understand, Mr. Heatley." He took a few more notes, then clicked his pen closed and placed it back the pocket of his suit jacket. "I would like you to talk to somebody."

Heatley grabbed his pack of cigarettes and took another one out. "You mean a shrink?" he said through clenched teeth as he flicked his lighter open. He lit the cigarette, and snapped the lighter closed again. "Forget it. I'm not crazy."

"Mr. Heatley, most of the people in therapy are not crazy. They just need someone to talk to, as I believe you do after your lengthly solitude." Edmunds looked as if he were getting ready to leave, smoothing out his jacket and tucking the clipboard back under his arm. "It doesn't even have to be a psychiatrist, Mr. Heatley. Let me get your assistant in here, and you can talk to her."

Heatley shook his head. "No way is that traitorous bitch coming anywhere near me."

"Mr. Heatley, while you are in this hospital, you are in my care and your health is of the utmost concern to me. I assure you, you will be fine. Now, shall it be Joan, a psychiatrist, or perhaps some medication until you've managed to calm down?" Edmunds slid the glass door open, and paused to wait for an answer.

Heatley hung his head, resting it against his palm, and not wanting to answer the doctor at all. "Fine. Joan, then. Send Joan over, but," he looked up at the doctor, "send in that pretty nurse and a bottle of scotch first." He held up the intravenous tube that was connected to his arm. "Connect it to this damned thing if you have to."

"Yes, Mr. Heatley. And thank you." Edmunds slid the patio doors closed, and left the room.

A few moments later, Dora came back in with a bottle of scotch, a bag of ice, two tumblers, and a mischievous look on her face that Heatley might have appreciated more if he wasn't staring quite so intently below it. "Mr. Heatley requires some special care?" she said as she crossed the room. She leaned over to place the tumblers on the table, grabbed a few cubes of ice for each glass, and poured both glasses half-full.

Heatley watched her with an increasing appreciation for the best health care money could buy. "Are you allowed to drink on the job?" he asked, with one eyebrow arching its way up his forehead.

"I've been hired on as one of your private care specialists, Mr. Heatley," she said. "Or didn't you recognize the uniform?" She pointed with a bright-red fingernail at each of the the double "H"s that were embroidered on what Heatley assumed were her double "D"s. "Should something happen to me again and again, and I were too tired to work, there's plenty more where I came from."

Heatley took this as the invitation to approach her that she had intended, and he grabbed her in an animalistic embrace. His attention had been focussed on her exposed flesh, and through his tunnel-vision he failed to see the syringe she produced from her cap. He barely felt it break his skin, and he was well on his way to unconsciousness before she could stop him from falling. He fell to the floor with a meaty flop. Blood trickled from his nose. Dora grabbed a napkin to wipe his drool off of her breast, then grabbed one of the tumblers and downed it in one gulp. She looked at the old man on the floor, and poked at him with the toe of one of her shoes. She shook her head at him and said "Too easy" before grabbing the other tumbler and the bottle, and headed back out the door to the sound of applause and cat-calls. "Yeah, yeah. Naughty nurses," she said. "I hate you guys. Somebody get me my clothes. I'm taking the rest of the day off." She almost cracked a smile as half of the male staff stumbled over each other to help her out. Almost.

The Caning.

Being paid to not work all day was something Sherman always believed only happened to executives, men in expensive suits, and people who could get away with never working another day in their lives anyway. He was none of those things, and had no idea what to do with this extra holiday that had suddenly been bestowed upon him. After he was tired from skateboarding all morning, he couldn't think of anything better to do than buy some beer and think about where it was he was going to drink it.

The man working the counter at the liquor store had a smug 'The skateboard in your hand means you are underage. This is a no-brainer' look on his face, and it took a few minutes of careful scrutiny at the identification Sherman had produced from his wallet before he begrudgingly allowed him to purchase a fifteen-pack of Pilsner, which he tucked into his backpack. Sherman stepped out of the store and walked down to the nearest one-way street headed west. He lived further east, and the one-way traffic would allow him to see any police cars headed his way. He dug through his backpack and took out one of the cans, opened it and began the walk home.

Front Street wasn't the front of anything that Sherman could see. The front of the houses and shops were all visible from the street, but the same could be said of virtually every street he could think of, so he doubted that had anything to do with the name. Maybe it was a front for something else, he thought. Maybe this was the place where the mob could open up a laundromat and use it as a front for whatever other business they were doing there that had nothing to do with stealing one sock out of every load and then selling them by the pound to second-hand stores. The thought was fleeting and Sherman poked several holes in his theory before he reached the first intersection along his way, Seymour Street. He quickly tipped the Pilsner upside-down to empty its contents, making sure that his lips were in their way, and threw the empty can into a garbage bin on the corner. At the other side of the intersection, there was a public recycling container, offering a place for more environmentally conscious pedestrians to dispose of their containers. Sherman looked back across the street to the bin he had just tossed the Pilsner, and thought about going back for it. Why could he never remember that the city had installed the recycling containers a few years ago? He looked around to determine the police situation again, then grabbed himself another beer from his bag before continuing down the street.

The block was mostly filled with homes that had been renovated and rezoned into businesses, the kind of area that blurs the line between residential and business areas when heading toward the downtown core of a city. Heritage homes that many people dreamed of living in had cheap neon signs hanging in the windows advertising a nail salon here, a lawyer here, a notary public there. Sherman doubted that he would trust a law office that used cheap, tacky neon signs to advertise its services, but when he thought of the sleazy lawyers and private investigators from the movies, he understood. This is what their offices looked like in real life. He was half-inclined to walk into one of the lawyer's offices and claim that he wanted to talk about breaking his contract with his employer, just to see if they could be as sleazy on the inside as they were in the movies, but left that idea as something he would just have to laugh about with his friends later on, probably without ever going through with it.

The neon sign theme continued down for another few blocks. Neon church signs, a plague on salvation, offered to get you off the hook in ways that even the lawyers couldn't. That the sleazy lawyers and seedy churches were so close together was not a coincidence, but more a natural merger of convenience between the two. Much as the jokes regarding the locations of veterinary clinics and Chinese restaurants prevailed among suburban kids, this merger had happened over the course of the last several years without anyone taking notice. Sherman didn't know why he rounded the corner onto Church Street; it defied the conventional wisdom regarding only walking down one-way streets with open booze. He turned left at the corner, anyhow, and found himself so distracted by the gaudy neon signs that he didn't see Old Blue until it was too late.

The cane smash across his shins half a second before he would have run into her, had she not stepped aside. She had seen him coming, of course. She moved about the city with a predatory disposition that belied her age. Although she had seen him coming, and realized that he was not going to notice her in time to move out of the way, it ran against what she believed to be right for her to get out of the way of somebody else. She believed that she had the right of way, at all times, no matter what, even when petty things like the law came and had its representatives in blue explain to her that she was wrong. She believed her way was right, and that if there was a discrepancy between what she knew to be the answer and what anyone else told her, a divine cane-to-the-shins would just have to help sort things out. Edna had just the cane for the job, which she had named Bessie at some point, for reasons she could no longer recall. What made things worse for Sherman was that she also believed she recently had all her beliefs completely validated. Because of her due diligence and the conviction she had in her actions, she was going to see the return of a prophet at the very church she attended. As such, this was no ordinary whack to the shins that she gave to Sherman. This was a step-to-the-side-and-take-up-a-comfortable-stance-complete-with-two-practice-swings-before-letting-loose-with-righteous-fury type of swing.

Whoosh.

Crack!

"Aaaaaaaaaaaaaaaaaaaaaaaaaaaaaaaaaaaaaaa!!!!!!" Sherman fell to the ground and dropped his beer, curling up to grab his shins. "You crazy bit-" -whack- "Aaaaaaaaaaaaaaaaaaa!" The second blow had been been directed at his shins as well, but he had unfortunately covered them up with his hands, so his knuckles took the brunt of it. He felt two of them break, and beer started to soak into his hair as it poured out on the sidewalk. His screams must have been enough to satisfy the old lady, because he could hear her heels clicking down the sidewalk as she walked away, humming something that he didn't bother trying to recognize.

Sherman stood back up, and looked at his throbbing, mangled fingers. He could tell they had broken when they were hit, and didn't need to see the awkward angles they were splayed at to know he was headed for the hospital instead of somewhere fun for the day. He tried to support the broken digits with his other hand, but he even that much contact with them hurt, and decided to let the already swelling pieces of his right hand be pressed on by gravity alone. He held his hand limply in front of himself. As it turned out, gravity was a force strong enough to cause his fingers pain, and he resorted to cupping one hand with the other again. He was still dazed from his encounter with Old Blue, and he wondered if he should plan some sort of personal retribution or if he should just admit to the police that he had been attacked by an elderly woman. The hospital was only a few blocks away, and Sherman headed toward it with a grimace on his face while attempting to limp on both legs.

As Sherman rounded the last corner before the hospital, which by fluke had been built diplomatically equidistant from the churches and the law offices, he felt relief and dread that the pain he would be feeling soon would be related to the straightening of his fingers, and he was so focussed on this that he didn't see Joan coming out of her office building. She, in turn, had her nose buried in a file she was reading, and did not notice Sherman until they had collided. Sherman's hand knocked the file out of Joan's hands, and Joan's file sent a bolt of pain running through Sherman's hand. Sherman almost screamed again, but couldn't muster another one up at the moment. Instead, he bent down onto one knee and threw up, the mess of beer and bile landing on Joan's paperwork.

Joan stared at him, unsure of what to do. "It would have been more traditional to offer to pick that up for me," she said while battling her gag reflex, which was trying to show its appreciation for what Sherman had done.

Sherman kept his broken hand tucked into his chest, and picked up the file by one dry corner, sickly fluid pouring off it as it drooped down, and offered it to her. A passer-by stopped to take a picture of the boy with the pained grimace on his face and the malformed hand who was down on one knee offering a vomit-covered document to the beautiful girl in the business suit who looked as if she were about to chastise him for everything that he was. "Bad Monkey!" was the most popular caption attached to the picture while it circulated the Internet for a few months. Sherman and Joan both received it from virtually everyone they knew.

Sherman let the folder drop to the ground, then stood back up and wobbled at Joan with his face pale and his jaw agape. Joan went from thinking he was homeless and being disgusted with him to realizing that he was just a skateboarder. She remained disgusted with him. He could have been wearing a three piece suit and stepped out of a Rolls Royce and she would still have been disgusted with him. After all, he had just thrown up on her file and tried to hand it back to her. She wasn't completely heartless, though. She saw from the pain on his face and his mangled fingers that he needed to see a doctor. "Oh, dear. Come with me," she said as she grabbed him by the shoulder and started to lead him away. She looked down at the folder that lay miserably on the sidewalk, then into the window of the Heatley building. Kelly Davenport, a new co-worker, was looking out his office window and laughing at her. She pointed at him and then down at the folder. He shook his head 'No' at her and she nodded 'Yes' back at him. He hung his head down, grabbed a garbage bag and went in search of some latex gloves. "I'll take you to the hospital." Sherman wondered whether this offer would have been extended to him had their encounter been further than a block from the hospital. "Are you okay?" she asked feebly. "What happened to you?"

Sherman wasn't feeling up to answering questions at the moment, but he knew he wouldn't have much choice when he got to the hospital. He thought now was as good a time as any to come up with a story that didn't involve being assaulted by a senior citizen. What should be the cause of his injury? "I g-got m-mugged," he said.

Joan looked him over, observing that he still had his backpack, his skateboard, and a chain led into his back pocket, indicating a high probability that he was still in possession of his wallet. "Mugged. Okay. Well, let's go," she said. She made a motion as if she were going to put her arm around him, but pulled it back before she actually touched him.

They walked to the hospital, Joan looking over her shoulder to make sure that Kelly was doing his distasteful duty. He was kneeling beside the vomit-covered folder with his sleeves rolled up, one latex-gloved hand holding a small garbage can, the other hovering over the mess, trying to figure out the logistics of lift and spillage. His tie had been removed and replaced over his mouth and nose as best he could, and the top button of his shirt had been undone. Satisfied that the sensitive files would be protected from the prying eyes of whoever might pick up such a thing in the streets, Joan turned her attention back to Sherman just in time to miss her coworker losing his battle with his own gag reflex, and soiling what his mother had thought to be a pretty snappy tie when she had seen it on sale. He removed the tie and threw it in the garbage can, then picked up the folder and threw it in as well, as disgusted with himself as he was with the situation. He went back into the office, and attempted to pass the garbage can off to the janitor, who refused to accept it on account of its unsanitary nature.

Joan didn't have to try and make small talk with Sherman for very long as they were only a block away from the hospital, and she was unconcerned with what he had to say anyway. Had her folder been handed back to her sans-regurgitated covering, it was unlikely she would have personally walked him to the hospital at all, but the opportunity to pass on the more distasteful of the two chores had presented itself, and she had acted on it. "When opportunity knocks, you answer the damn door," her father had been fond of saying. She had learned little more than Sherman's name when they got to the front entrance of the hospital.

Sherman was amazed at how much he was reminded of walking into a shopping centre. From the security guard to the information desk, the food court to the gift shops and coffee bar, he felt the grasp of consumerism reaching for him even when he should have been thinking of anything except what it was he was going to buy. "It's like a bloody mall in here," he said to Joan, who was busy reading something on her cell phone. "It's gross."

"Yeah, gross," she said, flipping her phone closed and dropping it into her bag. "Do you want a coffee while you're waiting?" She began digging through her bag. "I'm dying for a latte." She pulled out her wallet, and got in line at the coffee bar. "Go and get yourself started, and I'll be there in a minute. What do you want?"

Sherman was a little to the left of being impressed with his rescuer/assailant, and told her "Coffee. Black," through clenched teeth before heading off to get in a line of his own.

"That's a lot of no fun," Joan said under her breath. "Hell, at least he's a cheap date."

"What was that, ma'am?" piped out of the girl behind the counter, skinny, pigtailed, freckled, and looking to Joan every bit too young to be working anything except the see-saw at a playground.

Joan liked to think of herself as a mature individual, but she did harbour some resentment when it came to being called "Ma'am", a title which she still equated with somebody much older than she was. "I'll have a small black coffee and a double-tall-sugar-free-vanilla-latte, with lots of foam, cinnamon sprinkles on top, and make it really hot, but not burnt, please." She wished that her order could have a simple name, like

"Ted" or "The Yuppie", but despite her idea submissions to various coffee companies, complete with promises to fuel up with them instead of their competition for ever and ever, she never heard back from any of them. Every now and again, she would look up at the menu boards in vain for one of her name ideas, but she did so less frequently now, having all but given up. Her last vestige of hope came from thinking that one day, one of the people at one of the coffee shops she frequented would just know her drink and give it to her, but the employee turnover at the local shops prevented this dream from being realized. She handed over eight dollars absent-mindedly, shaking her head at the offer of any change from the freckled girl, and walked over to the bar to await her drinks.

Her phone rang, playing a cheap-sounding rendition of a piece of classical music that came pre-installed on her phone. She didn't know the name of the piece, but she felt that it made her appear more cultured when her phone rang. She dug through her bag until she found it, which took precisely two seconds longer than she had the ringer set up before she could locate it. The display told her that she had one missed call: Work. Of course it was work. She thought about calling back to tell them that she was at the hospital with a boy who had broken his hand, but thought better of it. If it was important, they would leave a message, and she was reasonably sure they could deal without hearing back from her until she returned, and she wasn't sure how much she wanted to return to work anyhow. The drinks appeared on the counter while she had been fussing with her phone. She grabbed them and went over to the waiting area to look for Sherman.

She found him at the reception desk, where he was telling the woman who was working there exactly how he felt about being asked to fill out forms when he was obviously incapable of holding a pen at the moment. Joan stepped in before the conversation could escalate into something that she really didn't feel like being in the middle of. "I'll help him out with this," she told the bitter face that was only visible by looking over the top of the counter. Heaven forbid she would actually stand up and face people who were in need of assistance. She grabbed the forms with one hand and Sherman by the backpack with the other and led him over to a few empty chairs. She sat him down and began going over the list with him. She clicked her pen open and started at the top. "Full name," she said.

To her surprise, Sherman snatched the papers from her and said "My name is Sherman Klein, and I'm left-handed." He reached over and took her pen from her as well.

Joan watched him start to fill out the forms. "Why... I mean... What was the big deal with the receptionist then?"

Sherman looked up from his scribbling. Apparently, even though his left hand was the one he would normally have used for writing, he hadn't practiced that particular activity enough, as he had the penmanship of a child. "It's the principal of the thing," he told her. "When she asked me why I was here, and I showed her my broken fingers and said 'I broke my fingers', she handed me these forms and asked me to fill them out."

"And you could have filled them out no problem," Joan said plainly.

"Yes, but she had no way of knowing that I'm a lefty. This hurts like hell, and I don't think that anybody dealing with pain like this in their fingers should be asked to fill out paperwork." Sherman was obviously feeling hard done by.

Joan tried to hide her contempt for what she was being told, with marginal success. Having better things to do with her day than hang out in the hospital waiting room, and figuring the distasteful chore of cleaning up the files from on the street was done by now, she began work on her exit strategy. "So, you'll be fine here, then?" she asked. "Do you need me to stick around?"

Sherman looked up from the paperwork, the pain in his fingers twisting the grin on his face into a grimace. "Yeah, I'll be fine, but can you tell me one thing?"

Joan was digging for her phone again, and didn't look up as she replied. "Sure, what is it?" She hoped that this ruffian wasn't going to ask her out.

"Does my medical coverage through the Heatley Company start right away? I just signed my papers this morning." He pulled his copy of the contract out of his bag, and passed the wrinkled papers over to her.

Joan stopped rummaging through her bag, and gave Sherman a perplexed look. Did this guy really work for the company? "I, umm..."

she began, trying to hide her surprise. She took the papers from him, and looked them over. "There's usually a waiting period for that sort of thing," she told him. She glanced over the contract to make sure that all the necessary signature blocks had been signed, the initial boxes were initialed, and the date boxes dated. It looked legitimate, and it also looked like the Heatley Company had purchased an adult video store. She suddenly felt self-conscious. Just reading the words adult video store, and being with this person who worked there made her feel as if she had done something sleazy.

"Yeah, but I've been working there for long enough to have coverage, it's just that you guys haven't owned it for very long." He finished with the hospital forms and handed Joan's pen back to her. She tried not to be too obvious about wiping it off before she put it back in her purse. Sherman got up and took the forms back to the receptionist, who looked them over quickly before telling him to go have a seat and someone would see him shortly.

Sherman returned to his chair to find Joan standing up, looking like she was going to be ready to leave as soon as she could come up with an excuse that didn't sound like she just didn't want to be there anymore. "Taking off then, are ya?"

"Well, it looks like I'm not going to be able to do you any more good here, and I do have to get back to work. They'll be waiting for me. I'm kind of-"

"Don't sweat the excuses, Joan. I'll be fine," he told her. "But can you see if I do qualify for any sort of benefits for this?" he said. He held up his twisted fingers as if she might have needed a reminder as to what he was talking about.

"Sure. No problem," she told him. Rooting around in her purse for another moment, she produced a business card and handed it to him. "You can call me on this number and I'll get the answers for you." He took the card from her and she tried to be subtle about wiping her hands off by smoothing out her suit jacket, which she knew she was going to go home and change in case it had any funky smells or pieces of anything undesirable on it from their earlier encounter. The encounter flashed into her memory and she immediately decided that she needed to have a shower and send her clothes out to the dry cleaner. She hadn't decided whether she would ever pick them back up.

After pretending to read the card with interest, Sherman put it into his pocket, hoping it would remain intact so he could get back in touch with her. "Thanks for walking me down here," he told her. "And for the coffee," he added. He wasn't entirely sure if this woman would be considered to be his boss. Certainly she was higher on the food chain than he was, but she was still somebody's assistant, he thought. Still a flunky. He rented out porn for the company, and she picked up the dry cleaning. Didn't she? She probably got him the coffee because it was what she was used to doing for other people. Just a mindless corporate drone, doing the mindless work that the bigwigs couldn't be bothered to do for themselves. Sherman found himself feeling contempt for her, not because of who she was, but because she probably got paid a lot more than he did, and the jobs she did were most likely mundane and easy compared to most of the minimum wage employees of the Heatley Company. He didn't think any of this thought process showed on his face, but he hoped that if it did, it was convincingly disguised as pain.

Of course, Joan watched his face contort in thought and wondered what was ticking away in his mind. *He's probably excited that I gave him my number, the little pervert,* she thought, feeling a moment's regret that she had given him her personal card, rather than the generic Heatley Company contact cards she had on her. "Well," she said awkwardly, "I do have to get back to work. Take care, Sherman," she extended her hand in what she thought was a friendly gesture, and found herself blushing when his eyebrow shot up and his face contorted into a full-blown Billy Idol of a sneer. He held up his mangled hand, and in the most insulting gesture Joan had ever seen, he extended his broken middle-finger at her, a bruised and swollen digit that shook with the pain and effort required to extend it as far as it would go. Although the movement itself was a failure, the meaning behind it was an epic success in Sherman's opinion, as it caused Joan to leave the waiting room as quickly as she could manage. Sherman was just about to go to the bathroom, where he planned on having another beer, but the moment he had his backpack in his hand, he heard a voice call out "Sherman Klein?" He looked in the direction of the voice, and saw a nurse who might have been working the last two hours of a month-long shift, and probably wouldn't appreciate any smart-ass remarks. He kept his mouth closed as she led him over to a small examining room and told him to wait. The doctor would be with him in a few minutes.

Sherman waited for the door to close, then reached into his bag and grabbed out another beer. Experience told him that the wait in this room would be just as long if not longer than the wait in the main waiting room, so he should probably try to relax and enjoy his stay a little bit. He was just leaning back into the chair when the door opened again without so much as a single knock and the overworked nurse made another appearance. "I just forgot my- WHAT THE HELL?" Sherman watched her eyes go from the beer in his hand to his open backpack, where she saw the rest of his stash. "Alright, you little shit. Give it up. Now." She didn't wait for him to comply, instead swiping the open beer from his hands and reaching into his bag and deftly picking out the rest of the case. "Little bastards," she said to the door as she turned back to leave the room. The typical smart-ass smirk that Sherman would usually be sporting was nowhere to be seen. The pain in his hand and the loss of his beer had rendered it temporarily inert. He reached into another, smaller pocket and retrieved a deck of cards, hoping to play some solitaire while he was waiting, but realized as soon as he had the deck out that there wasn't a chance in hell he was going to be able to shuffle it.

"Damn."

Edna's Disappearance.

Edna was elated as she headed back to her apartment. With no appointments that day, neither doctors, hairdressers, nor church, she was free to do whatever she wanted, and what she wanted to do was to call the other ladies and tell them what she had heard. She didn't have a cellular phone, claiming that she didn't hold with such things. Truth be told, she didn't understood how they worked and wasn't prone to embracing change. Her phone at home, a dark red rotary job, was connected to an answering machine that could tell her who had called. It even had a little display on it that would tell her how many messages were waiting for her, so she didn't even have to pick up the phone if the light told her that there were "0" messages. Today the light was flashing "1" at her.

She took off her shoes and coat in favour of some slippers and a sweater. She held up her cane, inspecting it for any damage that might have been caused by any of the wayward shins it had come into contact with, or any bloodstains that might rub off on anything else she owned. It was clean, but she put it back into her cane basket and withdrew another one from it. She then dipped her fingers into the basin of holy water and flicked her fingers at everything that had been outside. Satisfied that everything that had been soiled was now pure again, she made her way over to the telephone table, sat down, and pressed the listen button on the answering machine. Static popped its way out of the antiquated speaker, followed by a high-pitched, warbling beep. The message came a few moments after. "ongratulations," the voice began, "You have been randomly chosen as the winner of a trip for two, for an Atlantic cruise." Edna's ears perked up and her heart sang out. This was, hands down, the best day of her life. It was a sign from God saying thank you to her for being one of the devout. It was a bonus reward, in addition to the one she was sure to receive when she arrived in heaven, where she would surely arrive to cheering and fanfare and ticker tape parades. She felt as if she was going to burst, or float away, or have a heart attack.

Edna picked up the phone and dialled a nine. Her vision was going swimmy, and she felt it was the longest nine she had ever dialled as she waited for the rotary dial to swing back. The next two numbers, a couples of ones, were easier but she wasn't feeling any relief from this. Having completed the dialling, she reached for a cigarette while she waited for an answer. After what seemed like ages, the other end picked up "9-1-1. What is your emergency?" the voice on the other end asked her.

Edna had lit the cigarette to try and calm herself down, and didn't immediately reply to the woman as it would only have her think more intently about what she was pretty sure was a heart attack. Thinking about it would only make her more skittish and panicky than she already was. She figured she should be able to pray her way out of this, and told herself that calling 9-1-1 had been an overreaction, a precautionary measure that was entirely unnecessary, and she just needed to calm down. "I'm fine," she said.

"Are you certain, ma'am?" asked the operator. "Is there someone else with you? Is someone threatening you?"

"No dear," she took another drag of her cigarette. "Just thought I was having a heart attack is all."

"And you're okay now?" There was obvious concern in her voice. "Ma'am, I'm sending out an ambulance to make sure you're alright."

"That won't be necessary, dear. I had a bit of a start, but I had a cigarette to calm myself down and I'll be fine in a minute."

"You had a cigarette to calm yourself down from what you thought might be a heart attack, ma'am?"

"Just to take the edge off, dear."

The sound of fingers tapping on a keyboard could be heard through the receiver. "Ma'am, I've sent out a unit to see you, and I have called your building to ask them to check up on you. They should be at your door in just a few minutes. I'll stay on the line until they get there, ma'am."

Edna shook her head in disbelief. If the building manager found out that she had called 9-1-1 again and it turned out to be a false alarm, again he might finally decide she had become too much of a liability and have her put in a home. A home! Her. Edna Sheldon was not going into a home. Especially not now, knowing what she knew. "I won't," she blurted, and hung up the phone. Although she knew that hanging up the phone wouldn't make the problem go away, there was a part of her that really, honestly, held some hope that the woman on the other end wouldn't make the call to the building or send the ambulance.

The possible ramifications of the phone call she had just made, especially after the incident from earlier this morning, sent Edna into a panic. The building manager had already warned her twice about assaulting his employees. She started feeling worse again, and reached for the phone to call the front desk to tell them everything was okay. There was a knock at the door before she could make the call. "Mrs. Sheldon? This is Stewart, from the front desk. Are you Okay in there?"

"Stewart." Edna muttered, exhaling a fierce cloud of smoke. Edna did not like Stewart. She did not like his thick-framed glasses. She did not appreciate his antics, even though all of her complaints about him had resulted in her being told that he was not acting inappropriately, it was she that was overreacting. She hadn't always felt this way about Stewart. She had quite enjoyed him when she had first met him, but that all changed the day he showed up to pick up his paycheque while wearing a hooded sweatshirt that had a picture of a crucifix with a large red circle around it with a line through it, and the words Bad Religion written in large red letters across the chest. The image of that sweatshirt fixed itself in her mind so vividly she didn't realize her eyes had begun to lose focus. The sound of a key in the lock barely registered with her. The pounding on the door and calling of her name was hardly noticed.

"Mrs. Sheldon!" the voice came again, "Do you have more deadbolts on the inside of this door?" Edna didn't reply. When something finally did penetrate the haze that was overtaking her it was a sound she couldn't place, and would not have been able to recognize even if she wasn't currently preoccupied with thoughts of dying, as she had never had her front door broken down with an axe before.

Stewart was attracting quite a crowd in the hallway, albeit one that wasn't willing to come right out and watch the young man in the suit beat down the crazy old lady the hallway's door with an axe. The witnesses to Stewart's frenzy were all safely behind their own doors, which they had opened just a crack. An eyeball, and in some cases a camera lens, were all that was visible from the hallway, the rest of the tenants' bodies safely protected from harm by the indestructible piece of quarter-inch-thick brass chain that held their doors fast in place. When the paramedics came on the scene, they held their place at the end of the hallway and yelled for Stewart to put down the axe.

Stewart was in mid-swing when he heard the paramedics yelling at him. The axe was over his head, barely missing the ceiling as he swung it, and it occurred to him he must look like a madman. No wonder they didn't come closer. He put down the axe and backed away from it, pointing at the door to Edna's apartment. I've almost got it down!" he called out to them. "Crazy old bat must have six deadbolts on the door!"

The paramedics had already called for backup, and they cautiously approached the door, keeping cautious eyes on Stewart for any further axe-wielding antics. It looked to them as if he was no longer a threat, that he probably was just a kid in a panic, and they began to call for Mrs. Sheldon through the holes in the door.

"Mrs. Sheldon! Are you in there? Are you okay?" they repeated a few times before actually looking through the gaping holes in the door and saw her lying flat on the ground. One of the paramedics reached over to grab the axe and finish breaking the door down, while the other one reached into one of the holes already in the door and lifted a few latches, moved a few deadbolts, and pushed it open.

Edna had not responded to any of the questions they had asked, answered the repeated call backs from the 9-1-1 operator, or acknowledged the noise and commotion of the axe chopping its way through her door. The paramedics had their doubts as to whether or not she was going to make it until they crouched down over her. Her eyes bolted open and she howled "Raaaaaaaaaaaaape!" as loud as she could. It was really, really loud. The paramedics covered their ears and looked about themselves, slightly embarrassed. It was a mistake to take their eyes off her, even for a second, and with a renewed vigour she swung the cane she was still clutching at the paramedic who had been looking into her eyes with a penlight in his hand. He was sent sprawling to the floor. The old blue-haired woman bolted up into a sitting position, and the other paramedic had flashes of The Exorcist running through his mind as her head slowly turned to face him.

Trying as hard as he could to hold in a hysterical fit of laughter, yet afraid to come any closer than the doorway, Stewart yelled into the room. "Nobody's trying to rape you, you stupid old cow!" It wasn't the first time he had called her such a name, but it was the first time he said it to her face instead of gently coughing insults into his hand. It had been his intent to get her attention, to have her forget about her "rapists" and give the men some time to regroup, recover, escape, or perhaps sedate her.

The sound of the elevator bell announcing the arrival of the elevator car on the floor again went unnoticed in the commotion. The various doors in the hallway which had been opened even the tiniest crack all had eyes looking in the other direction, down the hall, because that was where the action had been. Had it been seen in a movie, the music would have changed and the camera would have travelled down the hallway from the commotion to the elevator just before the doors opened, telling the audience that something good was about to happen. The elevator doors opened, revealing five almost identical men in identical suits. Bill Griffin stepped forward, tilting his head as he appraised the situation. A subtle gesture with his hand brought another man forward, who dropped to one knee as he produced a rifle seemingly out of nowhere. He brought the sight up to his eye, and took a quick but careful aim at Stewart. The gesture to bring him forward was also his fire order so he didn't hesitate. He simply made sure he had his shot and he took it without a word.

Stewart braced himself in the doorway, leaning forward with both hands on the door frame, which prevented him from actually being in Edna's apartment. It was a protective posture which allowed him to have his head inside the room while his body remained outside and ready to run back down the hallway if Old Blue should make a move at him. He simply hadn't considered that he might be shot in the ribs by a well-dressed man stepping out of the elevator. It was not the kind of thing that he had ever been concerned with up until the exact moment it happened. He felt the puncture of the needle in between two of his ribs followed quickly by the solid impact of the base of the tranquilizer dart. "Uungh" was all he said, but if the tranquilizer dart hadn't taken effect so quickly, he would have had much more to say. It wouldn't have been anything that could be repeated in polite company.

Having grunted his displeasure, he began succumbing to the chemicals that had been injected into his system. He crumbled into a heap on the floor, his head rolling loosely in the direction of the five men, and although he was barely cognizant of their approach, he thought he was doing pretty well when he tried to yell for help. He was cognizant that nobody responded to his cries, though he didn't know he hadn't been able to produce any more noise than one makes when they drooled. As the room faded to black around him, he watched several pairs of highly-polished shoes step over him.

The paramedics were having what was probably the strangest call of their careers so far. The kid with the axe and the old lady yelling rape before assaulting them had been the stuff of anecdotes told at the bar over drinks after work, but when the kid had suddenly fallen down, and three armed men stepped into the room with two more keeping guard on the place just outside the door, the paramedics suddenly found themselves in the middle of a call without precedent. They had no clue what they should do. Despite their training, which had covered possible hostile actions, police action, and many other possible scenarios, not even their combined twenty-six years of experience had a single point of reference for what to do when approached by what looked to be five Secret Service agents armed with tranquilizer guns. Ordinarily, the protocol was to let the authorities deal with the conflict, and then the paramedics would clean up after them. Ordinarily though, the authorities would not have been shooting down the witnesses, tranquilizers or not.

Or would they? Wasn't there a new Chief of Police? There was something in the papers recently about unorthodox and experimental methods. Some sort of controversy involving him whatever city he had come from, resulting in the city needing to make a decision between transferring him or facing a lawsuit. The details of the article currently escaped the paramedics, but from that room they were the only things to escape, as Griffin pointed at one of the paramedics, and then the other, and as the two other agents stepped forward, they each drew up pistols and fired once. The paramedics looked at each other, each hoping that somehow the other had been missed and would be coming to the other's rescue. It was not to be, and neither man was concerned about it for very long, as the drugs took hold of them and they fell to the ground in drooling heaps.

Bill spoke into his cufflink, then held his hand over his ear to ensure he heard the response correctly. Edna was conscious, and her face was contorted somewhere between indignant and terrified. She was doing her best to regain her composure after her episode, but felt herself slipping again when the adrenaline started to wear off. She looked around the room at the carnage that had invited itself in, the paramedics and Stewart unconscious on the floor, her door smashed to pieces, and five armed men in dark suits. She wanted to put up a fight, but could no longer find the strength to lift her cane.

"Leave the other three. Blue is coming with us. Hospital." He spoke casually, as if nothing out of the ordinary had happened. Looking at the old lady on the ground, he decided that she was possibly not in the greatest of shape. "Too bad we didn't bring the doctor. Hope she makes it." He turned and made his way to the door, leaving the other two men to bring Old Blue with them.

The other men, knowing the reputation of the woman they were being tasked with, looked at each other. One of them pulled back his suit jacket, revealing his pistol and gestured quietly towards it. The other man shrugged a "Why not?" back at him. Edna watched this exchange through blurring eyes that still burned with a rage that had kept many an authority figure at bay. She tried to reach for her cane again with one feeble hand, moving at the same pace as her drool, when the pistol was drawn and fired at her. She was already on the ground, so she merely slumped down, the tranquilizer taking down her ability to communicate to her assailants "I'll get you bastards for this."

Legally Dead.

When Heatley came to, scattered memories came trickling back to him. He remembered that he had been betrayed, that something was rotten in the Heatley Company, and that he was not in a position to do anything about it. He wanted nothing more than to keep his eyes shut and force himself into oblivion, but curiosity kept creeping up on him, making him open his eyes, just a touch.

A bright blur was all he could see the first time, and it gave him a headache. The bright blur was there the second time as well, but the headache it provided was less substantial. The blur remained the third and fourth times that he opened his eyes, but it was getting clearer. He could begin to make out shapes. A bright square that must have been a window. A smaller, rectangular one that was less bright was probably the television. Other screens and medical supplies were probably there, but he couldn't see nurse who had sedated him. He closed his eyes again and listened to the room.

His heart monitor was beeping erratically. He was in trouble. He flailed his hands about, hoping he would hit a call button for a doctor, a nurse, a cop, or anyone else who might be able to help him. He felt what he thought must be a glass vase as it fell over. The scent of various flowers briefly filled his nostrils, the sound of the vase shattering as it hit the ground rang in his ears, and for a moment he followed the pieces scattering to their various halts along the ground. The heart monitor was still erratic. He heard a cough, followed by "Is that my no-good brother making all of that damned racket?" He tried to melt into the bed to no avail.

Frank realized he hadn't been listening to one erratic heart monitor, but two of them beating relatively normally. It didn't helped him relax, though. Instead of thinking he was going to die, he was going to live and he was trapped in a room with his sister. Given the option, a quick and scary trip into the Netherworld didn't seem like such a bad alternative. He knew that saying "No" wouldn't help his cause at all, just the same as his continued silence was bound to give him away. The closest he was going to find to a peaceful solution, short of finding out if there was a machine keeping him alive and pulling the plug, was to own up and see if Old Blue could bitch their way out of this.

"Sis?" He hoped that he sounded surprised. Pleasantly surprised would be even better.

"I knew you weren't dead," she said. "Damned papers can't get anything right."

Heatley didn't have to wonder whether or not he sounded surprised now, as he was practically gagging on his own stomach at this news. "Dead? Me? Who said I was dead? What paper?" He turned towards the sound of his sister's voice, but his vision hadn't quite cleared up yet, and there was a curtain in between the two of them. The curtain was plain white, so he couldn't tell that he couldn't make it out properly.

The sound of bare feet slapping down one at a time, combined with the sound of something being wheeled along the floor (some form of laminated or tiled affair, or something similarly easy to clean blood off of was his guess), told Heatley that his sister was on the move, that she was not nearly as medicated as he was, and that she was therefore capable of beating him senseless. The curtain was pulled to one side in a series of jerky movements. It could have been drawn back dramatically in one sweeping motion by someone younger, but the way Edna had done it had a much creepier, horror-movie feel to it. Add to that the way her voice croaked out the words "Your paper was the one that broke the story," and Frank Heatley was left with a wretched feeling that started off as dread and went downhill.

"Dead. How long have I been dead?"

"Three months now," Edna told him. "You had a lovely funeral. Lots of people turned out."

"Probably all from the company. Didn't have many real friends. Wait! Why am I referring to myself in the past tense? I'm not dead!" He broke into a coughing fit that sounded as if he were about to disprove this last statement.

"Well, you should probably try to convince the rest of the world about that one. They've not been treating me as well as they could have since your passing."

"That's because you're a bitch, Ed." Frank laughed, stirring up another of his near-death-inducing coughing fits, until she brought her fist down on his stomach, at which point he stopped laughing, but just kept coughing.

A thought suddenly occurred to Frank. "How did they kill me? I mean, my funeral…"

"Suicide," she told him. "Shotgun blast to the face, and they got a closed casket to hide the fact that you weren't in there."

"But wasn't there an investigation? Didn't anyone step up and say that I wouldn't have - couldn't have - done that to myself?"

Edna's face went cold. "Not one."

"Not even you?"

Edna laughed at this. "Of course I told them that you couldn't have done it, but they wrote me off as a family member in denial, or a crazy old lady, or something like that."

"Can't hardly blame them for - ooof!" wasn't exactly what Heatley had intended to say, but it was all he managed to say before his sister hit him in the gut again.

She leaned in, and lowered her voice to her most fearsome God-might-not-be-watching-you-right-now-but-I-sure-as-hell-am voice. "They've had you killed, and took over your company. They. Took. Everything."

"But I'm not dead!" Heatley protested.

"Oh, but you are dead, Mr. Heatley." The voice came from across the room, and was followed by the sound of a door closing. "Trust me on this. After all, I'm a lawyer, and I know dead."

"Shouldn't I be trusting a doctor to tell me when I'm dead?"

"Nonsense, Mr. Heatley. If you hear a doctor telling you that you're dead, he's not doing a very good job, because you shouldn't be able to hear him once you've left this plane of existence. A lawyer, on the other hand," he smiled, twisting an expensive-looking pen open, and wrote something on an elegant notepad he had pulled out of the breast pocket of his well-tailored suit. "Well, Mr. Heatley, when a lawyer tells you that you're dead, it means that all of the loose ends have been tied up, and the only thing left for you to do is get on with the dying."

"But why-"

"Why didn't the company just have you killed?"

"Yeah. I mean, what's the point of the charade?"

"Mr. Heatley, we're businessmen, not murderers."

"But you had me killed on paper. You took away my life."

"Just business, Mr. Heatley. You weren't doing anything but hanging out in your condo for the better part of a year before you had your accident."

"Accident!" Edna scoffed. "Ha! You call what you did to him an accident?"

"Mrs. Sheldon, I assure you that we tried to make what happened to your brother appear to be an accident. It was supposed to look like Mr. Heatley had been drunk and attempting to put a condom on the end of his rifle with his mouth when he accidentally shot himself in the face-"

"You bastard!" Heatley cried.

"But, due to the second-rate capabilities of both the investigators at the scene, and a communication problem in which the results which I wished to be reported did not-"

"You mean that you wanted it to be reported that I was blowing a rifle?"

"That blew you back. Yes, Mr. Heatley. Unfortunately for me, the end result was a simple suicide instead of the more elaborate plan I had for preserving your memory, but c'est la vie and all of that."

"That's all you have to say about having me killed? What about 'I'm terribly sorry' or 'I really am an asshole, aren't I, Mr. Heatley'?"

Edna hobbled back over to the bed where she had woken up and looked around. She began with all the places that she would normally have put her cane, and then thought about where it is that someone else would put an old lady's cane if they didn't know any better. She continued to come up empty.

"Mr. Heatley, there aren't words for me to express how I feel right now, but let me assure you that the satisfaction I will get out of this particular job well done far outweighs any guilt I should perhaps be feeling about your plight, or" he gestured to Old Blue, who was opening the cupboards and muttering to herself, "the plight of your family."

"You mean that you're going to keep her here, too?"

"For now, Mr. Heatley, yes. Until we figure out what to do with the two of you."

"You bastard!"

"Mr. Heatley, you don't know the half of it." He wrote down another few notes about something Heatley suspected he should not like at all, then turned on one heel and headed straight for the door, pausing when his hand was on the doorknob. He glanced back over his shoulder back at Heatley. "Have a good life, Mr. Heatley. The rest of the town thinks you had a pretty good run, after all."

Heatley's continued cries were muted to everyone who was not either in the room, or observing it through the video surveillance system as the door shut behind the young lawyer. The security staff who were watching the exchange between them turned down the volume when Heatley started yelling, but they could still sense how loud it was from their booth. One of them reached forward and pushed the power button on the speakers, then turned back to his microwave dinner, while his partner went over to the coffee pot, and poured himself a fresh cup. The old man and his sister weren't going anywhere anytime soon.

Frank and Edna sat on their beds, silently trying to figure out how they were going to get themselves out of this mess while throwing the occasional glare across the room, each letting the other know they were the one to blame for their predicament. Finally, Edna got up and grabbed two bottles of water and a bowl of strawberries out of the fridge, more perks of the private care that Frank had set up for himself. She passed one of the bottles over to Frank, who thanked her quietly, and twisted it open, then drank half of the bottle in a few thirsty gulps. Edna opened hers after a few moments of nothing bad happening to her brother, and took a few cautious sips. She handed him a strawberry, but his eyes glazed over and he fell back before he could even lift a hand to take it. "Uh knew ih," she said through the cotton that seemed to be building up in her mouth. She held up the water bottle to look for indication that it had been tampered with, but the label was blurry and her hand felt like a water balloon on the end of her arm. The bottle slipped through her numb fingers, and slapped itself on the floor. It rolled to a stop against one of the legs of the hospital bed. Moments later, so did Edna.

You'll Be Hearing From My Lawyer.

Sherman felt he had enough to be upset about for one day before he found out that he wasn't going to be getting his beer back from the hospital. He felt his fingers pulsing against the splints.

"Sorry, hospital policy," the woman behind the information counter told him. "Any prohibited materials confiscated on hospital property are not to be returned."

"But beer isn't a prohibited material. I'm over nineteen."

"Sorry, but alcohol is prohibited on hospital property. Because you were drinking it in the examining room, the nurse was within her rights to confiscate it."

"And what happens to it now?"

"Well, if you would care to call a lawyer and begin an appeal, you might be able to get it back, but the cost of the initial visit to your lawyer will be, on average, five times more than the beer that was taken from you, so the likely result will be one of our staff winning your beer in a weekly raffle, and consuming it, probably in a Mr. Turtle pool, probably Saturday night around six. Probably."

"So all I have to do to get my beer back is have a lawyer contact you about it?"

The nurse at the counter was taken aback by this. "Er, not exactly. If you chose to start an appeal, your beer will be placed in an evidence locker in the basement. There's no guarantee that you'll-"

"Put it in the locker, then, lady," Sherman said, in the most threatening voice he could muster up. "You'll be hearing from my lawyer." He had always wanted to say that to someone. Sherman tried to storm out of the office, but even with the painkillers he had been given the pain in his hand prevented him from making any sudden movements of the door-opening variety. He settled for slowly leaving with a dirty look shot back over his shoulder at the woman who had refused to return his beer.

The Heatley building was only a short detour on the way back to his apartment, so Sherman decided to head that way and ask for Joan. Although he was uncertain if he would be able to get the Heatley Company to send a couple of shark lawyers out to the hospital to get his beer back or not, he knew he would much rather find someone working a desk at the company who might be able to help him with some straight answers than try to call them from home and put up with the automated answering service that every company on the planet seemed to have turned to. Making his way out of the hospital through the thankfully automatic doors, Sherman crouched down and began fumbling with his backpack to get his sunglasses, cursing all the while and wondering how he was ever going to be able to jerk off if just getting his sunglasses on was causing him so much effort and pain. I'm just gonna have to really want it, he thought to himself.

Kelly Davenport, who had been given the unfortunate task of cleaning up Sherman's vomit, had done a good job of it. There wasn't a trace to be seen. Kelly believed he was entitled to get his job with the Heatley Company, and thought it was the embellishments he included on his resume that had secured him an office with a window his first day on the job, rather than finding himself confined to a cubicle like so many of the other people he had graduated with. He had spent most of his school years fighting an inferiority complex by joining every sports team that would take him, then fighting everyone who was smaller than him on the field. He had become used to being treated with a level of what he had mistakenly thought was respect. He managed to convince himself that the same level of respect would continue at the Heatley Company. It had never occurred to him that there might be resentment towards him at his new job, the kind that is reserved for the spoiled children of rich CEO types who get their jobs the same way that they get everything else in life: not by degree of effort, but by having daddy hand it to them.

Being given a corner office was something that Kelly thought came with the territory, just as sure as he knew that he would get promoted again and again until he was his dad's right-hand man, if he could only stick with it. He had been using his mother's maiden name as cover, but when he had walked into the office and run into David Meyers, he had said "Hi, Dad," without thinking about it. Joan had taken an immediate dislike to Kelly, and did her best to ensure that he didn't enjoy his time with the company. That was why she had recommended they give him the corner office. It wasn't a particularly large office, and it was built with restrooms on the opposite side of the too-thin walls. It was awkwardly-shaped, having only one position for a desk that didn't make it look foolish, placing it right beside the wall it shared with the bathrooms. The urinals could be heard flushing automatically every three minutes. That wasn't the worst part, though. The office was located directly behind a bus stop, and because of the position of his desk, Kelly found himself witnessing a wide variety of bodily functions most people wouldn't undertake in public. The sun struck his window a manner that made it highly reflective from the outside, and people from all walks of life found themselves unable to pass by such a large mirror without fixing their hair, adjusting their breasts, picking their teeth or their noses, and at least once a week he would nearly give himself whiplash as he turned his head quickly away to avoid seeing someone use the corner of the bus shelter and the building as an impromptu bathroom. Sadly, the only one of these actions that might have been desirable for him to observe, the boob-adjusting, wasn't an activity that anyone he found attractive ever participated in.

Kelly found himself folding memos into paper airplanes based on schematics he had spent the better part of the morning looking up on the Internet, save for the time he had spent cleaning up vomit from the sidewalk. He still couldn't believe he had been used in a janitorial capacity, but Joan had told him upon her return that it had to be him that cleaned it up because he was the only person working on the first floor with a high enough clearance to even accidentally glean the contents. Although Kelly suspected that he might have been sold a line, it was one he was willing to deal with, and after he had finished the distasteful task of cleaning up the sidewalk he went back in pursuit of creating the ultimate paper airplane. He was reasonably sure that it would take him the rest of the day at the minimum, and if he called one of his friends to come in and 'consult' with him about it, he could ride out most of the week on the endeavour. He threw the newest model towards the window, gently, like the site recommended, and rolled his head to follow as it wound around the room once, twice, three times before taking a sudden turn and hitting the glass with all the force of a toddler swinging a feather. As it fell to the floor, joining the pile of its predecessors, Kelly bore witness to yet another nose-picker. He opened up a spreadsheet on his computer, and recorded another mention under "Nose-Pickers" for the week, and had begun to record a few pieces of information about the offender's demographics when his door opened.

Kelly jumped in his chair and was just about to yell "Don't you bloody knock?" but the knocks came just before he could say it. This behaviour irritated him to no end. How was he supposed to feel like his office was his own when people could just barge in on him? Didn't they know who he was? Sofia, the secretary who had opened the door, poked her head into the room.

"Mr. Davenport?" The way she said his name was calculated to placate him, from the tone of her voice to the strategic positioning of the uppermost done-up button on her blouse in relation to her bra.

"Yes, Sofie. What can I do for you?" It worked.

"It's Sofia, Mr. Davenport," she said, the smile in her eyes wasted on him as his didn't ever meet them. "There is a - gentleman - here to see you."

"Yes, Sofie. Very well, then. Um…"

"Shall I send him in?"

"Yes, of course. Send him in."

Kelly always tried to sound like he carried some authority in their relationship, but Sofia wasn't fooled. She was highly intelligent, and stunning to look at as well. This combination gave her distinct advantages over many of her coworkers, and she knew that the lacy top of her exposed bra served as a great equalizer. Not equal to her, of course. It made her superior to most of her coworkers, who were in turn made equal to each other. She could reduce the IQ of the majority of her male coworkers and render most of them into submissive drones. Although she was not inclined to advance herself in the company by allowing others to use her body, she found nothing wrong with using it on the job herself if it helped her along her way.

"Yes, Mr. Davenport. Right away, sir." Her bra left the room quietly, her face following right after it.

The door didn't even close before Kelly opened up another important-looking document on his computer and a bedraggled skateboarder with splints along the fingers of his right hand came stinking his way into the office. With no small degree of disgust, Kelly recognized him as the same person who had taken the time out of his day to vomit outside his office window. He had an entire category to himself on Kelly's database, as nobody had done that before. Kelly got up and begrudgingly made a move as if to shake hands, but Sherman just held up his splinted fingers and smiled. "Of course, of course," Kelly said. "Have a seat, Mr. umm…" He looked down at his desk as if there should be a piece of paper or a note in his appointment book that would tell him the name of this person who had just walked in off the street.

"It's Klein," Sherman told him, dropping his voice and attempting a Bond-esque demeanour. "Sherman Klein."

"Well, Mr. Klein-"

"Call me Sherman."

"Of course. Well then, Sherman," he continued, irritated beyond reason, and barely trying to conceal it in his voice. He leaned back in his chair and clasped his hands on his lap to try to hide the fists he was forming with them. "What is it that I can do for you?"

"I need to speak to Joan."

"Well, Joan is unavailable at the moment. Is there anything I can do for you?"

"I want a lawyer."

Kelly leaned further back, separating his hands momentarily to let some of the blood flow back into them, and then clasping them again behind his head. "Mr. Klein-"

"Sherman."

"Sherman. Well, Sherman, we are not a law firm."

"I know that."

"Well then why would you come to see a lawyer?"

"I figured the company keeps them on retainer, I think it's called, and since I work for the company I thought that I'd-"

"Now wait just a second," Davenport was experiencing something that he was fairly certain was akin to an aneurism. "You work for the Heatley Company?" Kelly had a specific mental image with regards to his colleagues which was mostly designed to suit his own ego. A highly trained, highly motivated group of exceedingly intelligent and beautiful people, with himself at the top, and everyone else looking up at him as if life would be meaningless without him as their leader, guru, and sex-god. Kelly Davenport was never one to sell himself short.

"Yes, I signed my contract this morn-" but Kelly's hands were already flying across his keyboard looking for an explanation, preferably one that explained that this fellow did not work for the company, but was instead employed in some menial capacity through some outside contractor.

"Ah, never mind. I see a note here," Kelly felt a rush of relief flow over him. "It says here that you're employed by one of our newest assets, 'The Master Beta' if I'm reading that correctly."

"That's the one," Sherman said.

"And you say that you signed your contract this morning?" Kelly smiled a smug little smile that Sherman was convinced he shouldn't like.

"Yeah. Gary, the guy who owned it while it was called 'Gary's Empornium,' he gave me the contract this morning, and I-"

"Did you read the contract, or did you just look for the little green arrows and sign where they told you where to sign it?" Kelly asked, ninety-nine percent sure that he already knew the answer.

"Um… The thing with the arrows," Sherman admitted. "Why?"

"Because as you'll notice here," Kelly said, pointing at a paragraph on the contract, "it says that you're entitled to representation by the lawyers of the Heatley Company only under specific circumstances, listed here, and only after a probationary period of ninety days has expired." The smug smile that so many of his peers secretly hated him for exposed itself as he added "Here, let me put some more green arrows on there for you, so you can see it better."

Sherman was unimpressed, and decided to look up Davenport's name back on his computer at work to see if he could sneak some embarrassing late charges and perhaps arrange for some phone calls home from the store. Nothing said uncomfortable like having your wife or girlfriend answer the phone call about your overdue porn rentals. "I'd like to speak to Joan, please, if you don't mind."

Kelly felt the pang of fear that accompanies every request from someone with a complaint to see the supervisor of the person with whom the complaint originated. He immediately began recounting the details of their conversation in search of any legitimate complaint that Sherman might have, but didn't come up with anything that he felt could not be countered with having been asked to clean up Sherman's vomit before lunch. "Certainly, Mr. Klein," he said with a smile. "If you'd care to wait here, I'll go get her right now." He got up from his desk to find Joan, as he didn't want to call Sophia in. It was one thing for him to have another complaint against him, and entirely another for his coworkers to know about it. He liked to keep himself in excellent standing as far as they were concerned, never entertaining the idea that he was only fooling himself.

The moment the office door closed behind Davenport, Sherman switched chairs and started perusing the computer for anything that he might be able to use against him should the opportunity arise. Fortunately for Sherman, Davenport was enough of an egomaniac that it just hadn't occurred to him that he should lock his computer to protect himself against someone as insignificant as he appeared to be. As well as a web browser opened to a page displaying a "Girl of the Day," there was also a word processing program open to a document entitled "Cutting Corners." Sherman glanced up and down the page in front of him, and his eyes grew wider and wider with every sentence he read.

Ladies and Gentlemen,

For the last several months, since the unfortunate passing of this company's founder, Frank Heatley (wait for laughter), we have seen the first real growth of the company due to business decisions that did not include simply buying a successful existing business (wait for applause). Frank Heatley did not have a formal education, a natural aptitude for business, a clear vision, a lot of friends, family (besides a sister he couldn't stand), or common sense. What he had, my friends, was a winning lottery ticket, which gave him the ability to purchase some ofthese things (wait for murmurs of agreement). Since his 'passing' the company has struggled, not because of any vital role he had played, but because the company has finally been able to shift gears, and begin to set into motion some brilliant plans that could not be set into motion so long as he was in charge. Today's meeting will not outline all of these new plans, but the information we currently have available is in the folders you have in front of you (wait for people to notice large envelopes in front of them). Over the course of the next two hours, we will be going over two of the larger operations, some of the most ambitious plans we or any company have ever come up with: The Konfessional 3000, and the Betting Zoo (wait for ooos and ahhhs).

Sherman read on about the details of the Konfessional 3000, how a unit would be located in each of the Heatley Company buildings, and kiosks would be installed at strategic places that had not yet been brought into the fold of the company, such as the strip club down near the outskirts of the town that was still run by a gang of bikers who didn't seem too keen on selling it. When he got to The Betting Zoo, Sherman didn't think his eyes could possibly open any wider. He thought his head would eventually explode if he kept reading, but he couldn't look away. The memo went on at some length into the history which led to the concept of The Betting Zoo. The Heatley Company had some time ago acquired a medium-sized zoo on the outskirts of the town, a popular enough place that made a meagre profit, mostly through the sales of high-markup trinkets at the gift shop. Also purchased at around the same time was a local animal shelter. Normally run by the city at the cost of both taxpayers and donations, the shelter had been purchased by the Heatley Company after Frank had been shut-in for a three-week period and had done nothing except watch documentaries about various animal species on specialty cable channels. The shelter had been used as a tax write-off for the company, and Frank had insisted that the quality of the food be brought up, that new additions be made for the animals to give them more space, and that the shelter be designated a "no-kill" shelter except in the case of illnesses which could not be treated by the veterinarians in town. The shelter had, for obvious reasons, been operating at an incredible loss to the company, even as a tax write-off. This was, according to the memo, no longer to be the case.

The concept of the Betting Zoo had begun to develop shortly after the old man had locked himself away "for good". David Meyers, acting

CEO of the company while Heatley was indisposed, had gone over the financial considerations of having an animal euthanized in one corner of the Heatley Company and weighing it against the cost of feeding the animals in another, and came up with a plan that he quite liked. If an animal from the shelter was sick, or determined to not be a candidate for adoption, it would be brought over to be used as a feed animal for the animals at the zoo, preferably under cover of darkness, and without a paper trail. The cost savings of hiring a driver instead of a veterinarian alone seemed to be enough to make it worth while, and the reduction of the cost of food for the larger animals at the zoo would buy a lot of icing for any size cake. On paper it was written up as "Euthanisation By Environmentally Sustainable Methods," and it opened an unintended floodgate of opportunity for the company one night when one of the delivery men had been so entertained by the flailing of one cat in order to preserve its life from being terminated by a hungry bear that he had recorded the ordeal on his cell phone. Although the picture was grainy, and most of the action became so blurry that it was difficult to see what was happening, the final few frames of the video were clearly a deranged cat heading straight through the air towards the camera, and the sound of a man screaming.

The delivery man, nearly six feet tall and almost always wearing thick workwear that covered everything from his wrists to his toes, was initially embarrassed about his encounter, and had no intention of showing the video to any of his friends, but found himself showing the video to almost everyone who asked him about the scratches on his face that ran from just above his lip back to his ear, because nobody initially believed his story when he told them a bear had thrown a cat at him. Although it was not an entirely accurate description of what had occurred, the video footage certainly lent some credibility to his story, and a few of his coworkers had asked him for a copy of the video. He provided them with copies on the sole condition that they not distribute the footage to anyone outside of the Heatley Company, being mortified of what might happen if he violated the terms of his contract. The video distribution had, of course, gone company-wide within the week, and there were rumours of it having been leaked outside the company as well, which were later proven to not only be true, but understated. It wasn't long before the company had to send a couple of experts to debunk the theories by animal rights groups who were claiming that the cat in the video had been tossed into the bear's habitat to see how long it would have lasted in a gladiatorial match.

And that's where the idea came from. The very people who spent all of their time trying to prevent the cruel treatment of animals had, inadvertently, planted the seed, and even, according to some sources, initially coined the term "Betting Zoo" that was to be the name of the reality television show produced by the Heatley Company in the near future.

That was as far along as Sherman got skimming the document when he heard the door open up again. Kelly walked in, followed closely by Joan, too engrossed in their own conversation to notice Sherman gracelessly spring out of Kelly's chair. They might not have noticed his shifting about at all had it not been for Sherman's unfortunate landing in the chair he was originally sitting in. It began to tilt backwards, and Sherman flapped his arms outward in an attempt to keep his balance, bringing his right hand (the wrong hand, in his opinion) clumsily down on the corner of the desk. A signal was sent from the broken bones in Sherman's hand to his brain, informing him that a good yell would be both appropriate and therapeutic, and Sherman obliged with a good burst of profanities choice enough to have himself permanently banned from most places of worship.

"So you're making yourself at home then, Mr. Klein?" Joan asked him as she and Kelly made their way over to the desk.

Kelly looked resentful as Joan sat down in his chair, forcing him to either sit down on the other side of his own desk, move another chair over to sit beside her, or simply stand there. By his estimation, the most important-looking posture he could go for was to stand behind her, looking over her shoulder, possibly leaning against the wall nonchalantly, maybe with his arms crossed. He opted for this position and made sure to look as bored as he possibly could. He held a hand up in front of his face while Joan and Sherman began to talk about his request for a lawyer, examining his fingernails for any sign that his manicurist should be reprimanded, and only looked up when he heard himself mentioned. It wasn't by name, though.

"Can we speak alone please, Joan?" Kelly had just felt himself addressed by a request for his absence, and he lost his bored composure, and put on his irritated face again.

"Certainly." She looked up at Kelly, and made the slightest gesture towards the door with her head.

"But it's my office," he said in protest. Joan's eyes squinted with such subtlety it would have been easy to miss. "Fine," Kelly said, and headed for the door. He moved with a full-body pout that reminded Sherman of a small child who had just had his swing bullied out from under him by someone much to big to argue with.

After the door closed behind Kelly, Sherman looked across the desk at Joan. "Okay, seriously. What the hell is going on with this company?"

Joan felt anxiety start to build up in herself right away. "What are you talking about?" she asked, her voice almost not making past the lump in her throat.

Sherman looked back at the door, making sure it was closed with Kelly on the right side of it. Satisfied that they were alone, he turned back to Joan. "I'm talking about all the weirdness that's been happening since the the death of Mr. Heatley.

Although she knew Sherman wasn't in a position of authority, Joan felt she was tied to a chair under a heat lamp in an otherwise dark room, being asked where she was around 7:35PM on December the 8th last year. "I have no idea what you're talking about Sher-"

"You know damned well what I'm talking about, Joan," Sherman hissed at her. "I'm talking about the Betting Zoo. I'm talking about the Konfessional 3000. Oh, right - and I'm also talking about Heatley not actually being dead."

Joan turned green, then pale, and then a pale-green. She stood up, then sat back down. "I... I... What do you want?"

Sherman leaned forward, put his elbows on the table and looked at his hands in disappointment when he realized that he wouldn't be able to fold them together to make a rest for his chin without significant discomfort. He sat back a little until his forearms were resting on the desk. "I want a company lawyer to get my beer back, for starters."

Joan reached under the desk for her purse, but she wasn't sitting at her own desk so it wasn't there. "How about I just replace what they took from you?"

"No deal. I'm working on principle here, and I want my beer back. You can't just take the easy road out with these things, Joan. I want my beer back."

Joan picked up the phone, but paused before dialling any numbers. "What did they take from you?"

"It was a fifteen-pack of Pilsner."

"How about I buy you two of them? Will that do?"

Sherman briefly contemplated the true value of living a life based on principles. "Add a carton of smokes and you've got a deal," he told her.

Joan put the phone down, thankful that she had bought herself a reprieve. "Done." She picked it back up and hit a button that Kelly had labelled "Errand-Boy" on his speed dial, and sent in the request for two fifteen-packs of Pilsner and a carton of cigarettes. "That's right. And take it out of petty-cash, bring the receipts back to the front desk, and tell them to have it all held there. A Mr. Sherman Klein will be there to pick them up soon, and he'll be needing someone to drive him home, or wherever he wants to go. No, a taxi will be fine. I don't think he'll be requiring a limo for-" Sherman caught her attention by waving his hands at her, and she looked up to see him nodding "Yes" at her. "On second thought, make that a limo. Yes, wherever he wants to go."

Sherman sat back with a grin as Joan hung up the phone. "Okay," he said. "That takes care of my immediate problems, now how about the rest of it?"

Joan looked at Kelly's computer screen, wondering what she was supposed to do. In the movies, anybody who had become aware of a conspiracy would find themselves driving a car with no brakes, or the victim of a random mugging. Even though she wasn't sure about how for the company was willing to go to cover their tracks, she was certain that she wasn't going to have anything to do with escalating things to that level. "What do you think the rest of it is, Sherman?"

"Is Mr. Heatley still alive?"

"It's complicated, Sherman."

"I'm sure if you examine the question, you'll find it's a yes-or-no type. One of the least-complicated questions you can be asked, as long as you know that one of the answers is the truth, and the other one is a lie. Even if you didn't know the answer, you still have a fifty-fifty shot at getting it right."

"Well, Sherman, legally he's dead. All taken care of, right down to the reading of the will and the dividing up of his estate."

"That's legality, then. How about the real world? Is Heatley still breathing somewhere? Locked in a dungeon or laying down in a permanent chemically-induced coma?"

"No!"

"Hanging out in a detention cell in some prison somewhere?"

"No, he's-"

"Being forced to eat bugs to survive in a broom closet, with a bucket to piss in and drinking water out of the mop sink?"

"What? Sherman, you're being-"

"Well, what is it, then?"

"He's been - at home, so far as he knows. At least until recently."

Sherman had been feeling pretty good about the interrogation so far, believing himself to have the advantage over Joan, but this last response had sent him for a loop. "What do you mean, 'so far as he knows'?"

Joan took a few deep breaths. She had no reason to tell Sherman what was going on. In fact, the more she told him, the more likely it was that she would get in bigger trouble with the Choir Boys, and she had no idea what the ramifications of telling him the truth might be. She just knew that she would feel better telling someone else what was going on, to unburden herself from keeping all this bottled in. Since her meeting with Heatley that morning, she had been in a constant state of near-panic. "Sherman, can we meet somewhere after I'm done work for the day?"

"Are you asking me out on a date?" Sherman asked.

"Good god no!" Joan said, and recoiled in her chair at the question. "I don't want to talk here. I don't think the office is - a safe place to discuss this. For either of us."

The phone rang, and Joan picked it up in the middle of the first ring, her nerves running so tight that her reflexes were in high gear. "Yes? Okay, thank you. I'm sure he'll be out in a minute or so." She hung up again, and turned to Sherman. "Your beer and cigarettes are here, and there's a car ready to go."

"That was really fast," Sherman said.

"It came from the staff bar on the second floor," she said. "We're a company of more vice than virtue, if you hadn't guessed." She took an orange Post-It note from Kelly's desk, and scribbled her name and phone number on it, then handed it to Sherman. "That's my cell number. I'll probably be off in another hour or two." She looked around the room again, and Sherman wondered what the odds were that the office was being monitored, and by who.

He took the Post-It and put it in his wallet. "I'll talk to you later then. My beer is where?"

"The receptionist will have it at the front desk. She's got the car for you as well. It will probably be at the front door," Joan told him. She hung her head down, burying her face in her palms.

"Thanks." Sherman got up and made his way to the door. When he pulled it open, Kelly almost fell into his office, having been trying to listen in on their conversation. Sherman gave him a good sneer as he walked past, then made his way to the front desk.

Choices.

Heatley and his sister woke up within minutes of each other, and found themselves with only each other for company. This wasn't a good situation for either of them at the best of times, which this was definitely not. They were also both hooked up to various monitors, and an IV needle was stuck in each of their right arms. A television was on a cart at the foot of their beds, in between them. Attached to it, held on by masking tape, was a note that said in really large letters "Push play."

Heatley found a remote control fastened to his hospital bed, bolted down on a pivoting metal plate. He looked it over for and pushed the "Play" button. David Meyers' face appeared on the screen. "Hello, Frank, Edna. My apologies for having to address the two of you like this, but I'm a busy man these days, far too busy to wait around for a couple of elderly people to wake up from their nap time, and certainly too busy to wait around for you both to calm down enough after seeing me to hear me out. I'm sure that even if you don't agree with me about the difficulties in dealing with yourselves, you'll at least have enough experience in dealing with each other to agree with me."

"You son of a bitch!" they yelled at the television simultaneously, while Meyers stood silent on the screen.

"I will attempt to leave appropriate pauses for you to yell at me on the screen to make yourselves feel better, as I'm sure you both just did." He paused again, and Enda swore at him. "You see?" He laughed at his own joke, while Heatley insinuated aloud something obscene about Meyers' mother. "I really hope they're recording the cameras in your rooms right now, as I'm sure it will provide us with hours of entertainment." He paused again, but neither Frank nor Edna would give him the satisfaction of saying anything. He continued saying nothing for fifteen seconds before Heatley swore at the screen again, and then Meyers burst out laughing. "Did I get you again? God I hope so. Anyhow, that's enough fun for me. I'm a busy man, as I said before, so I'm just here to place an offer on the table for you. The Heatley Company is doing better than ever since you passed away, Frank, and we're inclined to keep our profits going up as high as we can for as long as we can, as is the nature of being in business.

"With that, we're proposing that we come to some sort of agreement that keeps most of us happy, with the possible exception of Edna, who, to the best of our understanding, has been disproportionately unhappy since birth, especially for someone who has had everything handed to her, even before you won the lottery, Mr. Heatley. According to our records, she married into money quite young, didn't have any children, and collected quite a handsome sum from the life insurance policy her husband had purchased for himself several years before his... questionable accident."

Edna's heart monitor began working harder than it had previously, trying to keep up with the erratic variations of unhealthily rapid beating it was suddenly forced to contend with. It was performing an electronic version of a jazz drumbeat, jamming until the wee hours of the morning on the buzz of red wine and methadone. "I had nothing to do with that, you bastard!"

Meyers, of course, had paused for her reply. "Now, Edna, nobody is saying anything about you being involved in your husband's accident, but it's not every day that a man is found drowned in his own bathroom sink while apparently trying to wash his hair. I'm sure it happens all the time and we just don't read about it." He looked away from the camera for a moment, then stared unblinking straight back at it. "Having the two of you aware of what has been happening here at the Heatley Company is problematic, at best, and there has already been several meetings to help us decide what the appropriate course of action will have to be, given our inappropriate situation. Of course we know that what we have done so far is wrong, if you want to look at it from standpoints as mundane as legality or morality, but from a business perspective, we have done what is best for the company, and as a business, that has been our guiding star.

"What we are proposing, for the time being, and I will be down some time in the next few days to discuss it with you, is this: Frank, you will be returned to your apartment. Your real apartment, if you choose, but with limitations on your contacts. Joan will be happy to continue to take care of your needs, of course, but if you have trust issues with her, I'll appoint someone else. Your communications, from your web-browsing to your phone calls, will not only be monitored, but relayed through the company. You probably won't notice the difference, as we've been doing that to you for months now. Any attempts to make contact with anyone outside of the company will result in your privileges being revoked. If you give us any grief about the conditions we've set up for you, we can always look into more - unpleasant options for you.

"Edna. Edna, Edna, Edna.... What can I say to you? I'm afraid you've become a liability that we just can't afford to have running loose, and we can't send you back to your old way of life because your way of life is a little bit too -"

"Pure." She interjected, even though he hadn't left room for her to say it.

"righteous for us. I'm afraid we're going to have to consider other options for you. We could have you sent to a missionary colony somewhere in South America, or placed in an institution for the mentally insane. We're in the process of purchasing one right now, for tax reasons, and we could ensure that you are made comfortable by means of the best medications money can buy." He did pause this time, although the only protest that Edna made about this was an involuntary scoffing noise. "Another option we have for you is to be placed full-time in the same residence as your brother. The penthouse is large enough for the two of you to live quite comfortably without seeing each other any more often than you like."

Heatley that spoke up. "I don't want to live with her! She's intolerable!"

Meyers looked away again, this time continuing to speak without looking back at the camera. "While the two of you decide what's best for you, we'll be keeping you here for observation. I'm sure that you've noticed that each of you has a ketamine drip attached to you, with a manual trigger. This isn't because either one of you seems to be in any pain. It's more of a test. You see, each of you is in possession of a trigger for the other's ketamine drip, so if either of you grows weary of the other's company, you can-"

Neither Frank nor Edna heard any more, though, as they simultaneously triggered each other into unconsciousness.

Wombattle-Axe.

Sherman and Joan met up on a park bench by the water. When he had asked her why they didn't meet up at one of their apartments, she had declined to answer on the phone. She found him sitting down on the bench, drinking something he had stashed in a paper bag. His skateboard was laying upside down over his feet.

"Tell me you're not drunk," she said as she sat down beside him.

He wiped his mouth with the sleeve of his sweatshirt. "Not really," he said. "Just enough to keep the pain in my hand in check. So, why are we meeting on a park bench, when I'm sure there's a dozen places the Heatley Company owns where you could haggle us up some free drinks?"

She looked over both of her shoulders before answering. "They might be watching me."

"Watching you? Who? Why?"

"The company might be watching me. They're getting paranoid now that Heatley..." She trailed off, looking out at the water.

"Now that Heatley what?"

"He's figured it out. Or, at least, he had started to figure out something was wrong, and now the proverbial cat is out of the bag, causing the proverbial shit to hit the fan."

"Understand I'm not the biggest fan of this idea myself, but why don't you go to the cops?"

Joan smiled at him. "You didn't actually read your contract, did you?"

Sherman shook his head at her. "It was a little bit thick."

"So were we for signing it," she told him. "Do you happen to have yours on you still?"

Sherman dug through his backpack and pulled out his copy of the contract, which was still in its manila envelope, impressively stained and crumpled for something that had been in his possession less than twenty four hours. He handed it over to her, and she took it from as if it was a soiled diaper he found in a dumpster behind a gas station. She opened up the envelope with as little contact with the thing as she could manage, and pulled out the contract. She flipped to the third page from the end, and handed it back to Sherman. "What does the small print on the bottom of the page say?"

He looked at the fine print she was talking about, and his eyes widened. "Immortal Soul Clause?" he read aloud. "What the hell is that all about?"

"Read it and find out, like you should have done in the first place."

"'In the event of any conflict that the employee may have with the employer, attempting to resolve said conflict by any means other than that of arbitration via Heatley Company approved mediation, including arbitration commencing after the termination of the employer/employee relationship, shall be penalized by forfeit of the employee's Immortal Soul. The Heatley Company shall retain legal entitlement to said soul until such time as the company is satisfied with the outcome of the conflict.'" He shook his head. "What the hell is that all about?"

"Just the company making sure that they keep us too scared to try and seek legal action against them."

"Well," Sherman said, "As an atheist, I don't hold with this immortal soul crap, so if you've got information on the company, give it to me and I'll go to the police."

"Are you sure?" Joan asked.

"Of course I'm sure. I live just a few blocks from a coffee shop, which is just as good, if not better, than living a few blocks away from a police station."

"No, are you sure about the soul thing? I mean really sure. If you have any doubts that you might be wrong, you might be making a pretty big gamble with this."

Sherman thought about this, and couldn't decide how strong his convictions were. He had certainly never been religious, but he had spent much of his life as an agnostic, always joking that whatever deity happened to meet him at the end of the line would be the one he believed in, passing through the gates with a 'Hey, I thought it might be you,' and a high-five. "Well, I'm not a hundred percent, no." He shifted uncomfortably on the bench. "If somebody could come out and explain why the Big Bang happened, or how space just goes on forever, I'd be sure. It's the big questions that leave a little doubt, you know?"

"All too well. Is it a chance you're willing to take?"

"Is this even legal?" he asked, staring in disbelief at the papers in his hand. "It seems like it's got to be bullshit."

"It's a legal document, and we've both signed it. The company bought a church recently, too. I didn't get it at the time, but I think they were looking to legitimize this clause."

"Well, what are we supposed to do, then?"

Joan thought it over before answering. "We need to get the old man to void our contracts, because he's the only one who's probably going to do it, but the only way we're going to get him to do that is by getting him out."

Sherman tucked the papers back into his backpack, zipped it shut, and got up to leave. "We're gonna need a plan."

"Of course we will, Sherman." Joan looked at him in exasperation for his statement of the obvious.

"Do you have anything in mind?"

"No," she said. "Until you came to the office, I was basically alone in the company thinking that they had gone too far. I was a willing part of all this until I saw the look in Heatley's face the other day. He was terrified. There are even a few members of the board that have put forth the economical method of dealing with this situation by means of ketamine overdose."

"You mean…"

"Yes. The two of them. Heatley and his sister are both being held, and the company doesn't want to keep paying to keep them comfortable. It's not financially sound, especially since they both seem to be in good health despite their advanced age. Hell, some of them think that Old Blue is too mean to die."

"Old Blue? That bitch is Heatley's sister?"

"You've met?"

"You could say that," Sherman said, holding up his hand. "She's the one that did this to me." Joan tried to hide her laughter by covering her mouth with her hand, but without success. "It's not bloody well funny, Joan."

"I know, I know. I'm sorry, it's just that-"

"It's just that I got sent to the hospital by a ninety-year-old basket case wombattle-axe from hell."

"How very succinct of you," she said.

"Doesn't that mean short?"

"I was being sarcastic."

Sherman kicked his skateboard onto its wheels. "Right. I'll talk to you later, Joan. I'm going home."

"What are we going to do?" Joan asked him.

"I don't know yet, but I'll think on it over a few drinks and get back to you." He jumped on to the board and sped down the path, leaving Joan on the bench, with a couple of pigeons lurking nearby, expecting to be fed.

Back to Work.

Sherman showed up early to work the next day so he could talk to Gary before he left. There was only one customer in the store, which wasn't unusual in the morning. The average customer preferred having their identity covered by a cloak of darkness, and there was a stigma, even among those who worked in the business, about those who decided they needed pornography before lunch.

Sherman said good morning to Gary, then went down to the basement to put his skateboard and backpack away. The Konfessional 3000 was already installed, and sat eerily in a corner of the room. He took his things back upstairs and placed them behind the counter. "Can you believe that thing they put in downstairs?" he asked Gary.

"Anything for a buck, Sherman. You almost have to admire it."

"Yeah. Almost," Sherman said. He turned up the radio in the store, then stood behind the counter next to Gary. "Gary, what do you know about the Heatley Company?"

"Not a lot, I suppose. Just the basics you get from TV and the local news, that sort of thing. Why?"

"Just wondering if maybe you had heard anything about them that the public might not have. You know, with your doing business with them and everything."

"I didn't really do business with them. I just sold mine," he told him, and began counting the till for the beginning of Sherman's shift.

"Did you talk to Frank Heatley about it at all?"

Gary stopped counting. "Frank? No, he died a month or so before the company approached me about buying this place."

The sole customer in the store came up to the counter, holding a DVD case in his hand. "Is this one any good?" he asked, nervous and fidgeting behind dark-tinted glasses. He handed over his membership card.

"I haven't seen it," Sherman told him. He looked at the back of the box.

"It should get the job done, though," he said with a smile. He typed the account number into the computer. "Five bucks," he told the man.

The man handed over a twenty-dollar bill, and Sherman rang it through and grabbed his change. He found the DVD for the man and handed it to him. "Have a good one, sir."

"Yeah, thanks," he said tucking the DVD into his coat pocket and heading for the door. He opened it slowly, looking around before he exited. Sherman always wondered why it was that so many of their customers appeared to be afraid of running into real girls. The coast must have been clear, and the man stepped out into the morning sun, presumably to head for a darkened room.

Sherman turned back to Gary. "So the Heatley Company bought this place after the old man died?"

"Yeah. I think this was one of the first places they bought after he passed away. Guess the company values are a little different without him around."

"I guess so. They're probably pretty happy that he's gone." Sherman hoped he didn't sound like he was probing too much.

"Why the sudden interest in the company, Sherm? You thinking about staying on for a while after all?"

"Depends on a couple of things, I guess. I mean, you did say they're gonna give me a raise based on my experience, right?"

"They're supposed to, yes. After I'm gone, there might even be some sort of management possibility for you. If you're interested, that is. I put in a good word for you."

Sherman looked around the store again, making sure there was nobody else around before he spoke again. "Sure. Maybe. Is there anyone else here? I mean like the installation guys for that thing downstairs or anything like that?"

"Nope. Just you and me, and the occasional guy coming in here that's not terribly social. What's up, Sherman?"

Although Sherman had worked for Gary for a number of years now, he was unsure of whether or not he could be trusted anymore. Hadn't Heatley been betrayed by people that had worked for him for a lot longer than just a few years? People that he had entrusted with far more than a day's worth of profits from an adult video store. People that he had treated really well. People that should have had no reason to wish any harm to come to him. He decided that he was being paranoid, and would take it on faith that Gary wasn't with the conspirators. "I heard some rumours about the company."

"Rumours? Like what?"

Sherman lowered his voice, and looked around the room again. "I heard that the old man isn't dead."

Gary burst out laughing, which Sherman didn't take as the most positive sign as far as finding an ally went, but at least it was better than being knocked out with chloroform and being woken up to the sound of power tools while strapped to a table in a slaughterhouse. "And where did you hear that from?"

"It's just I heard it from someone I was inclined to believe."

"And who might that have been, Sherman?"

"She's a friend. Kind of."

"A friend, eh?"

Sherman laughed. "No, not like that. Not at all. She's not my type, and even if she was, I guarantee I'm not hers."

"So who is she, then?" Gary asked.

"She's the old man's former assistant. Well, according to her, she's still his assistant, in a way. She goes through the motions of doing her old job, and has been telling the him that everything is fine, but now he's figured out that the company has declared him dead, and—"

"You're an idiot, Sherman," Gary said, shaking his head at him. "I don't understand your generation and your 'everything is a conspiracy' attitude. Not everything is a conspiracy, the world isn't out to get you, and you can't believe every damned thing you read on the Internet."

"Yeah, but-"

"But nothing, Sherman. Remember your insistence that the American government was behind 9-11?"

"Yeah. There was some compelling-"

"And what about the moon landing 'documentary' you saw, that made you believe that man never landed on the moon?"

"There's a lot of inconsistencies about-"

"Sherman, it's all bullshit. Deep down, you know it." Gary signed off on the paperwork for the morning's till drop, and placed it in a bag with the money, then put the package in the safe. "Can I use your phone, Sherman? They screwed up the lines here when they were installing that booth downstairs."

"No problem." Sherman fished his phone out of his pocket, and handed it over to Gary.

"Thanks. They should have it fixed by this afternoon sometime." He started to dial a number, then stopped. "Aw, crap. Sherman, can you get me my day-planner from the basement? Should be on the filing cabinet."

"Sure thing, boss man." Sherman said, and headed down the stairs. As soon as he reached the landing, the lights went out. He turned around and looked up the stairs, seeing the silhouette of his boss, a man he had thought he could trust, close the door to the basement. He heard a soft click as the door was locked behind him.

Back To Work - The Sequel.

Joan woke up, but wasn't terribly happy about it. She knew her job at the Heatley Company was about to take a drastic turn, as Heatley knew he no longer needed an assistant, and the company hadn't specified what her position with them would be once she had become redundant in her previous capacity. She had been hand-picked by Heatley prior to completing her degree, and she left school once it looked as if this was going to be something she could do long-term. It now looked as if there could be significant repercussions for her involvement with the company, as well as the potential backlash for her help in bringing the conspiracy to light. *Either way*, she thought to herself, *I'm screwed.*

All this had begun to run through her mind before the first drop of caffeine had coursed through her veins or the first drop of water had left the shower nozzle. "Shit," she said aloud to the bathroom mirror, and found it made her feel a bit better. She tried saying it again. "Shit." It worked. "Shit shit shit shit shit!" she yelled, and then briefly thought about punching her reflection in the face. She held back the punch, however, not because she had realized she would only be hitting herself in the hand, but because she had seen in Apocalypse Now, and countless other movies what happened to people who got frustrated and took it out on mirrors.

She stepped into the shower with the water set to that anomalous temperature that manages to scald second-degree burns into the burliest of men while providing a soothing experience to the daintiest of females, and stood under the head, uselessly wiping the water off of her face. She grabbed her loofa, and was just about to start the actual cleaning part of shower time when she ran out of hot water. She jumped out of the shower as quickly as she could, then reached back in to shut off the water, and wondered how long she had been in there. She hadn't run out of hot water since she stopped living with a roommate.

Joan looked at her alarm clock while she got dressed and was shocked to see she was going to be late for work for the first time in longer than she could recall. She finished getting ready as quickly as she could and ran out the door, startling herself as she saw Old Blue's apartment door. She had been so distracted she hadn't even noticed it when she got home the night before. Most of the days when she left for work and saw her neighbour's door closed, it was an almost joyous occasion as it meant she didn't have to have one of their little exchanges, which generally consisted of Joan being on the judged end of a judgmental scowl that she felt she didn't deserve. This time, however, the door had obviously been broken down, and there was yellow tape crisscrossed over it from top to bottom. Joan felt something she knew she deserved. She felt guilty. Guilty for having been a part of the conspiracy that had gotten way out of hand. Guilty for the elderly pair that were being held captive, giving each other ketamine injections every time they grew tired of each other, which Joan assumed meant that at any given time, one or both of them was rendered unconscious.

She took the elevator downstairs, and found the personnel in the lobby to be in an unusually good mood. Karl, the young doorman, was smiling blissfully as he opened the door with panache, bowing deeply. "Good morning, Ms. Miller," he said as she passed by. "Lovely day, isn't it?"

"Why are you in such a good mood, Karl?" It didn't matter to her what the weather did. It wasn't going to be a beautiful day at the office no matter what.

"No reason," he said with a wink. "Nothing to do with medical emergencies at all. Nothing to do with a certain neighbour of yours being taken away in an ambulance last night, that's for sure. Terrible tragedy." His smile grew as he spoke.

"You mean Edna? What happened to her?" Joan hoped pleading ignorance might get her the official company line on Old Blue before she got to work, so she would be able to prepare herself.

"Guess the old bat had a heart attack last night, and they had to break into her apartment to take her away." He obviously had no idea what had really happened, or why it was that Stewart wasn't at work today.

"My god!" Joan did her best to feign surprise. "I saw her door and wondered what had happened. Is she going to be okay?"

"Some guys in suits came by earlier this morning and said that they don't think she's going to make it," Karl said, his smile not dissipating in the slightest. "Like I said, it's a beautiful day."

Joan was repulsed by his callousness without admitting to herself that she probably wouldn't have thought it such a bad thing if Edna had simply died. "So she's probably going to die," she said, thinking about the implications of this. More specifically, she was thinking about how she might be implicated if word got out that she was involved. "Thank you, Karl." She ignored whatever he said next as she left the building and began her walk to work.

Her mind was brimming with conflicting options about what she should do. The easiest way out was to go to the police, as she wasn't sure herself that there was anything to this Immortal Soul clause in the contract she had signed, but she didn't want to take the chance. Next on the list was whether or not to tell the Choir Boys that Sherman was aware something was wrong, which would no doubt add him to the list of casualties the company seemed to be amassing in their efforts to keep their conspiracy quiet. Of course, he might tell them that the reason he knew what he knew was because she had told him, and then what? The best way she could think of to end this waking nightmare was to go through with her plan to work with Sherman to free the old man, and hope to strike a deal with someone to avoid charges. That was how it worked on all of the law shows she watched.

She arrived at work before she arrived at a conclusion. She had been so distracted she didn't even notice she was on auto-pilot when she arrived, saying good morning to Sophie at the front desk and proceeding straight to the elevator. It wasn't until the elevator doors closed in front of her face that she actually had time to fret. She felt the car start moving up, and her stomach fell at the movement, as it always did when she was on an elevator, but this time she felt it keep falling, instead of catching up to the momentum. She felt it fall past her intestines, squeeze its way between her kidneys, and she was positive it had split itself in half and was running down her legs. She wondered whether or not she might have peed herself. She patted her inner thighs as discreetly as she could to avoid the prying eye of the security camera. Her hands came back dry, much to her relief.

The elevator doors opened up and she stepped out onto the office floor. She looked for her clipboard, hoping she could set herself back on the autopilot that had served her well enough to get her to work that day, but the hook it usually hung on was empty. She looked around the office, to see if anyone was running up to her with her clipboard in hand, apologizing to her for not having it ready for her, or saying 'You were late so we took care of this for you!' but was disheartened when she didn't see anyone coming her way. What she thought she saw was people looking at her with suspicion or contempt, possibly both. They looked away when she tried to meet their eyes. She hoped it was just her imagination.

Joan made her way to Meyers' office and knocked on the door. She could see through the window that he was on the phone, but he waved her in with his free hand. He made short work of the conversation once she sat down across from him, and hung up. "Joan. Good to see you. Are you feeling okay? It's not like you to be late."

"I'm… fine, Mr. Meyers. I'm fine. I don't know what happened. I guess I just slept through my alarm." She found it unnerving to not be able to see what was going on behind her. In her mind, the entire office was gathered at the window looking in, some of them pressing ears against it to try and listen to what was going on while somebody else called for security to come and take her away. She tried to catch their reflection in the plaques he had hung on the wall behind him, to no avail.

Meyers leaned back in his chair, an all-leather affair that probably cost more that she made in three months, no matter what sort of raises that had given her since she signed on as co-conspirator. "Joan, we need to discuss your role in the company."

"Mr. Meyers?"

"Well, you're a valuable asset to the company, Joan, and we'd hate to lose you just because your position with us has become… superfluous. I feel it would benefit us all for you to remain with the company, perhaps keeping your former position, but working for me instead?"

A laugh broke out from Joan before she knew it was coming, making it quite impossible for her to stop it. "Mr. Meyers, forgive me for being blunt about this, but I'm nobody's personal assistant anymore." This could be her big break. She was about to either get fired or promoted, and she wasn't sure which one she preferred at the moment. Getting fired wouldn't get her out of the Immortal Soul clause, but she would be free and clear of the company when they finally got caught. Getting promoted might put her in a better position to have her contract voided, as she was positive that the higher-ups didn't have their souls on the line.

Meyers didn't see things that way, however. "I'm afraid you are, Joan. That's what you were hired for, and you're not qualified to work on the board with the big dogs, like you're probably hoping for. No, I'm afraid you're going to be my assistant, and that's that."

"Like hell it is," Joan didn't normally think of herself as being a threatening person, but she felt the tone in her voice had reached a new level. "I'm afraid you're just going to have to fire me, Mr. Meyers. I'm not going to do it."

Meyers leaned forward and put on his own threatening voice, which was significantly more practiced than Joan's. "You are aware that our... unique circumstances prevent us from terminating your employment, Joan, are you not?" His voice held an eerily steady tone.

"Yes, Mr. Meyers."

"And you are aware that it is mutually beneficial for us to work together. A conspiracy such as the one we have entered into, together, cannot be allowed a weak link."

"Yes, Mr. Meyers." Joan's voice was wavering now, as she felt a threat just around the corner.

"One weak link is all it takes for all of this," he gestured around his office, "to be taken away. All of it. So we can't afford to have a weak link, can we, Joan?"

"No, Mr. Meyers."

"The company will not tolerate it, Joan. Now, do you know how I take my coffee?" He smiled at her to let her know that he knew he had just won their argument.

"Whole milk, two raw sugars." Joan knew it, too.

"Excellent. I'll be in the boardroom in five minutes, and I'll be taking my coffee in there. That will be all."

Joan couldn't believe the promotion she didn't get, and wondered how far the company might go to protect their interests. They had already kidnapped two people, declaring one of them dead, and she suspected that Edna would have the opportunity to read her own obituary sometime soon. She felt the need to call Sherman, to tell him they had to act fast. She got up and left the office to get Meyers his coffee, and thought about how she was going to be able to get the old man out if she was being watched by the company.

As the door closed behind her, Meyers picked the phone back up and pressed number five on his speed dial. It rang once. "Sir?"

"She'll be in the boardroom in five minutes. Get her out quietly. Use the service elevator."

"Sir."

Meyers hung up without saying another word, and debated whether or not to take the trip down to the boardroom to get his coffee. He opted against it, assuming that Joan would have done something disgusting to it before bringing it to him. He opened a calendar program on his computer, and began looking for a good time to have a meeting with the Choir Boys as well as the conspirators. He had to get the message out that there wasn't going to be any tolerance for anybody changing their minds about what they had done, or were doing, or were going to do. Joan was going to have to be his sacrificial pawn. "Let's see how they like it when I take out one of their own," he said to the empty office. He reached into the bottom drawer of his desk, the kind that was built into expensive desks and was large enough to accommodate a bottle of scotch and a few tumblers on top of everything else that an executive might need throughout the course of a day on the job. He poured himself three fingers of the scotch, and looked in the desk drawer to see if there might be an ice cube tray in there as well. His search was in vain, though, and he called Sofie at the reception desk.

"Mr. Meyers?"

"Yes, Sophie. Did you inquire about that ice cube maker I wanted installed in my desk?"

"Yes, Mr. Meyers. I believe we made an appointment to have someone come in and look at that for you next week. Have you considered the bar fridge idea we talked about?"

"Bar fridges are for college kids and door-to-door salesmen in hotels," he snapped at her. "They look cheap, and I don't want anything in here to look cheap."

"Yes, Mr. Meyers." David felt that he couldn't hear those words enough. It was a boost to his ego every time he heard them, and he was a big fan of receiving boosts to his ego. He hung up the phone and put his drink down on the desk. He didn't notice the Choir Boys in the boardroom closing the blinds to prevent anyone else from seeing what was about to happen.

Sherman's Escape.

Sherman reached for his phone, then cursed himself when he remembered that he had given it to Gary. Why had he trusted him like that? Right. There was no reason not to trust him. He wondered how it was that the Heatley Company had managed to turn Gary from being the mom-and-pop-porn-shop type to the conspire-to-kidnap-my-employees-in-the-basement type.

He ran back up the basement stairs and started to bang on the door, yelling for help and hoping, for the first time since he started working there, he would get the attention of a customer. He stopped for a moment and tried to hear what was going on in the shop. He could make out Gary's voice, but couldn't hear who he was talking to. He figured he was on the phone, probably talking to someone from the company about what had happened and asking what he should do about it. Company goons would probably be on their way to pick him up any minute now, adding him to the company's list of detainees. "Great," he said aloud as he realized the very real possibility of being placed in a holding cell of some kind with Old Blue, and Heatley, and - would Joan get caught, too? He had forgotten about her, but he told Gary that she had been the one who told him about the conspiracy. He sat down at the top of the stairs, and tried to be thankful that at least there would be someone born within fifty years of himself sharing his cell.

He thought he heard the front door open and close, and he was about to start yelling for help again, but he could hear the alarm system beeping. It was being armed, and he was alone. Fortunately, the alarm system was only equipped with motion sensors on the main floor, so he could move about freely in the basement so long as he didn't try to get through the back door (which was not only alarmed, but also chained shut despite fire regulations to the contrary). He stood up and turned on the lights, then made his way down the stairs, hoping there was something down there he could use to get out of the basement. The basement used to house an office area for the store, but it hadn't been used for anything except a place to store old boxes and miscellaneous supplies for a long time. The Heatley Company was not a big fan of wasting space, and they had decided to expand the store to incorporate the existing basement, but they hadn't announced what it would be used for. Given the company's decision to install the Konfessional 3000, Sherman thought it was likely that they would renovate the entire area and put in a peep show booth, or a private video viewing room. He shuddered at the thought of having to clean any of it up.

The desk that was originally for managerial purposes was still down there, but it had fallen into disuse at least a year ago, and was now covered in old paperwork as well as random bits of everything that didn't have a proper place to be put away. The idea was that the desk would be unusable until it was cleared off, making sure that everything got put away in short order, but ever since Gary purchased a laptop computer to replace the aging machine he had lost beneath a pile of paperwork, the managerial duties had been done upstairs during the inevitable slow periods during the day. He abandoned the desk along with everything inside it. Sherman opened the main drawer, hoping to find a screwdriver or a multi-tool, anything that might help him remove the door handle so he could get past the thick chain that was preventing him from getting out. Finding nothing useful, he slammed the drawer closed and opened up the top one on the right-hand side of the desk. He didn't find anything useful there, either, although there was a ragtag assortment of stationery there that he might have found useful dozens of times in recent months, had he only known to look there for it. Instead, every time he needed a pen, or some tape, or any other office supplies, he would make up a quick sign that said "Back in 5 minutes" in thick black marker, tape it up on the door, and run down to the convenience store to pick up whatever he needed. That worked fairly well until he needed to buy tape, at which point he simply locked the door and hoped that nobody came by.

He closed the drawer, then made short work of checking the others, as they all appeared to contain nothing but paperwork, before he started pushing piles of junk off of the desk to see what was underneath them, becoming more desperate with every one that failed to yield positive results. He lifted an overturned box that was on one corner of the desk, and found a telephone underneath it. He picked up the receiver, and was disappointed to find that there was no dial tone, but not surprised.

He hung the phone back up and pushed it off the desk out of frustration, enjoying the sound it made as it hit the ground. It was satisfying enough that he placed his arm outstretched on the desk and swept everything else off it in one swoop, creating a mess on the floor that looked not entirely unlike the mess he had cleared off the desk, with one important difference: there was a key on top of the pile now. He picked it up and ran to the back door of the store, and tried to fit the key in the padlock, astounded at his luck when it fit. He opened the padlock, and was removing the chain from the door handle when he heard the front door open, and the beeping sound of somebody turning off the alarm system. Sherman wasn't sure if he was extraordinarily lucky that whoever had shown up had done so when they did because the alarm wouldn't go off when he opened the back door, or if he was in deep trouble now that whoever was here, and he had to assume it was the Choir Boys, was going to be just a few steps behind him. He waited until he was sure the alarm had been turned off, then pushed the door open as quietly as he could. He held the door handle from the outside to prevent it from slamming shut, then ran like hell down the alley, turning down every corner he could to hide.

Allies.

Frank and Edna had been racing each other to pull the trigger on each other's ketamine drips for hours, and it looked like they would soon be running out, and quite possibly addicted. Dr. Edmunds, who had set up the initial apparatus for the siblings, was unaware the Choir Boys were going to be switching the trigger mechanisms and would have advised against it, or refused to set it up to begin with had had known, which was why he hadn't been told what was going to happen. Shortly after one of their tied games of quickdraw, Heatley and Blue woke up to find out that they were no longer alone in the room.

"Wha- who's there?" Heatley asked the room. The constant barrage of ketamine to his system was causing him a considerable amount of disorientation.

"It's Joan, Mr. Heatley," she said.

"Joan?"

"That hussy that lives next door me," Edna had woken up as well, much to the chagrin of both Heatley and Joan.

"Yes, Edna. I'm a hussy. A shameless, godless hussy. Shall I give you some ketamine now?" she said, and pressed the button she had swiped from Edna's hand before she had woken up.

Heatley had started to laugh before he realized that he still had his trigger in his hand, and promptly passed out again, at which point it was Edna's turn to laugh. "What the hell?" Joan said, looking at the trigger in her hand, and realized what had just happened. "What kind of sick joke is that?" She moved over to Heatley's bedside, Edna cackling all the while, and took the trigger from his hand. She pressed it, putting Edna to sleep, and waited for Heatley to come back around.

When Heatley came to he found Joan sitting by his bedside, watching the television. "What do you want, you backstabbing bitch?" he croaked at her.

"Mr. Heatley, I'm so sorry," she said, and turned off the TV. "This whole thing, this-"

"Conspiracy of assholes? The people I trusted to take care of my business who went turncoat on me without even giving me the decency of a hostile takeover?"

Joan felt pangs of guilt hammering at her with every syllable that came out of his mouth. "I'm so-"

"Sorry. Yes, you said that. Now, what the hell do you want?"

"Mr. Heatley. Please, let me explain what's going on." Edna started to wake up with a groan. "Sorry, Edna," Joan said. "I just need some alone time with your brother," and she pushed the trigger again, putting her back to sleep.

Heatley tried to suppress his smile, but it eventually forced its way out. "You always did know how to win me over, Joan." His anger rose up at her again. "Now, what the hell is going on here? What do you want?"

"We're in trouble, Mr. Heatley. You, Edna, myself and one of your other employees. Things have gotten - out of hand."

Heatley looked around the room. He had expected to find somebody else there, perhaps Meyers, or one of those Secret Service-looking security types. It infuriated him that he had been so oblivious to what had been happening in his company he had unknowingly funded his own kidnapping. He made a personal vow to employ more personal oversight in his company when he got out of this room. "I need a cigarette," he told her.

"Of course, Mr. Heatley. I took out your IV while you were asleep."

"And Edna?" Heatley said, looking at the bandage on his arm where the needle had been.

Joan blushed. "I thought we might keep hers in, for now."

"Good then. Now, help me get out of this thing." He reached out, and she took his hand, pulling until he was out of bed. Heatley saw his clothing on a table beside the bed, and pulled on his underwear and pants underneath his hospital gown, then slowly made his way over to the balcony. He stepped outside to the balcony and began to shiver almost immediately.

"Are you okay, Mr. Heatley?" Joan asked. It was a nice day out, and she didn't feel any chill in the air at all.

"Am I okay? How the hell do you think I'm doing? I'm not exactly happy to see you, either, for the record." He grabbed the ashtray from the table outside, and stepped back into the hospital room.

Joan followed him, closing the door behind her, watching as he lit up his cigarette. "Mr. Heatley?"

"What do you want?"

"Well, you know you're not allowed to -" Joan started, but trailed off. What did she care, after all?

"Let them kick me out," he said. "It's too cold outside for me, and I own this goddamned building, as well as everything in it. Hell, the people who have me trapped in here still work for me. I think." He sat down beside the window, looking out at the city. "I mean, even you still work for me. Not that I want you as an assistant anymore, mind you. I'd fire you in a second if anyone would listen to me."

Joan pulled out another chair and sat across from Heatley at the table. "Mr. Heatley, they've taken over. They don't work for you anymore, and you don't own anything anymore. You're dead, as far as everyone outside is concerned. And I will be too, I assume." She looked out the window and started to tear up.

"What are you talking about?"

"I'm here because they found out that I was trying to do something about this. To help you."

Frank blew a puff of smoke across the table at her. "Bullshit."

"Really, Mr. Heatley, I was. I was working with someone else in the company to try and-"

"Who?"

"You don't know him. He's new to the company, and-"

"So a brand new employee I've never met and my personal assistant who lied to me for months are working together to try and take down a company-wide conspiracy?" He took another long haul on his cigarette. "Why should I believe you?"

"I'm sure that your smoking is going to be bringing them in here any minute now, Mr. Heatley. It will probably be fairly obvious to you that I'm not with them anymore once they come in."

As if on cue, the door opened. David Meyers entered the room, followed by Dr. Edmonds. Meyers looked quite cheerful. "Well, how are our guests doing?" Meyers asked no one in particular.

"Doing well enough to stab you in the face with my IV drip, you bastard." Heatley had never been a master of subtlety.

"Well, I'm afraid you won't be feeling much better about me any time soon, Mr. Heatley," Meyers said. "Joan, when you're done trying to make peace with Mr. Heatley, we need you back in the office."

"I knew it! You bitch!" Heatley swiped the ashtray across the table, spilling ashes into Joan's lap. She sat there looking at the ashes, watched as the plastic ashtray fell to the ground, hitting the clean linoleum with a collection of harmless, hollow-sounding tick noises as it bounced itself clumsily to a halt.

"David!" she yelled. "Mr. Heatley, I - I didn't - they must have been listening in on our conversation. They're trying to pit you against me!"

"Pit me against you? That's rich." Heatley got up from the chair and walked over to where his shirt was still laying. He took off the hospital gown, put on the shirt, then crossed the room again and went back to the patio door. "I'm not coming back in until the lot of you are gone. I've got nothing to say to any of you. I'm dead, after all," he spat. He stepped out and closed the door behind him. Looking back in the room, he came back in and shut the blinds, then stepped out between them.

Meyers and Dr. Edmonds stood watching the blinds as they gently swung, displaying decreasing triangles of the balcony. Meyers turned to Joan. "Gotcha," he said with a wink. He turned and left the room as she unleashed a hurl of insults at him that he had, as a result of working with the Heatley Company, heard before.

Joan went out to the balcony where she found Heatley staring over the railing. "Mr. Heatley, please believe me. I'm not with them anymore. I'm just as much a prisoner here as you are."

He spat over the railing, and watched his ball of spit fall until it was out of sight. "I don't know whether I should believe you or not, Joan. What I do know is, no matter how I look at it, you're not exactly innocent here."

"I know, Mr. Heatley. I just got caught up-"

"You could have stopped this. You could have said no to them, told the police about what was going on before any of this happened. Or told me." He turned to face her. "Why didn't you stop it?"

Joan didn't know what to tell him. Of course she had known what the company was doing was wrong, but it hadn't stopped her from going along with it. "There were some meetings after you locked yourself away, Mr. Heatley. We were all pretty sure you were just going to stay locked away for years, if not the rest of your life, and I - well, we - I mean they - thought that it wouldn't do you any harm to live life how you were, and the company could go ahead with some of their plans that had been shot down by you every time they were brought up."

"And the company thought it all had to be done now? I'm an old man, Joan. I smoke, I drink, and I barely ever leave the house. How long did they think I would last like that? They couldn't wait just a few short years?"

Joan felt guilt kick her in the ribs again and again while he spoke. She would never have agreed to the company's plans if she thought even for a second that she would end up being the one who would have to explain all of this to Heatley if he caught on. "It was Meyers who really pushed for it. He started off relatively small, while you were still in your apartment, making changes here and there, feeding the animals that were to be euthanized to the ones at the zoo -" Heatley's eyes almost exploded they grew so fast. "-and he was the one who started to implement the plan to kidnap you, without even telling anybody else what he was doing." She leaned over the balcony beside him, staring down at the street below. "He told me to keep quiet about what he was doing when I was making my reports to you, and he had proof that the company was making more money the way he was doing things than it had while you were in charge."

"I was still in charge," Heatley pointed out.

"Theoretically, yes. But you were locked away in your apartment, and didn't ever come out to check up on things, so all they had to do was start producing two daily reports instead of one. You'd see what you wanted to see, and the company did what it wanted to do. It really did seem harmless at the time."

"So what happened, then? Why didn't they just keep me where I was?"

"Well, Mr. Heatley, there were things that couldn't get done without the approval of the CEO, which was you, and Meyers started asking 'What if I was the CEO?' He came to a meeting one day, very top-level types only at the time. Well, top-level types and me, I guess. He said he had a plan." She stepped back from the railing, unable to stand beside the man she had betrayed any more. "He must have been looking into it for ages, maybe even before you had locked yourself away this last time, because he had everything ready to go as soon as he got approval from the board."

"Meyers." Heatley turned his back to the railing, and grabbed another cigarette out of the pack. "I'm gonna get that son of a bitch."

"Does this mean you believe me, Mr. Heatley?" Joan asked.

Heatley lit a match from a pack that sported a Heatley Company logo. "Maybe. Doesn't mean I trust you, though."

"You might as well start," came a voice from the doorway. "The little hussy isn't with them." Edna was holding herself up by leaning on the wall, and Joan wondered how it was she managed to cross the room without her cane after all the drugs that had been pumped into her system. "I heard them talking. I was pretending to still be out while you were out here and they were talking to her, Frank. She's locked in here, too." She looked at the two of them out on the balcony, then stepped out and grabbed a cigarette from her brother. "Now, how the hell are we supposed to get out of this place?"

Grilled Cheese With Bacon.

Sherman slowed his pace to a walk when he got to the mall, looking over his shoulder every few steps for any signs of men in suits that might be looking for him. He ducked into the first store he saw. He pretended to look at some shirts on a sale rack near the entrance, but he was really watching the people passing by the front of the store. He was suspicious of everyone that passed by, as they all appeared to be looking in at him.

"Can I help you, sir?" a voice came from behind him. He looked at the attractive young woman working in the store, then over her shoulder at a selection of lingerie that seemed to extend from right behind her all the way to the back of the store on both sides. He looked back at the shirts he had been trying to pretend he was interested in and realized they were women's nightwear. He also realized he was the creepy guy sweating profusely in a lingerie store while fondling the merchandise.

"Uh, no. I, uh, sorry," he said. He clumsily made his way back out the front door, and went into the next store, where he was immediately accosted by a man in a suit.

"Hello-" was all he got out before Sherman bolted back out the door, looking over his shoulder to see if he was being chased only to realize he had just run away from a suit salesman.

Sherman shook his head and told himself to find a place where he could calm down. He reached for his phone for the fifth or sixth time since he had escaped the basement, reminding himself yet again that it was still back at what was presumably his former place of employment. Even if he wasn't going to be fired, which he was positive he was, there was no way he was going back to find out. He quit, and didn't feel the slightest bit of remorse for not giving them any notice. *It's not like they gave me any notice about locking me in the basement, after all.* He kept moving down the hallway of the mall, trying to be more inconspicuous. He saw a sign for a pub disguised as a family restaurant at the opposite end of the mall and headed there, deciding that a beer and some food were a really good idea while he contemplated what he should do next.

The hostess was a slightly younger version of the servers, who were all slight variants of essentially the same physical form, and dressed in slightly different versions of the same non-uniform. It was the kind of place that was two steps away from a serious sexual-harassment lawsuit at any given point in time, which they managed to keep at bay without anyone ever figuring out how. The hostess was looking forward to being legal age to serve alcohol, so she could get the chance to earn the same tip money that the servers counted at the bar after their shifts. She asked Sherman if he was alone, if he wanted a menu, and a few other mundane questions as she led him to the table she had already decided he was sitting at. Sherman tried to find a discreet way of asking if he could have a dark, quiet seat with his back to a wall. "Can I sit over there?" was the best he could come up with.

She made a face at his request, but it was lost on him as he walked behind her, watching her backside as she changed directions and took him to the table that he had requested instead of the one she had picked out for him on her plastic map at the hostess' podium. "No problem."

She ran through the daily specials with an almost non-existent degree of enthusiasm, and told Sherman what his server's name would be, although he wasn't listening to her. He smiled and nodded at her whenever she stopped talking long enough that he believed she needed a response of some sort, and then she grabbed the three extra sets of cutlery at the table, telling him she was just getting it 'out of his way,' although Sherman suspected it was the kind of thing that was done to prevent the silverware from going missing.

When his server came by, he asked her for whatever dark beer they had on tap, and asked if they could make him two grilled cheese sandwiches with crispy bacon cooked inside them. Her face contorted as she tried to suppress her revulsion, but she said she would ask the cook. She didn't seem to think it would be a problem, so long as his arteries could stand it. He ordered a side of poutine to go with it instead of the regular fries it would normally have come with, and she walked away from him, shaking her head.

He sat at the table, watching the people who passed by outside the restaurant, and began to wonder whether or not he was in a Heatley Company-owned business or not. Would they have conspirators on staff? Would his name and photo be sent out to all the company stores in an email marked "Urgent!"? Did the company own a dairy, and would they put his face on milk cartons? He wanted to slouch in the chair, hide under the table, or just walk out and go home, but he thought that doing anything except just sitting where he was and having his lunch might fall under the category of conspicuous behaviour, and he was desperate to avoid drawing attention to himself. "Should have just ordered off the menu," he said. He wondered if he should try and get in touch with Joan first, or Karl.

His server came back, and told him that the cooks could make his request no problem. "And oddly enough, there's not even any health code violations in serving it," she said.

"Thank you," Sherman told her, and held up his glass in a cheers gesture to her.

"What did you do to your hand?" she asked him.

Sherman pulled his injured hand back and tried uselessly to hide it under the table. "Nothing. I got -" he almost said 'I got assaulted by a ninety-year-old woman,' but managed to catch himself in time to spare himself that particular bit of humiliation. "I fell skateboarding."

"Ouch," she said.

Sherman wondered why she had to know how he broke his fingers before she said 'Ouch' to him. Did it matter how they broke? Was the pain involved in breaking fingers not universally unpleasant, or did she just need the visualization to have any empathy for his discomfort? He decided he didn't really care. "It happens," he told her.

She left him alone with his beer, which he was too preoccupied to drink at the time. He found himself doing something that he hadn't done in years, which was looking around to see if there was a pay phone around that he could use, thinking he could call Karl. Knowing there was little if any chance that he could be involved in the conspiracy, he figured Karl was probably his best bet of finding, if not an ally, at least someone to confide in, or a safe place to hide until he figured out his next move. It dawned on him that he didn't even know Karl's phone number. Ever since he had begun to rely on having a cell phone, he had kept a simple method of keeping track of his friends' phone numbers: he looked for their names in the address book of his phone, and hit send when he found the right one.

Karl's number, so far as Sherman was concerned, was 3. Just hold down the number 3, and the preprogrammed speed dial would have him talking to Karl in a matter of seconds. The pay phone, however, was not very likely to connect him with Karl by holding down the 3 button.

When his server came back with with his food and a queasy look on her face, Sherman asked her if he could see the menu again. She brought it back in a few minutes, asked him if everything was okay so far, and left while he was still giving his answer. She didn't believe that everything would be good with the piles of grease she had been forced to deliver. Sherman skimmed the outskirts of the menu, not interested in anything in the way of food, but instead looking for Heatley Company logos hidden somewhere, or any fine print that might say something along the lines of 'A Subsidiary Of The Heatley Company' to help him determine whether or not he should be wary of the waitress, or suspicious of his food. Not finding anything, he put the menu back down and poured a puddle of ketchup on the side of his plate that would have been considered an unhealthy amount had it not been the most healthy item he was going to ingest during his sitting. He flagged down the server, who had been trying to avoid him, despite not having anything better to do on such a slow day and he ordered another beer, asking for his bill at the same time. She brought them both by a few minutes later, and while Sherman looked over the bill, his eyes were taken off of the window for just long enough to miss spotting two of the Choir Boys as they passed by, looking into each window they passed for their escapee.

One of them spotted him, and tapped the other on the arm, and they simultaneously lifted the radios embedded in their cufflinks to their faces. "Target acquired," they said over top of each other, and headed for the restaurant door.

Sherman, meanwhile, was arguing with the waitress why he was being charged for two complete platters, when he only received one portion of the poutine. She didn't feel like arguing with him, as she knew from experience that every word out of her mouth which wasn't an offer to correct the bill would affect the tip she would receive. "Let me just fix that for you then," she said, wishing that she had typed the code into the computer that told the cooks it was perfectly fine with her if they spit in his food. They were both facing the till at the bar, and didn't notice the two men coming up behind them until one of them had Sherman by the arm.

"Is this man causing you any trouble, ma'am?" one of them asked. The server didn't know what to make of the two suits who had grabbed Sherman. They had the distinct look of government agents from every television show her boyfriend insisted on watching, from their build to the coiled wire coming out of their right ears, attached to what she assumed was supposed to be a discreet radio system, that lost all of its discretion thanks to the close-cropped hair they were both sporting.

"No, no problem." She wanted to address them as officers, but that didn't seem appropriate so she let the sentence dangle, hoping they would fill in the blanks, perhaps flash some form of identification at her, and explain who they were and what Sherman had done. They didn't. What she did get was a generic-looking business card that simply said Choir Boys from one of the men. It had a contact email address on it, which she stared at while the other man escorted Sherman out the front door.

"Email this address, tell them what happened, and give them this reference number," he said, writing down a six digit code for her. "They'll make sure this gets paid." Without another word, or waiting for one to come from the server, he turned and left, joining his partner out front just as an unmarked black van pulled up, and absconded with the three men. She picked up her cell phone, and began sending text messages to everyone she knew.

New Beginnings.

"It's done," Roger told the rest of the room as he put the phone down. "We have the boy in custody, as well as Joan and the siblings. The situation has been… contained, for now." His smiled his massive smile that reminded some who had seen it of what must go through a cat's mind as it watched a mouse slowly fight back less and less.

There had been panic among some of the conspirators upon learning that Sherman had escaped, and the reassurances from Clemens that he would be captured again before there were repercussions did not provide them any solace. Most of those in attendance were relieved to have Sherman apprehended, but there was an elephant in the room that nobody wanted to talk about: What was going to happen to the detainees now? It was Roger's job to make sure that the rest of the room had plausible deniability when it came to decisions like the one that had to be made. His ability to do this sort of thing so dispassionately was one of the main reasons most of the other board members lived in fear of him. The sheer volume of him didn't help them to relax, either. "We will have to deal with the four of them, and soon," he told them. Several of the board members pretended not to have heard what he had just said, and they began shuffling papers about at random, hoping they could pack up and leave now.

The collective conscience of the room came out in a single voice, however. "What are we going to do about them?"

Eyes went everywhere. Some went to Dr. Edmunds, who had asked the question, some went to Clemens, who was now staring at Edmonds, but most took note of the plants in the room, or the remnants of the robin's nest that had been built on the window ledge earlier in the spring. It had suffered a catastrophic structural failure a few weeks ago when a window washer had dropped his squeegee on it. "Dr. Edmunds," Roger began, "it is for the benefit of everybody here that we do not discuss such things. Rest assured that this problem will be dealt with quickly and effectively, without any unwanted media or police attention."

The chill in Clemens' words sent a round of goosebumps through the room. Even the board members whose moral fibre levels were so low they were rendered incapable of giving a shit about anything except their bank accounts and making sure their wives never met their mistresses were hesitant to immediately dismiss the implications of what Clemens had just said. Once again, it was only Edmunds who spoke up. "You can't be suggesting that we have them ki-"

"Doctor Edmunds!" Clemens yelled at him. "You are dismissed from this meeting." His hands clenched into fists so tight that it looked like the skin on his knuckles were going to tear open. Edmunds gathered the papers in front of him and got up to leave. "I'll be wanting to see you in my office later, doctor." Edmunds left without a reply, but the words chased him out the door.

Clemens' knuckles loosened up enough to allow some blood to flow through to his fingertips, and he appeared to relax a little bit, insofar as he was no longer making threats at anybody who was currently sitting in the room. "Ladies and gentlemen, that will be all for today," he said, and the rest of the board members stood up and began to leave in a quiet shuffle. Clemens picked up a pencil from the table and snapped the eraser off of it with his thumb, then dropped both of the bits of it on the table. He stared at the pieces intently, and waited until everyone else had left the room before standing up to make his way out the back door of the boardroom which led into a private hallway towards his office.

Clemens stopped at the drinks trolley just inside his office door and poured himself a scotch large enough to incapacitate some men, and expensive enough to bankrupt others, then sat himself down in his lavish chair. He took a large sip of his drink, enjoying the burn as it washed over his tongue, and sat in an almost meditative silence for thirty seconds before snapping back up. His right hand reached out and pressed the page button for Edmunds while his left brought his drink back to his lips, then placed the tumbler down on a coaster that cost more than the average desk in the building. "Edmunds. My office. Now," he said, then released the page button without waiting for a reply.

Less than three minutes later, Edmunds came into his office, knocking to announce himself as he slowly entered the room, eyes scanning the room. "Mr. Clemens?"

"Doctor Edmunds. Please, have a seat." The big man's eyes indicated the chair across from him, and Edmunds walked obediently, but cautiously, over to it and sat down. Clemens swirled his drink around in his hand, watching the liquid as it formed a tiny whirlpool in the glass. "We seem to be having… an issue, don't we, Doctor?"

Edmunds shifted uncomfortably in his chair. "I don't believe so," he said, hoping to diffuse the situation as quickly as possible.

"Then what, exactly, would you call your little outburst in the boardroom? You must remember it, surely? It was no more than ten minutes ago, so far as I recall." He took another swig of his drink.

Edmunds found he was shifting again and tried to stop himself from looking as uneasy as he felt, although he felt it was a futile effort to try and disguise it from Clemens. "I don't think it was an outburst as such. I was merely concerned for the lives of my patients, as I am wont to do as a physician. You are familiar with the Hypocratic Oath, I assume?"

"I am familiar with many things, Doctor, and I assure you I am familiar with several uses for many of the tools of your trade that you have never thought of." He smiled as he watched Edmunds squirm in his chair. "I am also familiar with the terms of your contract with the Heatley Company, as I am sure you are as well." He reached into the top drawer of his desk, and pulled out a copy of the standard contract for employment with the Heatley Company.

"I've read it, Mr. Clemens. Is there something in particular you're hoping I remember out of this?"

"If you would care to open this to the page marked by the blue tab I've placed in there, and tell me what it says in the hi-lighted area?" Roger pushed the contract across the table.

Edmunds picked it up and opened it up to the page Clemens had told him to, looked at the paper briefly, and slid it back across to him. "You're talking about the Immortal Soul Clause. Yes, I know about that."

Clemens' eyes widened. "And?" he asked, slight surprise at the doctor's lack of concern in his voice.

"Have you ever heard people talk about doctors having a god complex?" Edmunds asked him.

"Of course I have."

"Well, it stands to reason that a man of science would have little use for the concept of religion, doesn't it?" Clemens nodded at him. "I'm an atheist, and I figure I don't have much to lose by the Heatley Company confiscating something I don't believe in that was written in a book of fairy stories, no matter how well it's been selling over the years." Edmunds was looking a little bit more confident, but Clemens quickly sent him reeling back.

"It also stands to reason, then, that a man who doesn't believe in the afterlife might want to prolong his current life for as long as possible, as once it's over, it is over." He said this with so little emotion in his voice that it was impossible to miss the threat lurking in the undertones. The words were a fin, indicating the merciless mass of razor-sharp teeth in the water.

"What is it that I'm expected to do here, Mr. Clemens?"

Roger drank the rest of his scotch in one gulp, then placed the tumbler back on the coaster. "Just what you have been doing, Doctor. For the time being. As a physician with the company, we are not asking you to violate your oath. You will continue to care for our patients as you have been, ensuring their comfort during their stay with us."

"And by 'ensuring their comfort' you mean keep them sedated? There's nothing wrong with any of them."

"I have to disagree with you, Doctor," Clemens said. "I'm sure that they are all suffering from some rather high levels of anxiety right now, and the care you will be providing will relieve them of that."

"Until they are no longer staying with us."

"Precisely."

"And what happens to them once they leave my care?"

"Doctor Edmunds?"

"Yes."

"Do you remember why it is that I asked you into my office?"

"Yes, Mr. Clemens."

"And would you say that you consider yourself a reasonably intelligent person?"

"Yes, Mr. Clemens."

"And yet you asked me what was essentially the very same question that got you invited into this private discussion. Your job does not require that you provide follow-up care for persons no longer in the employ of the Heatley Company. Are we clear?"

"Yes, Mr. Clemens." Any questions Edmunds still had he opted against asking, and he found himself relieved that at least he would not be the one asked to terminate the lives of his patients. What little relief he found in this, however, was countered by the anxiety he felt knowing that he would likely share their fate if he continued to ask questions.

"Excellent. Would you care for a drink? A toast to new beginnings, perhaps?"

Edmunds knew better than to refuse a drink offered by Roger Clemens. "To new beginnings. Yes, I would, thank you," he said.

Clemens reached out and lifted his empty tumbler to him. "Fetch me one while you're up then, Doctor Edmunds. Two fingers, no ice." Edmunds reached out and grabbed Clemens' glass from his desk, who looked disapprovingly at the doctor's small hands. "Make that three fingers, if you're pouring it to your scale," he said.

Edmunds thought about the various meanings of the words 'New Beginnings' as he got Clemens his drink and didn't like anything he came up with.

Something's Getting Burned.

Sherman had seen countless movies in which a person was abducted off the streets and forced into the back of a van, but he had never seen one in which the van was decked out in such luxury. Had it not been for the manner in which he got in, and perhaps the company he was forced to keep while he was there, he might have looked as if he was on his way to the prom, or perhaps being escorted to a private jet for some whirlwind tour with a rock band. There was one row of seats in the back of the van, with room enough behind it for luggage or (more likely, given his present circumstance) a few bodies and some digging implements, a can of gasoline, and something to beat the dental records out of an inconvenient ex-employee. An oak-topped mini-bar extended all the way from the back seats to a pair of rear-facing seats that had drink holders and control panels on their arms. The carpet was the thing that Sherman was happiest with, as it looked well-maintained and didn't show the slightest hint of bloodstains.

"So do you guys do this kind of thing often?" he asked his captors, trying to break the ice. It didn't even crack. "Where are you taking me?" Again, nothing. "Can I have a beer?" he tried. His luck changed, as one of the men gave the slightest twitch of a smile and reached into the mini-bar and grabbed him a green bottle of some imported beer Sherman had never heard of. "Thanks," he said, and opened the bottle on an opener mounted on the edge of the bar. The man who handed Sherman the beer nodded at him. Sherman had been placed in the middle of the back seat of the van, with one of the Choir Boys on either side of him. He wasn't handcuffed, he wasn't told to put on his seatbelt, he wasn't hit, he didn't have a gun pointed at him, and he was drinking a beer. He thought himself to be at least a little bit lucky, all things considered. He wished he had a window to look out, to try and gain his bearings on where he was, but the only window he could see was obscured by the severely tinted shield that separated the driver's area from the rest of the van, and two goons sitting in the seats across from him. He took a sip of his beer.

A few minutes later, the van rounded a corner and Sherman could felt the van begin on a downward angle. He heard the sound of a garage door opening, and as they moved forward the sounds of traffic outside became muffled. They came to a stop, the driver and passenger got out, and moments later the side door slid open. "Out," one of the men said, still wearing his sunglasses in the dimly lit garage.

Sherman nodded to him, and tipped his beer back, chugging the rest of it awkwardly as he made his way to the door. The Choir Boys grabbed him roughly and moved him hurriedly into a service elevator. All the buttons had been removed from the panel, except for the ones for the top three floors, all of which required a key to gain access. One of the Choir Boys pulled out a keyring so thick with keys that Sherman thought he must have his pockets specially tailored to prevent the keys from showing up as a jagged mass in his pants. It took him a moment to find the right one, which he slipped into the keyhole beside the top floor button and turned it. The elevator doors closed and after a moment they were brought up to the top floor. When the doors reopened, Sherman was escorted down what looked like the hallway to an expensive condominium. He was ushered down the hallway, and brought into Heatley's apartment. "Make yourself at home," somebody said behind him, and the door was closed behind him. A deadbolt locked the door from the outside.

Sherman looked around the unusual layout of the place. The foyer was large and luxurious, but furnished as if it was a living room, with bookshelves, a big-screen television, and couches. It reeked of cigarettes, and so Sherman lit one up. "Would have done it anyway, you bastards," he said to the empty room. He walked around the room, looking at the books and other items on the shelves, then made his way into the kitchen. He opened the fridge, and found it well-stocked with expensive beer. He grabbed two, figuring that making himself at home included giving himself access to whatever was in the fridge, then walked back into the living room. The remote control for the television was on the coffee table. He sat on the couch and turned on the TV. "You know what I've always wanted to do?" he said out loud, hoping that he was being monitored. He stood up and threw one of the unopened beers at the television. The bottle went through the screen with a triumphant shattering noise. Sherman twisted the cap off of the other beer with some difficulty and stated looking around for something to break the doors down with. On one of the bookshelves, he found a marble bust of Frank Heatley.

He placed his beer on the shelf and picked up the heavy bust, hefting it in his good hand. He walked up to the front door and threw it as hard as he could. It fell to the ground, hardly placing a dent in the heavy door. He picked it back up, this time gripping it with both hands as best he could, and brought it down on the doorknob, breaking it off and sending an agonizing bolt of pain through his fingers. He cradled his broken fingers uselessly and made his way back to the bookshelf to grab his beer. The doorknob lay on the ground, but the deadbolt prevented the door from being opened. Sherman heard some commotion in the hallway, followed by the sound of the deadbolt turning in the door. The door was pulled open and four of the Choir Boys came charging into the room. Sherman was trying to hold his beer and his injured fingers with his good hand, and didn't make any signs of resistance when they surrounded him. "Just making myself at home," he said. "You should see my apartment."

"We have. Some people are working on that shithole you live in as we speak, Mr. Klein," one of the Choir Boys said. Sherman suddenly felt diminutive. He was physically smaller than any of the Choir Boys, but he hadn't actually considered the real danger he might he might be in until now. The thought of these men going through his apartment filled him with a sense of foreboding.

"What the hell are you doing in my apartment?" he asked them.

The same Choir Boy was the only one that ever addressed Sherman, and he thought that this one must be either their leader or a terrible public relations worker. "We're making arrangements, Mr. Klein."

"What are you talking about? Arrangements for what?" His fight-or-flight instincts told him neither one was currently a viable option.

"Mr. Klein, you are suspected of breaking your contract with the Heatley Company, and we are making arrangements to have this taken care of without a lengthly and expensive trial." He turned to the rest of the Choir Boys. "Find anything else heavy enough to do damage, and get it out of here." He turned back to Sherman. "I'd suggest you sit down and watch some television, but it looks like you're not a fan," he said, indicating the broken screen. "Perhaps you should just settle in with a good book for now. And remember, we're watching you, so behave yourself."

The rest of the Choir Boys walked around the apartment, looking for anything that might be used to break down the doors, and brought it with them. Sherman watched as they found things he had overlooked, mostly decorative items from the bookshelves. One of the Choir Boys even took away a large hardcover edition of the Oxford English Dictionary. "I was gonna read that," Sherman said. The man glared at him, and joined the other three as they filed out of the room. The door closed, the doorknob falling off the other side as they left. The deadbolt locked again.

Sherman looked at his beer, and briefly considered polishing it off and getting another before deciding he would be better off keeping his mental faculties in proper working order if he was going to get out of this place. He set the bottle down on the coffee table and went to the kitchen to see if he might be able to find something useful in there. After going through the drawers, it was clear to him that somebody had beat him to the punch and removed all of the sharp knives from the place, leaving the rest of the cutlery, but nothing that could do the type of damage he was looking to do in any short amount of time. The cupboards underneath the countertop held a full complement of cleaning supplies, many of which were marked as poisonous and flammable. He wondered if they would just let him burn if he started a fire, or if they would try to put it out. Would the fire department get there on time to save him? Would there be an investigation? The decision to not set the apartment on fire should have been easy to make, as all the variables could end up with him being in a worse position at the end of it than he was before it started. He kept looking, but found nothing else. "Okay, then. Something's getting burned," he muttered to himself.

They're Listening.

Heatley and Joan both stared in disbelief at Edna, who was hobbling about without her cane. "I don't know how many times I have to tell you that I'm not a hussy, Edna. I'm just–"

"I'm not interested in how you perceive yourself, Joan." Edna spoke her name as if it were a profanity. Joan was surprised that she used it at all, as she was used to being addressed by a series of slanderous names by the old woman. Joan wasn't even sure which one of them had begun their animosity towards the other, though she suspected it was Old Blue, as she had a tendency to bring out what could categorically be called the worst in those with whom she came into contact.

"Mrs. Sheldon, I don't believe that this is the time for you to behave like this. We're going to have to work together if we want to get out of here." Edna finally found her cane, which had been placed on a counter on the opposite side of the room from her bed. It made her appear stronger when she picked it up, and Joan couldn't help but think of the damage she was reputed to inflict with it. Frank Heatley didn't have a magic cane to bring him up in stature, and Joan thought that he might end up being their weakest link in their escape. His bank accounts had been closed after his will had been honoured, and without money he wasn't capable of getting much done. Making coffee, pouring drinks, smoking cigarettes, and coming up with asinine financial endeavours were the extent of his specialties.

"Well, I've got Bessy here," Edna said, swinging her cane through the air. It came into contact with a fly, sending it arcing towards the wall. It fell to the ground and didn't move again. Joan wanted to believe that it had been pure coincidence that the fly had been hit, as Old Blue didn't even seem to notice, but she couldn't be sure. Perhaps she really was that vicious, and that might even be a good thing. "And you," she said, looking Joan up and down, "Well, I suppose you've got your feminine wiles. You're younger than us, too, so I guess you can help just by virtue of being more spry than my brother and I. This one, though," she said, pointing her cane at Heatley. "I don't know what he's going to be good for. Maybe a decoy."

"Hey!" Heatley barked at her.

"We could push him down a flight of stairs, and the noise he makes could bring everyone over to where he is while we make our escape." Joan and Heatley looked at each other, unsure of whether or not she was joking.

"I'm not useless, you know," Heatley said. "I've got-"

"Money is all you had, and you don't have that anymore." Edna was pacing the room with her cane in her hands. It was as if the cane gave her strength by osmosis, and she didn't need to use it to walk once she had picked it up.

"Mr. Heatley?" Joan felt the need to intervene. She knew they had to work together if they were going to make it out.

"What?"

"I don't want to sound too paranoid, but this room is probably being monitored, isn't it? I mean, after all, there were several cameras in your apartment."

"There was what?"

"The cameras in your apartment. I thought you knew, or at least would have suspected that they were watching you." She looked around the room, and dropped her voice to a whisper. "They've probably got this place wired as well, and if we'd like to talk about escape, we should do it from the balcony."

"Speak up, hussy!" Edna yelled at her.

Joan grabbed Heatley by the hand and led him out to the balcony, told him to stay put, and then came back for Edna. She reached out for her hand as well, but Bessy came down and rapped her across the knuckles. "Edna, I'm trying to help you-" her eyes darted quickly around the room again, "-patch things up with your brother," she finished lamely. "Turn up your damn hearing aids."

"If he wants to make things right, he'll throw himself down a flight of stairs to distract them so we can escape." Edna stood her ground, daring Joan to reach for her hand again.

Joan reached out with speed she didn't know she had and snatched the cane from Edna's hand, then ran for the door to the balcony. Relieved of her weapon, Edna's strength diminished slightly, but she hobbled after Joan, making her way out to the balcony where Joan was waiting for her with the cane held out in a gesture of truce. Edna grabbed it back, leaned forward on it and slapped Joan across the face as hard as she could. Joan had worked for Heatley for years, had become accustomed to the irrational behaviours he exhibited on a regular basis, had joined a criminal conspiracy involving his betrayal and kidnapping, and had thought she had become impervious to feeling indignant as a result, but being slapped in the face by a self-righteous old lady was an affront she hadn't been prepared for. Casting better judgement aside, she slapped Edna back. She felt as if she had just slapped the inside of a bag of Gummi-Worms, and she looked for something to wipe her hand on.

"You bitch!" Edna yelled at her, and she raised her cane over her head.

"Me bitch?" Joan said. "What about you? Isn't there something about 'An eye for an eye' in that book you put so much stock in? I'm trying to help you, and all you can do is yell at me as if I'm the cause of your problems. I'm not the enemy here, Edna, so save your bullshit for somebody who deserves it."

Edna stood trembling, although because she wasn't the most stable person on their feet at the best of times, it took Joan a moment to realize how angry she was. Just when it looked like Edna's vibrating limbs were about to break their gravitational orbit from her body and lash out at Joan, Heatley stepped in between them and grabbed Edna by her shoulders. "Edna," he said, his voice eerily calm. "We need you. We won't make it out of here if we're fighting each other. So save it for them." She lowered her cane to the ground, her eyes following it, and she stood in silence. Heatley turned back to Joan. "Now, let's talk about how we're supposed to get the hell out of here."

The Burn.

The Internet is a valuable resource for many things, and Sherman had spent a significant amount of time scouring it for documents that he felt might become useful, from the antiquated Anarchist's Cookbook to safety information guides that explained which commonly-found household cleaners could be dangerous when mixed together, as well as a Boy Scout Manual, an Army Field Manual, several books on survival in the outdoors, and other such things that he thought might help get him out of a bad situation if he found himself in one. Unfortunately, all the information he had collected was stored on his phone, which he did not currently have the good fortune to have on his person. What's more, he hadn't actually gotten around to reading any of it yet, preferring instead to read the comic books or science fiction novels that he kept on it. As a result, he didn't know if mixing the chemicals under the sink would create some form of poisonous gas, or if it might create a spontaneous explosion upon contact with oxygen.

He looked over the bottles again, as if he was attempting to mentally will some fragment of memory of a text he had never read, but of course nothing came to him. It occurred to him that he was at least fortunate to not be reading the chapter from the Worst Case Scenario Handbook on how to escape from a car that was sinking in a river while trapped in a car that was sinking in a river. He left the chemicals under the sink alone for the time being and looked around the apartment. There was a patch on the wall that appeared to have a newer paint job than the rest of it, and he was unnerved by the thought of another person being captive in the same room as he was in now, trying to escape and being caught by the Choir Boys. Was this where Heatley had been kept? Where was he now? He looked at the other doors, but they were all locked shut with deadbolts and Sherman knew he would never get one of them open before they figured out what he was doing and burst back into the room. He looked at the hinges on the doors. They were nothing special, just regular door hinges like he had in his own apartment, with no industrial design to prevent tampering. A few months ago, there had been a party at his apartment, and somebody had locked themselves in the only bathroom for a much longer period of time than is considered kosher to be in the only bathroom being used by over twenty people who were imbibing. After somebody had given up waiting and urinated off his balcony onto the sidewalk below, they had tried to open the door by picking the lock, but the door wouldn't budge. One of Sherman's friends, inebriated beyond reason, had passed out on the other side of the door, preventing it from opening, and they had to remove the hinges to get the door open. As far as Sherman could recall, it hadn't been that difficult, and the whole process had taken a few short minutes after they had found tools that could do the job. All he had to do was find something he could remove the hinges with, and buy himself the few minutes he needed to do it.

He walked around the room a few times, searching for the supplies he needed without picking anything up to avoid suspicion. If his plan was going to work, he was going to have to set up everything in less time than it would take the Choir Boys to realize what he was up to and come down the hallway again, which wasn't going to give him much time. After his fifth pass around the rooms, he figured he was about as ready as he was going to be.

He left open the drawers and cupboards in the kitchen he would need to get into, hoping that anyone watching would think that he was becoming more desperate and couldn't be bothered to close them, then he made himself a drink. He brought the bottle back into the living room and sat on the couch, then took a big sip out of the glass before he picked the bottle back up and threw it at the front door. He bolted up from the couch, taking one of the cushions with him in his good hand. He threw the cushion in front the door to protect himself from the broken glass he was about to throw himself down on, brought his lighter up and set the alcohol on fire. The door was ablaze in seconds.

Sherman got up and ran back to the kitchen and reached into the cupboards, where he grabbed a rolling pin and a honing steel (neither of which Heatley had ever used, but had simply had purchased for the appearance of a fully-stocked kitchen). He then grabbed a bottle from under the sink that had a warning label on it saying it was flammable and ran back into the living room. He threw the rolling pin and honing steel at the door he was going to try and open, then ran to the heavy couch and pushed it towards the front door, his broken fingers screaming at him to leave them alone. He could hear the Choir Boys yelling as they ran down the hallway. Once the couch was pressed up against the door, he dumped the contents of the bottle on the fabric, spilling the last stream of it into the flames. The couch went up in seconds, and Sherman was already running back to the other door. He picked up the honing steel and pressed it up against the pin at the bottom of the top hinge, then swung the rolling pin at it awkwardly a few times, hoping to make contact with the honing steel rather than the splints on his fingers. The pin flew out of the hinge after three hits, and he moved down to the middle hinge. It flew out after only two hits. Sherman could hear the Choir Boys yelling and banging at the front door. The smoke alarm went off, but was shut down almost immediately. Sherman guessed they wouldn't want any outside interference in dealing with this particular problem. He knelt down to the third hinge, and cursed out loud at himself for not thinking this far ahead. The honing steel was too long to fit underneath it.

He ran back into the kitchen, heard the sounds of fire extinguishers going off in the hallway, and began frantically searching the drawers for something he could use to get the last hinge off. He took a metal spatula out of the drawer and ran back to the living room. Some of the flames on the couch were going out as the Choir Boys held a fire extinguisher up to the hole where the doorknob used to be, and an axe split a hole in the door. He knelt by the last hinge again, pressed the spatula into the thin gap in it, and pried it upwards. It gave a little bit, then slipped out. He stuck it back in the gap. It fit in easier this time, and he held it steady as he picked up the rolling pin again and slammed it down. The hinge popped out further. Using the spatula with both hands, Sherman pried upwards as hard as he could, and the pin finally popped out. He wedged the spatula in between the door and the frame, slammed it once with the rolling pin, and the door popped off of its hinges, crashing into the room.

Sherman ran out the door, and was immediately disoriented by what he saw. He had expected to run into the next room of a condominium, probably a bedroom or a living room, and hopefully find a window with a fire escape, or at least a window that he could smash open to yell for help. What he hadn't expected to find was the large, empty floor of an office building complete with cubicles, desks and chairs collecting dust. The backside of the walls of the apartment he had just been in were unfinished, with no drywall or insulation. It looked like the room had been built as a movie set that was never intended to be filmed from the outside. He ran for the end of the fake apartment frame, rounding the corner just Choir Boys broke the front door of the apartment open. They yelled instructions to each other to find Sherman and to put out the fire. Another door led out of the office, a sign on it marked "Emergency Exit Only," and Sherman prayed it wasn't going to be locked, as this was an emergency.

He pressed the handle down with his good hand while still at a dead run, and it opened as his shoulder slammed into it. No alarm rang out, but the Choir Boys could be heard running around on the floor, and it would only be a matter of seconds before they were on his tail. It's not like there was an abundance of places for him to go. Although Sherman's instincts told him to head down the stairs, he chose to go up one floor and lay low in the hopes that his pursuers wouldn't think he was stupid enough to go further up into a building he was trying to escape from. He went up one floor and found himself facing the door to the roof. He pulled a few coins out of his pocket, and dropped them as straight as he could down the middle of the winding staircase, then laid down on cold stairwell just as the door he had come in through burst open again and two of the Choir Boys burst into the stairwell. All three of them were as quiet as they could be. "You check the roof, I'll go down," one of them said, and Sherman cursed himself for thinking he could get away that easily, just as the coins he dropped hit something on their descent. "Never mind that. Come with me." Sherman tried to hold his deep breath of relief until the men were making too much of a racket running after the coins to hear him.

He started slowly back down the stairs to the floor below the apartment/prison level and pulled the door open as slowly and quietly as he could. It led into another unused office area, complete with the backside of yet another false room. This one had a lot more electronic equipment being sent through its walls, though, and Sherman wondered if there was a way in. It was safe to assume there wasn't, but Sherman's curiosity got the better of him, so rather than just running away as most of him wanted to, he found himself looking for something to poke a hole through the wall. Would there be anyone on the other side? Would Heatley be there? The thought that there would be security cameras on the other side of that wall, like there must have been in the room he had been kept in, just watching for something to happen didn't even occur to him. He wanted out, and if there was somebody sharing his fate on the other side of this wall, odds were they would want out, too.

There was a fire extinguisher mounted on the wall, covered in dust, and he picked it up. Making the smallest hole possible in the wall would have been ideal, but time constraints in the shape of large men in suits were an issue, and he lacked the tools required to make the ideal size hole in the wall. Sherman stood a few feet back from the wall, then took a step forward, propelling the extinguisher forward with his good hand as he did so. To his surprise, it went clean through the wall when it hit. The extinguisher hit the floor on the other side, making far more noise than Sherman had intended. He placed his hands on either side of the hole in the wall, and poked his entire head through it. He was looking into what was clearly a mockup of a hospital room, but there didn't appear to be anybody inside. Three silhouettes could be seen on the balcony through the curtain, but it was impossible to tell who they might be. The doorway on the other side of the room opened, and Sherman found himself staring into the startled eyes of a doctor who had just entered the room. They paused, awkwardly looking at each other, each wanting to step backwards and pretend nothing had happened, but both knowing that wasn't a viable option.

The doctor backed away slowly, not breaking eye contact with Sherman until he was back at the door he had come through, and then only because his fumbling hand couldn't locate the doorknob behind him. Sherman, meanwhile, had been inching his face back into the hole it had appeared through, knowing with every painfully slow fraction of an inch he moved that he should already be running and that every second he wasted was another second the Choir Boys had to catch up with him. As soon as the doctor broke eye contact, Sherman quickly pulled his head back. He smacked the back of his head on the hole, then overcompensated by ducking away from it and smacked his teeth on the drywall on the lower part of the hole. The sound he emitted, although muffled, was enough to startle the doctor into leaving the room as fast as he could manage. The started yelling for security the moment he had the door open. Sherman ran back to the stairwell.

The Choir Boys could be heard running back up the stairs, leaving Sherman nowhere to go but up. When he ran out the door onto the rooftop, he realized how little he had planned ahead. *I knew I should have just gone down the damn stairs,* he cursed himself. There was a helicopter pad on the roof, but no helicopter. Sherman didn't understand why he thought that was significant. *It's not like I could fly the thing anyhow,* he told himself.

There was also no way he would have had the nerve to kidnap the pilot and force him to fly him somewhere else. There was only one other structure on the roof, and it looked exactly like the doorway he had just come out. Figuring it must be another flight of stairs, he headed for it.

There was a chain on the door handle, and Sherman hoped that it wasn't locked. There wasn't anywhere else for him to go, though, except possibly the top of the doorway he had come out of, using surprise to his advantage as he dropped down on the unsuspecting Choir Boys and knocked them out, possibly by cracking their skulls together as he came down from above them, stealing one of their radios so he could keep one step ahead of them. Sherman couldn't believe he had let his imagination get that far away from him. "Too many movies," he said as he reached the door, which he didn't have to pull on to realize it was chained shut. There was a sign on the ground, which must have been mounted on the door at one point. "Use Other Door," it said.

"Shit," Sherman replied.

The Hole.

Heatley, Edna, and Joan had completely failed to come to any agreement about how they were going to try to get out of their predicament. Joan refused to demean herself by trying to seduce any of their captors, citing on top of moral grounds that she had no place to try it. "Unless you want to watch," she said to them.

"Well, I-" Heatley started.

"Certainly not!" Edna cut him off.

"Besides," Joan went on, "it's not like anyone coming in here doesn't know that the whole place is being recorded, anyhow."

Heatley refused to be thrown down the stairwell as a distraction, no matter how many different ways Edna tried to make it sound like a good idea. "I've seen it in movies before," she said. "The Allied hero throws a rock and it distracts the Nazi villain long enough to let him sneak by."

"But I'm not a rock!" Heatley yelled at her.

"No, you'll be far more noisy, and your screaming will give away what they'll think is our position, and then Joan and I can escape."

"Mrs. Sheldon," Joan started, hoping to appeal to the old lady's sense of whatever it was that made one believe that throwing one's brother down a stairwell as bait was the wrong thing to do, "the idea is to get all of us out, and we won't be able to accomplish that if I'm naked in a broom closet with the security guards, or if your brother is paralyzed in a stairwell. How would you feel if I suggested a plan that involved you being the one who stayed behind while your brother and I escaped?"

"Neither one of you would make it without me. You're both spineless." She looked around the balcony, daring either of them to disagree with her, but neither one said anything. "See what I mean?" she said. "Neither of you can even muster up the stones to disagree with me." She slid the balcony door back open, and stepped inside, taking it for granted that the others would follow her. They did, Heatley stepping in right after her because he was used to falling in line behind his sister when she was being irrational, and Joan right after him.

Joan paused halfway inside the door looked at the city around them. "Why don't we just close the door and make a bunch of noise, call for help, or something like that?" she asked the others.

"I - the company, I mean. The company owns a good chunk of the other buildings around here. I'm sure that they've got somebody watching for just that kind of thing, if they don't have the balcony bugged as well. Hell, they probably do, and they already know everything we've been talking about." Heatley suddenly looked ten years older, which was an accomplishment for someone who looked as old as he had before this ordeal started.

"Mr. Heatley, sir, I-" she trailed off.

"Yes, Joan? Joan?" Heatley stood in front of her, waving his hand in front of her eyes, hoping she hadn't gone catatonic on him. She went to the counter and opened a drawer, fishing around until she came up with a pad and pencil. She scribbled down the words 'Hole in wall' on the paper and held it in front of the old man, who wished he had his reading glasses. He bobbed his head back and forth to try and find the optimum distance from the paper so he would be able to read what she had written, then grabbed the pencil from her and wrote down the words 'Too small' and handed the paper back to her.

Joan looked at what the old man had written, and shook her head at him. She took the pencil back, and wrote down 'We can make it bigger. The wall is thin.' She handed the paper and pencil back to him. The old man looked at the paper again, and wrote down the words 'Your writing is' above what he had written before, and passed it back to Joan, who swore out loud when she read it. She dug back into the drawers until she found a thicker marker, and wrote down on the paper 'There is a hole in the wall,' and held it up in front of his face. He looked at it, and his face lit up. "A hole in the wall?" he asked out loud. "Is it big enough for us to fit through?"

Joan buried her face in her hands. "Mr. Heatley... I was writing it down so they wouldn't know that we noticed that the hole is there. If they're listening in on us, the only way to keep things from them is to write them down."

The door opened up, and Dr. Edmunds walked into the room, followed by two workmen carrying a sheet of plywood between them. "We were, obviously, hoping that you wouldn't notice that right away, although this does prevent us from having to orchestrate finding a way to drug you all while we fix this." One of the workmen held the plywood over the hole, while the other one pulled out a hammer and began to nail it in place. "Just so you know, we are watching you. You have a certain amount of freedom right now, things such as your ability to remain conscious and mobile, even if it is within the confines of this room, but that could change if we feel that you have become problematic, and I am capable of keeping all of you in a trouble-free medically-induced coma for quite a long period of time." The two men made short work of getting the plywood in place, and they left without uttering a word to anyone.

Edmunds smiled at Joan and held his hand out. She placed the marker in his open palm, which he continued to hold out to her until she placed the pencil in it as well. "Thank you, Joan. Your cooperation is much appreciated." He turned on a heel and left.

Joan stood there, not listening to the bickering that had broken out between the siblings again. She stared intently at the plywood on the wall, knowing that their one hope for getting out of this place, in all likelihood, lay right behind it.

The Cupboard.

Sherman ran back across the roof to the door he had come out from, where he could hear the Choir Boys coming up the stairs. He had never been a fighter growing up, and didn't think too highly of his odds at beating two larger men into submission. Not when the two men were, presumably, trained in some form of hand-to-hand combat, and not when one of his own hands wasn't much good for much more than a story to tell over drinks later on.

He hid just around the corner from where the door would swing open when the Choir Boys reached the top. The two men ran out onto the roof, eyes looking everywhere around them. They kept moving as they ran through the door in hopes that if there was a trap set up, such as something rigged to fall on their heads as they ran through the door, they would be able to outrun it. Neither man wanted to be first or second running through, because if the first man was running fast enough to avoid what was coming, the second man would take the brunt of it, but there was always the very real possibility that the first man through wouldn't quite be fast enough. To split the difference, both men ran through the door as close to the same time as they could, bumping shoulders as they passed through the doorway, one of them splitting left, and the other running to the right, both of them looking around wildly and covering their heads and faces with their hands.

Sherman grabbed the doorknob and held it open as the men ran out, then tried to slip through the door as subtly as he could and it closed behind him. He quickly but quietly walked down the stairs, mentally mapping the levels he had already been on. He had been on the top two levels, but didn't know what was on any of the others. What he did know about the top two levels were not things that he was fond of: security cameras and prisons dressed up like condos and hospital rooms. He went down another floor as quickly as he could, then decided that he had best get out of the stairwell before the Choir Boys realized that he wasn't hiding on the roof, which shouldn't take them too long no matter how thick they might be. He opened the door slowly, hoping he wasn't about to poke his head in and find himself lurking around the Choir Boys' break room, or some place where they might be planning a search party in his honour.

For what felt like the first time that day, luck was on his side, and Sherman found himself on an empty floor. He didn't know that the entire Heatley Company wasn't in on the abductions and conspiracies he had recently learned about. Everybody involved with the company that he had met was in on it. He had no way of knowing that the Heatley Company executives had gone through exhaustive measures to ensure that their secret stayed in a relatively small group. The contractors had all signed non-disclosure agreements, after they had been told they were building a couple of movie sets on an unused floor of the Heatley Building. None of them questioned why they didn't just use the original apartment they were duplicating, nor did they care, as the company was paying them an extraordinary amount of money to build the place. After the hospital level had been built, and the penthouse built just above that, it was decided that the next floor down should be emptied as well, in case there was any noise, or if the old man lit his apartment on fire with a derelict cigarette. Sherman didn't know any of that. What he did know was that he exited the stairwell and found himself on what appeared to be an unused floor, where he could find some place to hide and gather his wits.

Walking briskly in between the empty cubicles, he found a cupboard by the water cooler that he thought might serve to hide him comfortably enough. He opened the doors and crawled into it. It lacked walls dividing it from the adjacent cupboards, so he was able to lie down. Despite the amount of dust he kicked up when he crawled into it, he found himself able to control his breathing enough to calm down. Knowing there was nothing he could do if he was caught, Sherman forced himself to keep his breathing in check when he heard the stairwell door open, and the Choir Boys who had been chasing him started searching the floor for him. He heard the squawk of a walkie-talkie. "Does anybody have eyes on him?"

"Negative."

"Keep someone at the bottom of the stairwells, and make sure all calls are dialled out through the switchboard."

"Roger that."

Sherman winced at this, unsure of how he might be able to escape. He felt a sudden and unfortunate pressure building up in his bladder, and even though he knew there would be a restroom somewhere on the floor, he had no clue how long he would need to wait before he could look for it.

"Did you check the bathroom?" he heard someone say.

"Yeah, it's empty." The voices were slightly muffled coming through the cupboard, but he could make them out well enough.

"Let's split up. You take the far stairwell, I'll take this one, and we'll sweep the next floor down. Ask everyone you see if they've seen someone running through."

"Yes, sir." Sherman listened for the sound of the doors to the stairwell opening and closing before he placed his hand on the cupboard door. He was just about to push on it and make a run for the bathroom when a nagging voice inside his head told him to stop. He was an only child, but he had played hide-and-go-seek with friends while growing up, and one of the oldest tactics, one of the ones that he had been caught with time and time again, was for whoever was 'it' to pretend to leave the room and lay in wait for him to feel safe enough to get out from his hiding spot. He would, almost without exception, get caught while in an awkward position, half-stuck trying to get out of his hiding spot. Memories of repeatedly getting caught by this tactic made Sherman pause. He wanted to push the door open just a crack and look into the room, but he wouldn't allow himself to do it.

Thirty seconds later, a voice broke the silence of the room. "Okay, he's not here," it said, and the doors opened again, and this time Sherman heard the sound of muffled footsteps in the stairwell before the door closed. He waited another thirty before pushing the cupboard door open just enough to peek through. The door to the stairwell was clear. Slowly, Sherman got out from his hiding spot. He was fairly certain that he should wait longer before making a move, but he was more than certain that it would be worse to get caught after having pissed in his pants. He took off his shoes so his footsteps wouldn't make as much noise, and placed them back in the cupboard before closing the door, then made his way to the bathroom as quickly as he could. In the silence of the empty office floor, he heard the doors in the stairwell open one floor below, and he froze in place. The sound of uncomfortable footwear on the stairs almost sent him running back to his hiding spot, but they grew quieter, not louder, which meant they were going down another floor.

He stepped into the women's bathroom not only because it was closer to him, but because it was stereotypically going to be cleaner and he was in his socks. There were three stall doors, and he opened the one in the middle. It was clean and well-stocked for an unused floor. He thought about adding it to his list of public restrooms to be used when nature called and he was downtown, but it was too close to the top floor of a building that lacked public access. Besides, the coffee shop just down the street was clean enough. "What I wouldn't do to be pissing in that bathroom right now," he said quietly as he relieved himself. Hell, I'd even love to be taking a crap in that filthy diner down the street right now, he thought. After he was finished, he reflexively reached out and flushed the toilet. It made a no-nonsense noise as it sent his subtlety down the drain. "Shit!" Sherman ran back out of the bathroom, and tucked himself back into the cupboard, listening intently for the sound of the Choir Boys racing back up the stairs, but the noises didn't come. Sherman felt every second ticking by as he lay there, gradually becoming more confident that the search for him was going down floor by floor, hoping it would eventually hit the street. He was exhausted, and eventually he felt the tension start to leave his body as the minutes turned into hours until, much to his surprise, he fell asleep.

Scapegoats.

The Choir Boys' search wasn't going well, in that they had only one objective and had so far failed to achieve it. "The only thing we know for sure, sir, is that he hasn't left the building," Rupert Pinkson told Meyers, who sat stone-faced at his desk.

"And you know this how?" Meyers asked him.

"Well, there's no way he could have got past us, sir. There's only a few exits to the building, and we've had them all guarded since the alert went out about his escape."

"Interesting choice of words, Pinkson," Meyers told him. "Escape." He typed something on the keyboard in front of him. "According to the online dictionary, that word would imply that he succeeded in getting away from you." He turned the monitor towards Rupert, who begrudgingly read the definition on the screen.

"Sir, I don't believe he has been able to leave the building, and my men are almost done sweeping the floors."

"If he doesn't turn up, my dear fellow, your men will not just be sweeping the floors, but mopping them as well. And not the floors here, mind you, but the ones in whatever prison they send them all to." Meyers turned the monitor back towards himself. "We are all culpable in this, although executives are notorious for being able to keep themselves out of trouble while the little people get themselves locked away."

Rupert felt the weight of responsibility for all of the Choir Boys drop onto his shoulders as the senior security officer for the company. He began to suspect that the company had planned to use him as the fall guy if anything should happen from the very beginning, and wondered how this had not occurred to him before. "I'll keep the men late, and once the sweep hits the main floor, we'll work our way back up to the top." He got up and began to leave, not bothering to ask if Meyers was done. "We'll find him, sir."

"See that you do," Meyers said.

Rupert didn't wait for the office door to be closed before he grabbed his walkie-talkie. "Pinkson here. What's our status?"

Reports came back, all negative. One of the Choir Boys announced that he had just saved a bundle on long-distance calling, but he didn't get the laughs he was looking for. The entire security team was now involved in the search for Sherman. "Team leaders, keep someone on each of the exits and stairwells, and have the elevators monitored. Everyone else come to the meeting room on the second floor once the sweep hits ground level." Rupert swore, then took the elevator down to the second floor.

It was less than ten minutes before the rest of the security team joined Rupert in the meeting room. While he would normally appreciate the sense of urgency with which they met him, he found the timing to be suspect. He looked around the table at the team, fifteen faces looking back at him. "Am I to believe that you guys searched the entire building in the last half hour?" His question was met with nodding. "The entire building?" More nods, with the addition of a few murmurs this time. "From top to bottom?" A few faces looked away.

"I thought so. Well, let me tell you guys what's going on here, just so we're all aware." Rupert didn't enjoy public speaking. In contrast to his physical presence, he felt intimidated when he was around groups of people, always feeling anxious about how he was being perceived by others, from his friends and family to complete strangers. Thanks to his size, however, he was never actually picked on. He often wondered what might happen if somebody were to actually fight back when he was supposed to apprehend them or remove them from the premises, or kidnap them off the street. He hadn't actually participated in the abductions beyond being the intimidating obstacle that would have to be dealt with should the potential kidnappee decide that they were going to resist. In order to cover for how insecure he was, he wore his sunglasses at all times. He had even had some made that were tinted just enough to to prevent people from being able to see his eyes while he was inside. He was wearing those now, though he wished he had worn something with a darker tint. The thought of going to prison was causing him to tear up.

To prevent the others from seeing how fragile he was feeling, he decided to yell at them a lot to put them on the defensive. "If you don't find this kid, and get him put back under wraps, and he manages to get out and tell the cops about what's going on here, we're screwed. All of us. And I'm drawing the distinction of us here as the people in this room, and our coworkers that are watching the exits right now. Meyers has assured me that the executives have found themselves a scapegoat, and I'm pretty sure that we all know who plays the scapegoat for rich people, don't we?" He looked around the room. "Is anybody here not clear on what I've said here?" A timid hand tried to make its way up at the far end of the table, but the brain it was connected to shamed it into not admitting ignorance.

"Okay, then. We're going to work in teams. First order of business is to clear the building of all the employees who aren't us. Not everyone at the company has been in on this, and we need to clear them all out so we can get this done. I don't think anyone but the real keeners will give you any grief about this, and it's only an hour before people would be going home anyhow, so let's get them out, then we start clearing floors. Teams of five to a floor, three floors at a time. One man on each door, three search the floor. Any questions?"

This time a hand did go up. Pinkson nodded at the man to speak. "Are we going to be getting overtime for this?"

"We'll be going to prison if we don't do this," Rupert told him. "Now, get out there and bring me that damn kid." The Choir Boys got up and filed out the door, organizing themselves in groups of five as they did so. Rupert sat down and began to have himself a serious fret, giving himself five minutes before he would start checking up on the teams.

Joan's Plan.

Joan stared at the plywood covering the hole in the wall and wondered if there was any way they could punch another one large enough to get through before they got busted. She went over to the small table in the corner of the room where Frank and Edna sat, not looking at or talking to each other. There were only two chairs at the table, so Joan crouched down to talk to the siblings. Her voice dropped to a whisper. "I have a plan," she said.

Frank looked at her with interest, Edna with disdain. She turned her hearing aids up anyhow. "We need to find a way to block the door long enough to get us through that wall," she told them, her eyes shifting over to the piece of plywood.

"They'll get in," Frank told her without lowering his voice. "They'll see what we're doing and bust through the door before we have a chance to get out, and who knows what they'll do to us after that."

"I get the feeling that we're running out of time, anyhow," Joan told him.

"I get the feeling," Edna cut in, "that the little hussy is right."

Joan decided to let the slight against her go, as it was the first time Edna had agreed with her about anything, and that was progress enough for now. "Do you want to hear the plan or not?" she asked him.

"Fine," Heatley said. "What do you have in mind?"

Joan lowered her voice again. "It's all going to have to happen at almost the same time, and it's going to take all three of us to pull it off. Frank, you're going to be in charge of blocking the door. Edna, you'll take out the cameras with your cane, and then you'll come and help me smash through that wall."

Edna shook her head at Joan. "Young miss, how do you plan to brace the door or break through the wall?"

Joan admitted that she hadn't got quite that far with her plan, that it was more conceptual at the time. "I just thought of it," she told the old woman. "We can look around and find what we need to pull it off, and then try to pull it off after the majority of the staff have gone home."

Edna and Frank looked at each other. The sense that they would put their differences aside and work together, at least for the time being, was tangible. "I'll walk around and see what I can find," Joan told them, "and with a little bit of luck, we should be able to do this tonight." She hoped that the elderly siblings wouldn't decide that it was time for bed before she found what they needed.

Joan started poking around in the cupboards, through the shelves, and in the closet. There wasn't a lot available to them, as the room had been stocked to look like a hospital room. There were various medical supplies, but nothing potent. She found a glass container full of syringes, all still sterilized in their plastic wrappings, and she walked back to the table. "There's needles here," she said.

"So what?" Edna snipped at her. "Are we going to poke them into submission?"

"We still have ketamine in those bags, right?" She didn't make any gestures towards the bags, in case there was somebody watching the security cameras that might be able to interpret her movements.

Edna's face smiled so broadly that Joan thought it might crack along her wrinkles. "I didn't think you had it in you."

"We should be able to brace the door by opening the closet and pushing the bed into it. I think it's wide enough to fit one end of the bed in, long enough to block the front door. If anyone gets a hand through, we can jab it full of ketamine." Joan was feeling surprisingly optimistic about the first part of her plan, although she didn't want to mention out loud that they would be ad-libbing everything as soon as they were out of the room.

"We can't do anything until the cameras are offline, and as soon as we knock them out, we'll probably only have a minute or so to get everything that door blocked and the needles loaded." Joan was having difficulty keeping her voice down, her mind racing with the possible outcomes, both successful and failing scenarios. She tried to focus on the possibility of them getting out of the room and being able to make contact with someone on the outside. All it would take would be one of them getting a phone call to the police and it should all be over. She wanted to believe the company wouldn't dare add murder charges to their growing criminal portfolios.

Edna got up and began changing around the network of tubes by the beds. "I'd like to have control of my own ketamine tonight," she said out loud. "I don't think I'll be able to sleep through the night without it."

It took a moment for Joan to figure out that Edna was actually on board with the plan, having first assumed that the old woman had changed her mind and dismissed her idea, instead opting to let fate take its course. She watched for a few moments as Edna moved the tubing around. Once she had finished setting up the apparatus for her own bed, she set up Heatley's, and that was what told Joan that she was on board. There was no way the spiteful old bat would set up her brother's bed for him. Joan got up and discreetly looked at what she had done to find that with the tubes set up and the brakes off on the bed, there was a single power cable connecting the bed to an outlet in the wall, which would disconnect itself when the bed was pushed towards the door.

Edna sat back down at the table. "I made your bed for you," she told her brother.

"Thank you," Heatley said after a moment of shock. It had taken him a moment to figure out why she would have done something nice for him. It was out of character by a long shot, and for a moment he thought she might have begun her travels down the road to dementia.

When Joan came back to the table, she quietly told them where everything they needed was located, but she couldn't move anything into a more convenient location for them for fear of stirring up suspicion. "All that's left to do now is wait until it's dark out, so we can assume that most of the employees have gone home." She stood up, and looked into one of the security cameras, raising her voice. "I don't suppose there's a hide-a-bed somewhere you guys can bring me? I don't much feel like sleeping with either of these two."

A few minutes later, the door opened and a sofa was brought in by two men in suits. The company hadn't thought they would ever need to house more than one person in their pretend hospital room, so they had only purchased two beds. Heatley was accustomed to having a private room, but the second bed had been added for realism.

"What's with the suits?" Joan asked. "Don't you guys have security monkeys to do all this work for you?"

The two men put the couch down without comment. They were relatively new to the company, and hadn't actually met Heatley before. They were both outside hires that Meyers knew from previous dealings to be morally destitute enough to not care what the company was up to so long as the pay was good, and that was exactly what the new vision of the Heatley Company called for. They were obviously unhappy to be delegated to do physical work, though, and they spent their walk back to the door brushing the unsightly creases from their suit jackets.

"You come back in here, and I'm going to throw a full bedpan at you bastards," Edna called after them. The two men looked at her, and she lifted a metal container up from beside her bed and took a few steps towards them, sending them running the rest of the way out the door.

"Why on Earth would you do that?" Joan scolded her. "Those men could have us all sedated, and then-" she cut herself short before saying out loud that their plan would be ruined.

"Relax, Joan. I didn't even use the thing." Edna tipped the bowl upside down, and a piece of lint spilled out of it, too small for Joan to notice. She tossed the bowl aside, ignoring the loud clanging noise it made as it bounced its way to a halt.

Joan walked over to one of the cupboards where she had located some linen while she was looking around, and grabbed herself a clean sheet and a pillow. "You think they're going to be bringing us a change of clothes at any point, or am I going to be stuck wearing the same underwear for the duration of my stay?" she asked.

Heatley walked over to the couch and sat down. Joan was initially put off by this, but she had to admit the couch had to be more comfortable than the chairs they had been provided with. He was also fully clothed right now, not wearing his hospital gown, so she didn't have to worry about sleeping where his naked ass had been. *Besides,* she told herself, *with a little bit - make that a lot - of luck, I won't be sleeping here at all.* With nothing more to do than wait for dusk, the three of them sat on the couch and tried to find something on television that they could agree on watching.

Down the Stairs.

Sherman bolted awake at the sound of the stairwell door opening up. He almost sat up at the noise, and would have hit his head on the top of his hiding spot, but some subconscious instinct prevented it. The edges of the cupboard he was hiding in let the slightest bit of light through them, not enough for him to see anything except the outline of the cupboard, but it was enough to orient himself back to his situation. The sound of footsteps falling in an irregular pattern said there were at least two people on the floor.

"You check the men's room, and I'll check the women's," a voice said from outside. The sound of the footsteps split up, and Sherman opened the cupboard door a fraction of an inch, watching the two men as they disappeared into the washrooms.

He started to push the cupboard door open, ready to make a break for the stairwell, but he froze. What if there's more than the two of them? He thought to himself. He poked his head out of the cupboard and saw another man standing less than ten feet away from him, facing away from where he was hiding and surveying the room. He slowly brought the door closed again, praying there wouldn't even be the slightest of noises as it shut. He lucked out. The sound of a toilet flushing filled the relative silence of the room, followed by a hand dryer.

"Find anything?"

"Just relief."

"You want relief, find that damned kid."

"We've been through the damned building twice now. The kid is gone." Sherman felt a hint of optimism when he heard this, which disappeared a moment later when he heard "Did you check the cupboards?"

The sound of footsteps grew louder as the Choir Boy in front of his hiding spot turned around and headed for the cupboards. Sherman drew his hand back, ready to smash the door open with his open palm, hoping that he would be able to hurt whoever opened the door, distracting him long enough to get himself out and - the sound of the cupboard door right next to the one he was hiding in opened. He was separated from prying eyes by a single piece of laminated pressboard.

"These things aren't big enough to hold a person," the voice said, and the door slammed shut again. Apparently, the Choir Boys never had to search for cleaning products before, and didn't realize that some of the cupboards would be double-wide.

"Forget it then. Search the cubicles and we'll hit the next floor," someone responded, and Sherman felt enough tension leave his body to require another trip to the bathroom. There was some muttering of discontent on the floor, but the only words Sherman could make out were "...overtime for this shit."

After the sounds of footsteps had been brought to a halt by the sound of the stairwell doors closing, Sherman left his hiding spot, put his shoes back on, and headed for the bathroom again. Having been hiding in darkness, Sherman could see fairly well even though the Choir Boys had turned out the lights when they left. The bathroom was dark, though, as it didn't have any windows, and he had to feel his way around to the urinal. He was quite disgusted when he located it with an outstretched hand. Certain his luck was going to run out soon, Sherman consciously didn't flush the toilet or wash his hands and kept a low profile as he left the bathroom.

He wondered if there was a window-washing platform conveniently located outside one of the windows on this level, but he dismissed the possibility as he didn't have a clue how to operate one, and if there was one on this level, it probably meant that whoever had left it there would have taken an eighteen-story plunge. He heard voices in the stairwell again, and ducked into one of the cubicles, cursing it for not being a better hiding spot. The voices and the sounds of footsteps passed by the floor he was on and kept going down.

He waited until the sounds disappeared, then ran to the other stairwell and opened the door as quietly as he could, pulling it open just wide enough to fit himself through, then gently closed it behind him. The slightest of clicking sounds that the door made when it closed sent his entire being into panic mode, but there were no other sounds in the stairwell, and he let go of the door handle. It felt like letting go of his safety blanket. He slipped his shoes off again before starting down the stairs at a faster pace than he thought prudent, but he was able to keep himself from breaking into a run. The doors for each level were marked with the floor numbers in large red letters, and Sherman kept wishing they would go faster. Fifteen, Fourteen, Twelve, he paused. Right, no thirteenth floor. Bad luck.

As if Bad Luck had heard him and put down whatever it was reading, a door opened somewhere above him, and the sounds of disgruntled voices and footsteps began heading his way, no doubt emanating from some highly irritated members of the security team. Sherman picked up his pace, hoping that the Choir Boys wouldn't be able to hear him over their own racket. He knew he was moving too fast, that he was outpacing the Choir Boys by enough that it would be safer for him to slow down and make sure that the path ahead of him was clear, but he couldn't make himself slow down. He was escaping.

He was no longer looking at the numbers on the doors, no longer thinking anywhere ahead of the next step below him, no longer conscious of anything except the movement of his feet below him, until he ran out of stairs and found himself face to face with a door marked with a large red 'P'. He had gone too far, but was afraid to turn around. He opened the door to the parking garage and hoped there wasn't someone waiting for him on the other side.

Breakout.

As soon as the sun had set, Joan announced she was ready to go to sleep and asked the others to get off the couch. She was more than a little bit upset that a change of clothes wasn't brought in for her, despite having made mention of it to the security cameras over an hour beforehand. It didn't bode well for the company's plan for her.

Heatley and Edna got up with some difficulty, making Joan feel ill at ease. She needed them to move quickly, and they acted as if they were really going to go to sleep instead. Edna walked to the far side of her own bed, and Heatley walked in between them. He made a move like he was going to get into Edna's bed instead of his own, at which point she jabbed her cane in his direction.

"That's my bed, you senile old ass!" she yelled at him, and she swung her cane back over her head. Even Joan thought she was going to smack Heatley with it, but at the same time he took shelter by crouching at the head of the bed, Edna turned quickly around and smashed the first camera with one quick blow that ripped it from the wall. Heatley immediately began pushing the bed towards the open closet door, the only preparation Joan felt they could get away with. He wedged it in place and put the brakes on as Edna moved to the second camera and took it out with a single blow as well.

Joan was so surprised by the coordinated effort of the siblings that she was found herself being the only one who hadn't sprung into action right away. She shook it off and ran for the closet, leaned over the bed and removed the hanging rod from its hinges, then ran into the bathroom with it where she began trying to smash her way through the back wall. There was pounding at the door within a minute of the first camera being smashed. Heatley had wedged a doorstop under the door, and was further bracing it with his foot while he held the deadbolt in place to prevent it from being unlocked. Edna grabbed the box of syringes and began poking them into the ketamine bag, filling as many as she could. Following Joan's instructions, she held each one up after she was done filling it and pushed out the air bubbles to avoid doing more serious harm to anyone she might poke with them.

"What do I care?" Edna had asked her. "These bastards deserve what they get."

"You could end up killing someone, Edna," Joan had told her. "Do you really want that on your conscience?" Edna had initially tried to shrug the comment off, but she had to admit to herself that she couldn't, in good conscience, do anything that would actually end up killing somebody. Even at her most vicious, when she was caning somebody silly, she had stopped well short of doing any permanent harm. Except for that one time, with the mugger. She shuddered at the memory of his bleeding head laying in the gutter. She had never told anyone about it, nor had she missed a single mass since then. His obituary, and all the newspaper clippings about the incident, were in a scrapbook at home. She made sure there was not a single air bubble in any of the syringes as she filled them.

Joan wasn't having much luck with the wall. Despite it being a single piece of drywall without anything backing it, it was taking her several attempts to punch the tiniest of holes in it. Growing up without being a tomboy and learning the necessary skills required to destroy things was suddenly a childhood misspent as far as she was concerned, and it perturbed her to think she might be the only participant in the escape plan unable to hold up their end. Edna saw the difficulty that Joan was having, dropped the syringes off with her brother, and went to help her out. "You've got a terrible swing with that thing," she told Joan, and began stabbing at the drywall with her cane. Together, they began to make a hole.

Heatley kept one hand on the deadbolt until he heard somebody yell that the key had broken in the lock. He pressed his ear against the door to listen in on what was happening on the the other side, when an axe came splitting through it six inches in front of his face. He picked up one of the syringes. A few more blows from the axe made a hole large enough for a hand to come through. Heatley stabbed it full of ketamine as it reached for the lock. A scream came through the door, but the hand made its way back through, the body it was attached to falling to the floor in a daze. "Get security up here now!" somebody yelled. Heatley grabbed another needle. When a face appeared in the door and said "You're going to regret this," to him, he poked it in the lip with the needle and pushed the plunger down as quickly as he could. "You bastard!" the face said to him before falling back into a relaxed stupor.

Heatley picked up another needle. "How's it coming, ladies?" he yelled into the bathroom.

"Not great," Joan called back to him. They had begun to poke an outline of holes in the wall, and once they had enough of them made, they planned on kicking their way through. It was Edna's idea, and Joan found herself wondering why she would be surprised to find out the old woman knew how to wreck things efficiently. "How's your end?"

Heatley looked through the hole in the door, and saw the single remaining employee talking to someone on the phone. "There's only one left, but he's calling for help right now. You'd better move fast." The man on the other side of the door hung up the phone, and stood staring at him through the hole. Heatley was surprised when his sister pulled him away from the door, but the man on the other side of it was almost in shock when the door opened up and one of his coworkers and a notoriously nasty old woman came through the door with syringes in their hands. He ran for the stairwell.

Joan looked at Edna, and then behind her at Heatley. "Grab some needles. We've got to go." Joan ran for the stairwell on the other side of the room, but Heatley and Edna made their way to the elevator. "We can't take the elevator," she told them.

"The hell we can't," Heatley told her. "Do you have any idea how old we are?"

Joan sighed as Edna pushed the call button for the elevator. "We'll split up, then. Somebody has to make it out, or to a phone. Whoever makes it out calls the police." Joan grabbed the handle to the door in front of her, then paused. "You didn't own the police by any chance, did you, Mr. Heatley?"

"I tried, but the bastards said they weren't for sale," he said with a huff.

Joan nodded at him. "Good, then. That means we can probably trust them." Joan didn't wait for the elevator to arrive before heading down the stairs.

The Elevator.

Edna was irritated when the elevator at her own apartment building wasn't waiting for her the second she pushed the button, so waiting what felt like hours for the elevator to arrive while trying to escape from being kidnapped was not especially good for her mood, or the well-being of anyone she would encounter for the next few hours at least. Frank knew the signs. She was twitching, she was blinking too much, and he could hear the popping noises in her hands as she gripped her cane tighter and tighter. She needed a nap. Under any other circumstances, he would have taken one of the syringes in his hands and stuck her in the ass with it, just to cool her down, but as long as her anger was directed towards their captors he was going to let it slide. If he still had any ketamine left once they got out of the building and called the police, he would use it on her then - if she hadn't calmed down.

When the elevator finally arrived, Heatley and Edna both stepped forward, crowding the doorway in flat contradiction to elevator etiquette. Heatley did it out of his growing concern at getting caught, Edna out of habit. Frank looked at his sister, who had lifted her cane in a striking position with one hand, and had a syringe poised in the other. Heatley took her cue, lifting a syringe in each hand, hoping he was ready to medicate anyone who might arrive with the elevator car. Frank and Edna both made preemptive stabbing motions as the doors opened, but there was nobody in the car. They bumped shoulders as they packed themselves in, neither one apologizing to the other. Heatley went to press the 'L' button, but Edna smacked his hand down before he could. "What the hell?" he asked her. "Whose side are you on?"

"They'll have the lobby blocked off for sure," she told him. "We should go to the parking garage and take a car." She used her cane to push the 'P' button instead.

"Oh, shit," Heatley said.

"What?"

"There's a camera in here. I totally forgot about it." He pointed at a black bubble in the back corner of the elevator, and Edna proceeded to smack it with her cane until it was cracked enough that it couldn't be seen through.

"They probably saw us hit the button," Edna told him. "They'll be able to push the button on any floor and stop us."

A thought struck Heatley, and he began patting down his pockets until he found his keyring. "No they won't," he told her. "Not as long as they didn't swap my keys out." He took a small key from the ring, and put it in a small keyhole at the top of the number pad. "Instant executive express," he smiled at her. The elevator won't stop for anyone else while this is turned." Heatley thought himself quite lucky that they would have left his keys with him, but the company was confident he wouldn't be in a position to use them, and it had been their intention to keep him thinking things were as normal as possible.

He had expected Edna to be impressed, and was caught off guard when she asked him why she didn't have one for her building. "You're on the third floor, Edna."

"And there are people that stop my elevator on the second floor. Young people. People that should take the stairs." She looked at him as though her case should be open and shut, in her favour.

"I'll tell you what, Edna. If we get out of here, I'll get you your own executive key."

Edna swung her cane in response, waiting to club anyone on the other side of the doors when they reached the parking level. When the elevator finally slowed to a halt and opened up, they had expected to find the Choir Boys waiting for them, but there was nobody there. The doors had revealed a dimly lit, mostly empty parking garage. Edna stepped out of the elevator first, swinging her cane out to the right side of the doorway, drawing her left arm back to get a good swing with the needle if she needed to. There was nobody to hit.

Heatley stepped out right after her. "Let's go," he said. "I've got a spare key hidden on my car."

"Do you really think your car is here, Frank?" Edna was disturbed by her brother's stupidity at times.

"Oh," he said. "Right." They walked towards the garage door. "There's a stairwell at the front of the building that leads into the parking garage. We should be able to get out through there." He took the lead, not because he felt he was in charge, but because he was more mobile than his sister. He made sure not to leave her too far behind though, as she was the more experienced of them when it came to physical violence. The sound of glass breaking brought them to a halt.

"What was that?" Heatley said.

In the dim light of the far corner of the parking garage, they could barely make out the shape of a figure leaning through the window of one of the vehicles. "That, my brother, is a car thief. Let's go meet him." She started moving towards the figure, who looked over and saw them. At first, it looked like the thief was going to make a run for it, but he leaned into the car first, rooting around, before heading right towards them.

"Mr. Heatley, is that you?"

Heatley stopped dead in his tracks. The only people who knew that he was alive, so far as he knew, were the conspirators, which made this person the enemy. Knowing he couldn't outrun someone as young as this, he readied the syringes in his hands, hoping to get one good stab in before he could be subdued. Heatley was standing underneath one of the few working lights in the garage with Edna right behind him as the thief walked towards them. As soon as Sherman's face was illuminated by the lights in the garage, Edna stepped out from behind Heatley. Sherman and Edna looked and pointed at each other and yelled "You!"

Joan's Last Flight.

Joan could hear the commotion of the Choir Boys as they came up the stairs from several floors away. She ducked into the first door she ran into after she heard it. She didn't bother looking for a hiding spot. Instead, she crouched below the window on the door so that nobody would see her as they (hopefully) passed by on the way upstairs. She could continue down the stairs after they had gone.

She stayed perfectly still, listening as they went by. It sounded like there were a lot of them, but finally the sound of footsteps faded away. She stood up, and opened the door again, taking the stairs as quickly as her oppressive high heels would allow. The large red numbers on the doors were getting lower and lower, but she found herself thinking that she would already have been on the ground level if she had only taken the elevator. "Halfway down," she said to the echo of her steps. "Why didn't I just take it halfway down." She was out of breath, and still had five floors left to go. "Five more, five more," she said.

"Four."

"Three."

"Two."

The next door was marked with a large red '1', and Joan breathed a huge sigh of relief as she pushed it open, only to find herself face to face with a tall man in a suit. "Ms. Miller, I presume," he said as he grabbed her roughly by the arm. The Choir Boy raised his arm to deflect what he believed to be a slap from Joan, smirking at her attempt to hurt him until he felt the needle pierce the palm of his hand. She pushed the plunger down as far as she could before he yanked his hand away. "What the hell?" he said as he lost his grip on her arm. He took a few steps back, grabbed out his walkie-talkie, and tried to call for help, but he only got out "Sheeth on th' maih fl-" before he fell over in a stupor. Joan ran for the emergency door on the side of the building and spilled out into the alley.

She inhaled her first breath of freedom deeply, and began choking on it. She had never imagined that the smell of garbage and urine would ever fill her with such joy, but that's what she felt after her eyes stopped tearing up. She ran to the street, turned away from the Heatley Building and began to yell for help.

Joan had loved the city, and believed it to be full of good people who would help each other out in time of need, so she was astounded as people turned their heads and looked away as she was calling for help. How many times had she been walking down the street, minding her own business, and had countless propositions of varying degrees of degradation offered to her? Where were all those guys that wanted to talk to her now that she was running down the street, asking for help? It was as if the more she wanted to be seen, the more invisible she became.

She stopped and asked a group of young men if she could use one of their phones. "It's local, and it's an emergency," she told them. "Please."

"Yeah, alright," one of them said, and handed it over to her. "Keep it short." She dialled 9-1-1, and waited for an answer.

"Yes, I need the police," Joan said into the phone.

"What the shit!" the owner of the phone said as his friends bolted off in different directions. "You did not just call the cops from my phone!" He made a move to take it back, but thought better of it. The last thing he needed was the police tracing his number back to a disconnected emergency call. "Don't you go anywhere," he told her. "I'll be right back." He ran into an alleyway, but Joan hardly noticed he had left.

The Garage.

Sherman moved quickly to his right to keep Heatley between himself and another thrashing by the crazy old woman who had assaulted him. "Mr. Heatley," he said. "I'm here to help you."

Heatley stood trembling. "How am I supposed to believe you?" he said. "Everybody is supposed to think I'm dead."

"I'm a friend of Joan's," Sherman told him. "I just got hired on, sort of. I worked at Gary's Empornium, and they kept me on after the company bought it."

Edna slapped Heatley. "Your company owns that filth?" She rounded back to face Sherman. "And you work there?" Sherman took a couple of steps back, contemplating how he was going to help Heatley and fend off his lunatic sister at the same time.

"A job's a job, Blue," he said, and immediately regretted the antagonistic manner in which he addressed her. "Ma'am. I meant ma'am. Listen, we need to get out of here. Anyone know how to hotwire a car?"

"I rather thought you might," Heatley said, indicating the car that Sherman had broken into.

"Just stealing a cell phone to call the police," Sherman said. He held it up to show them the phone he had stolen. "It's locked, but you can still make emergency calls if you can get a signal, which I can't do in the garage. Outdated piece of crap," he said, as he tucked the phone into his pocket. "We need to get above ground."

"We were just headed to the stairwell at the front of the garage," Heatley told him. "There's a door there, which hopefully won't be guarded. If it is, we have these." Heatley held up the remaining syringes full of ketamine. "It's put a few of them to sleep already." He held out one of the makeshift weapons to Sherman, just as the door from the stairwell burst open.

"There they are!" someone yelled, and five of the Choir Boys started running towards them. "Get them!"

Heatley turned to Sherman. "Run," he told him. "Get help, and we'll try to take a few down."

Sherman hadn't even finished nodding to the old man before he took off towards the opposite stairwell. "Good luck," he called back to the elderly couple.

The Choir Boys didn't bother much with the siblings. Four of them ran a wide circle around them in pursuit if Sherman, and Pinkson stopped to keep an eye on the two. He kept his distance, though, making sure he was an arm's length from Heatley, and added a cane's length to his proximity to Edna. He grabbed his radio. "Mr. Meyers, sir. We have Heatley and his sister. The men are in pursuit of the male escapee, no word on the girl."

"Hold Heatley and his sister, and make sure they get the boy," Meyers' voice crackled over the radio. "The girl has escaped, and the police are on their way."

"Say again, sir?" Pinkson went pale.

"The girl has escaped, and the police are on their way. We need to cover this up, and now… make her look like she's crazy."

"And what do I do about the rest of them?" Pinkson asked, positive he wasn't going to like the answer.

"Don't make a mess in the garage," Meyers told him. "Put them in a trunk first, then kill them."

"With what, sir?" Pinkson asked. "I'm unarmed."

"I beg to differ, Rupert. You have huge arms, and they should be more than capable of dispatching a couple of old people and some punk kid."

Pinkson looked at the elderly couple, who were staring back at him, terrified after hearing the orders for their own executions. "Negative, sir. I won't do it."

"It wasn't a request, Rupert. Now do it."

"I quit, Dave," he said into the radio. His arms dropped to his sides momentarily, then he brought the radio back up to his mouth. "Okay, boys, it's over. The cops are on the way, and unless you want attempted murder charges added to the list, I'd suggest letting the kid go." He tossed the radio off to the side, and pulled out his keyring. "I'll let you out through the front of the garage," he told Heatley and Edna. He began to walk to them to the main door.

Three of the Choir Boys who had pursued Sherman ran back past them on the way, shouting as they went by.

"The cops are here!"

"Lots of them."

"They're gonna have us surrounded!"

Rupert Pinkson was done with the company. He didn't try to run and hide, didn't look to pass the blame. He knew that if he wasn't caught now, he would be soon enough, and wanted to be as compliant as possible when they took him down. "I'm sorry," he told the two as they walked towards the garage door. "Things got out of hand in a big way, and I never meant for any harm to come to you." He had to walk painfully slowly to keep in step with Heatley and his sister.

"Rupert!" The three of them turned around to see David Meyers running towards them, brandishing a gun in his hand. "Step the hell back, Rupert," he told him. Rupert started to step away from the couple. "Wait, no. Is that needle still full of tranquilizer?" he asked Edna. She nodded. "Stick him with it." Meyers waved the barrel of the gun at her, and she made her way over to the big man. "You might want to lie down before I do this, dear," she said to him. Heatley was amazed. He hadn't witnessed his sister actually being nice to somebody in so long he had dismissed it as a possibility.

Rupert nodded his thanks to her before lying on the ground. She crouched down beside him and stuck the needle in his leg, then pressed the plunger, giving him half of the dose it contained before pulling it back out. She stood back up.

Meyers smiled at her. "Good girl. Now, toss the rest of the needles." He waited until both she and Heatley had dropped at least two of them each.

"Toss the cane, too, Blue," he said. "I'm not a complete moron, you know."

Edna dropped her cane to the ground. "I won't be able to keep up to you without this," she told him. "I'm just going to hinder your escape."

Meyers hadn't considered this. Of course it was true. There was no way he would be able to make an escape from the police if he had to bring Edna in tow. "Frank, pick up one of those needles," he said.

"You wouldn't dare," Edna said to her brother.

"On the contrary, sis," Heatley said as he bent over and picked one of the syringes up. "This is almost literally one of those gun-to-my-head moments that I've heard so much about, and you'd better lie down."

Edna slowly, painfully, laid down. Heatley apologized to her before sticking her with the needle, injecting her with a fraction of what it contained. She went unconscious with a snarl.

"Good then," Meyers said. "Now, Mr. Heatley, if you would kindly come over here, I have what sounds like an entire police force to contend with."

Heatley shuffled his way over to Meyers, who grabbed him by the neck and forced him towards the elevator doors. The distorted sound of a voice amplified by a megaphone could be heard from outside. "David Meyers, this is Officer Bratton of the Police Department." There was some feedback, a static squelch, and the brief sound of a siren as Bratton fiddled with the megaphone's controls. It had been some time since he had used one. "Is that better?" he said through it. "Can you guys hear this? Okay, good. David Meyers, we are attempting to call you, but we keep getting the switchboard, and there's nobody there to patch us through."

"Shit," Meyers said before hitting himself in the forehead with the butt of the gun. Continuing to hold Heatley by the neck, he changed directions and headed for his car.

The power in the building went off. Within moments, the emergency lights came on in the garage, providing just enough light to prevent Meyers from walking into any of the pillars in the garage. The sirens outside had gone quiet, presumably because everyone had arrived, and not because they had given up and gone home. "David Meyers, can you hear us?" came through the megaphone again. "David, we need you to talk to us. You have two minutes to pick up the phone, and then we're going to come in there."

Meyers pushed Heatley ahead of him the last few feet to the driver's side door of his car, then pulled out his key fob and unlocked the doors. "Get in," he told Heatley. Heatley got in the car and sat down as Meyers walked around and got in the passenger side. He handed the keys to Heatley. "We're getting out of here," he told Heatley. "Smashing right through whatever they have out there. Drive."

Heatley put the key in the ignition and turned it, but nothing happened. He looked at Meyers and shrugged at him. "Nothing's happening."

Meyers stared out the windshield in disbelief. "Are you telling me," he said, "that you don't know how to drive stick?" He slammed his head against the dashboard in frustration.

Bratton's Big Bust.

Bratton was exhilarated. He often dreamed of being in charge of a bust this big. It was his big, shiny, picture-in-the-paper, career-defining moment. He was surrounded by his peers, the SWAT team had shown up, the media had been told to keep back, and the crowd that had begun to form was approaching proportions he had only seen in movies. *And I get to be the hero,* he told himself, smiling. He took what he thought of as a heroic stance in front of his squad car, showing no fear.

"Officer Bratton?" someone asked from behind him.

"Yes," he said, looking around. There was a young man in a suit behind him. "What do you want?"

"Detective Smith." He extended his hand to shake Bratton's, but nothing was offered in return. "I want to thank you for taking care of this situation so far, and I'm here to relieve you of your command." He flashed his smile and a badge that Bratton hadn't seen before.

"Like hell you are," Bratton said. "What kind of badge is that?" He grabbed it out of the young man's hand for closer examination.

"I'm with the new Chief of Police's new division."

"What's it called?" Bratton asked.

"We're waiting on choosing a name until we come up with something that can be shortened into a badass acronym," he said. "In the meantime, if you need to ask the Chief about it, I suggest you call him now. Can I have the megaphone, please, Officer?"

Bratton hadn't realized how pumped up he was until he had been completely deflated by this news. He handed the megaphone over, pushing it hard into Smith's chest, hoping it hurt him as he did it. Before he let go of the megaphone, he flicked on the siren button again.

Smith turned off the siren, then addressed his team with the megaphone instead of the building. "Prepare for BlueBomb," he said to them. The unit hurried their way to the back of their armoury vehicle, where a team member swapped their weapons for them. They went into a formation that looked intimidating to everyone there, including the rest of the police force, all weapons pointed at the front of the building.

Bratton walked away from the crowds, away from Detective Smith, and towards the alleyway beside the Heatley building, where he planned on having a good official sulk behind a garbage dumpster until the crowd had dissipated enough for him to drive his squad car away without having to answer any questions. He in no way wanted to have to fake taking pride in the new unit, or explain why he was relieved of command. As he was passing by the door to the parking garage, the stairwell door beside it opened slightly. He was the first one to notice it, and he sprang into action, running forward before he Smith could tell him to stand down.

The door started to swing closed again, but Bratton had covered the distance quickly enough that he was able to grab the handle and prevent it from closing completely. He yanked the door open, the SWAT team forming a line behind him. Sherman, battered and bleeding from his recent encounter with four of the Choir Boys, fell limp halfway out the door. Bratton recognized him through the dirt, blood and bruising, and immediately pinned him to the ground, forcing his hands behind his back and cuffing him.

"You're all mine, you little bastard," he said, crouching low enough to spit right into Sherman's ear as he spoke. He forced Sherman up and hauled him back to his squad car. He didn't bother reading Sherman his rights, ignored the paramedics who insisted they have a look at him before he was taken away, and shoved him into the back seat.

Sherman wasn't in any shape to put up a fight, but he was cognizant enough to recognize the officer who had arrested him. He was leaning towards Bratton to insult him, but Bratton saw it coming and slammed the door on him, breaking his nose as he did it. Sherman lay in the back of the car, wishing he had a free hand to cover his face with. When he was able to sit himself up in the car, he leaned his head back and blew as much blood as he could out his nose, through the wire separator in the car and onto everything of Bratton's he could manage, despite the pain it caused him.

Even through the commotion Sherman was able to make out Joan's voice as she was yelling at Bratton. "Why is he under arrest? He was one of the victims here!" Bratton would have none of it, though, and while the rest of the force was preparing for the raid on the Heatley Building, Bratton grabbed Joan and walked her to the other side of his car. "What the hell do you think you're doing?" Joan yelled at him.

Bratton opened the back door, and forced Joan into the car as well. "Just keeping the peace, ma'am, and you're under arrest for interfering with a law enforcement officer in the execution of his duties." He slammed the door on her before she could utter a word of protest, but she had the presence of mind to not have her face in the way. Sherman couldn't help but admire her foresight.

She looked over at Sherman, his face a bloody mess. "Were you blowing nose blood all over the front seat of the car?" she asked.

Sherman sneered. "Maybe."

She wanted to laugh at him, but the tension was still building outside. She shifted around awkwardly in the seat until she could see what was going on. "What the hell is a BlueBomb, Sherman?"

"De ell ib I know," he bled at her.

They were about to find out, though.

BlueBomb.

Heatley didn't know what to say to Meyers. "I've never had to drive a standard," he told him. "Hell, for the last fifteen years, I haven't even had to drive myself anywhere."

Meyers stared at him in disbelief. "You haven't driven in fifteen years?"

"They've got all these rules and so on about drinking and driving now, so I just kind of gave it up," he said. It made perfect sense to him at the time.

"Press down on the clutch," Meyers told him.

"What's a clutch?"

Meyers screamed in frustration and banged his gun against the dashboard. A shot rang out. The bullet went through the windshield, ricocheted off the cement wall of the garage, and took out the light above them. They sat in darkness for a moment. "Get out of the car," he yelled at Heatley. "We're trading places."

They both stepped out and began to walk around the back of the car when the garage door opened. "David Meyers! This is Detective Smith with the Police Department. Let Mr. Heatley go and come out with your hands up."

Meyers threw one arm around Heatley's neck, and held his gun up at the police. "Step back or the old man gets it!" he yelled back at them. He started making his way back to the stairwell by the elevator, keeping his back against the wall. The doorway opened, and more black-clad officers come through. He was trapped. "I mean it," he said. "Turn the power back on, and get your men out of here, or Heatley dies."

Smith spoke something into his radio, and within moments the power in the building came back on. He ordered his men back into the stairwell.

"Wait!" Meyers called out to Smith. "I want one of your men, unarmed, to get the elevator down here, and put his helmet in the way of the door so it doesn't close."

Smith spoke into his radio again, and a lone officer came out of the doorway, holding a second helmet in his hands. He pressed the call button for the elevator and waited for it to come down, then placed the helmet in the way of the doors as he was instructed. The main group of the specialized unit moved into a line, forming an intimidating barrier that covered the entire garage doorway. Meyers waited until the officer at the elevator door had disappeared back into the stairwell, then made his way to the elevator. "If that door opens again, I'll do it," he said, pointing the gun directly at Heatley's head for effect.

He was almost inside the elevator. "I'm taking the old man with me, and if the power goes out, he's done. Got that?"

"I understand, Mr. Meyers," Smith told him. He spoke into his radio again, but nothing happened after, which suited Heatley just fine. He assumed that Smith had told the team behind the door to stand down.

"I want a helicopter on the roof in ten minutes. No cops in it. I want the company chopper there, with my usual pilot. Any funny business, and, well, you know." Meyers wondered if he could think up a new threat, but he didn't have many cards to play at the moment.

"Yes, Mr. Meyers. I'm making the call right now." David was beginning to wonder how so many criminals got themselves caught. This whole manipulating the police thing seemed to be so easy.

"Good, then." He pulled Heatley back towards the elevator, not daring to move his eyes off the wall of officers who had started to move in on him. He didn't think it would matter once he got to the elevator, as there was no way they could follow him into it, and his confidence started to build up again as he got closer to the elevator doors, which kept on trying to close, hitting the helmet, then opening up again. Two steps away from the elevator door, he took the gun off Heatley's head for a second and pointed it at the cops.

Smith smiled as he said "BlueBomb," into the megaphone. The entire line opened fire on Meyers.

The Speed Of Urine.

The speed of sound is reportedly much slower than the speed of light, but neither Meyers nor Heatley could tell you which they noticed first, the sound of automatic weapons or the muzzle flashes. To the best of Meyers' knowledge, the speed of smell has never been factored into the race, but one of the first things he was cognizant of was the smell of urine once the hail of gunfire had commenced. He dropped to the ground, letting go of both Heatley and his gun as soon as the firing started, and curled up in the fetal position. He stayed there, frozen in place after the firing stopped, barely aware that he hadn't been hit. He figured that Heatley must have taken the majority of the bullets that were meant for him. The old man was unconscious in front of him. He hadn't noticed that Heatley wasn't bleeding.

Smith was the first officer on the scene. "I told you that would work!" he called out to someone behind him. "Keep the media back," he added. "We don't need this getting out. You've just been BlueBombed, Meyers," he said with a smile as he kicked David's weapon away from where he had fallen.

Heatley got up with help from one of the other officers on the scene, who quickly ushered him away to be examined by paramedics, while Meyers lay down in a puddle of his own urine, staring up in confusion at Smith. "What?" he started. "Why?" he continued.

"Why aren't you dead?" Smith finished for him. "The BlueBomb, Mr. Meyers. The BlueBomb." He ordered one of the other officers to cuff him, and leaned down in front of Meyers, who was still staring in bewilderment. He ejected the magazine from his gun, and held it down in front of Meyers' face. "The BlueBomb is a psyche-out," he said. "Blanks. We scare the target into submission, and in your case, by the smell of things, we may have scared the shit right out of you." He turned to the other officers. "Great work, guys," he told them. "Now, let's get this guy the hell out of here. Drinks are on me once your paperwork is done, and if you don't want to do the paperwork tonight, buy your own damn drinks."

Epilogue.

Heatley was released from the hospital two days later. His new doctor wanted to keep him there longer, claiming a man Heatley's age should stay there at least a week after his ordeal, but Heatley had been adamant about getting out as soon as possible.

"Yes, Mr. Heatley, I understand," he said. "But please, take my card, and call this number if you feel you need anything. Day or night, I mean it." Being Heatley's personal physician had extraordinary benefits, and he didn't feel like doing anything untoward that might jeopardize the sweet gig he had stumbled into. "Your car is here," he said.

"Thank you, Doctor," Heatley told him. He stepped out of the examining room and made his way to the elevator, making a note to contact his sister soon. She was still recovering from an unsightly ketamine addiction and was less than her usual hospitable self these days, which had caused no end of inconvenience for the hospital staff. His car was waiting in front of the main doors, just like he wanted it to be. Life was back on track.

In the few days since he had been officially declared alive, he had ordered everything back to the state they were in before his passing. He had the charges against Joan dropped in return for her assistance in getting things back in order, although she was no longer his personal assistant. He was, understandably, leery of trusting her in that capacity, but he had offered the job to Sherman, who seemed to be of good stock despite having slightly substandard personal hygiene. Sherman had promised that it would pick up once his fingers had healed.

Having canceled the television contracts for the Betting Zoo, which Heatley had declared an abomination, he began a campaign to fund a series of no-kill shelters in the city, which brought an era of respectability to the Heatley Company that it hadn't experienced in several years. His new driver opened the door for him, and Heatley sat down beside Sherman. "Hello, Sherman," he said with a smile as he buckled his seatbelt.

"Hi, Mr. Heatley."

"Please, call me Frank," Heatley said. "You might be wondering why I called you in on a day off."

"Joan told me to expect it," Sherman told him. "I believe she said that there was no such thing as a day off."

"In the past, my friend," Heatley told him. "In the past. Your weekends are officially your own after today. I just need you to sign something, and you are free to go about your day."

They sat in relative silence for the rest of the drive, and when the car came to a halt, Sherman found his door opened for him before he could even unbuckle his seatbelt. "Uh, thanks," he said, and wondered if he was supposed to give a tip for something so trivial. Heatley gave the man who opened his door a few bills, making Sherman feel awkwardly poor, instead of his default of feeling generally poor.

"I've got it, Sherman," Heatley told him over the car. "Make sure you split that with your partner," he told the valet, who nodded his appreciation at receiving even half of what Heatley had given him.

They walked through the front door of the office building, another person tipped generously by Heatley, and continued on to the front desk. "Mr. Heatley," the receptionist said. "Mr. Vasquez is ready for you."

"Thank you, Samantha," Heatley nodded to her, and they walked through the office door. Sherman couldn't help but feel bad for her, being the only person that had addressed Heatley who hadn't received a tip for their effort (then again, she also hadn't opened a door for him), but Sherman only had a few dollars worth of change on him, and thought it would probably be insulting to offer it to her.

They were greeted inside the office by Mr. Vasquez, who was wearing a suit that was all too reminiscent of the Choir Boys for Sherman's liking. Heatley didn't seem to mind, though. "Please, have a seat, gentlemen," he said, gesturing to two chairs across from his desk.

They sat down, and Mr. Vasquez brought an ashtray out from his desk. He pushed it across the table, and grabbed a lighter out from his suit pocket. "Mr. Heatley?" he asked.

Heatley smiled at him and pushed the ashtray back. "Thank you, but I quit," he said, and he reached into his own pocket and grabbed a toothpick from a small container. "My new vice," he said to Sherman. "To help me get through."

"You're probably wondering why I've asked you here," Heatley told Sherman. "And I'm sure you'll be happy with the answer. Mr. Vasquez?"

"Mr. Heatley," Vasquez chimed in, "we are here today to discuss the amendments made to your will." He took a moment to file through the paperwork he had on his desk, dividing it into three separate piles. He handed one to Heatley and one to Sherman.

"In accordance with the wishes of Mr. Heatley," he began, irritating Sherman with the formal language, "his estate will be divided, upon his passing, between his sister, one Mrs. Edna Sheldon, and one Mr. Sherman Klein, equally." Sherman would have fallen down if he wasn't already seated. As it happened, he slumped backwards in his chair.

"Mr. Heatley," he said.

"Frank," Heatley corrected him.

"Frank," Sherman corrected himself. "I don't know what to say."

"Don't say anything, just sign the papers," Heatley told him. "I already have."

Sherman reached for the pen being proffered to him by the lawyer, and signed on the dotted line. "Thank you so much," he said, and he patted Heatley on the back.

Heatley started to nod 'You're welcome' to Sherman, but the toothpick he had been chewing on slipped back into his throat when Sherman slapped his back and he began to choke. Both Sherman and Vasquez noticed Heatley's distress and moved in to help. "Do you know the Heimlich Manoeuvre?" Vasquez asked.

"I've seen it on TV," Sherman said. Heatley continued to convulse, slapping himself in the throat, and fell to the ground. He wasn't breathing.

"If you screw up, and you're not qualified to be giving him CPR, or whatever he needs, you can be held liable for whatever happens to him," he said.

Sherman let go of Heatley. "Well, what do I do, then?" he asked.

Vasquez looked him in the eye, as Heatley fell out of his chair. "We call 9-1-1, and hope they lead us through. You have to cover your bases." Vasquez picked up the phone, and pushed a button. "Samantha, be a dear and call 9-1-1, would you?"

Sherman began an improvised resuscitation based on what he had seen on television, yelling at him to stay with him until he felt Heatley go limp.

Sherman looked over to Vasquez, who was looking flabbergasted. "Congratulations," he said. "You're rich."

Sherman held the old man in his arms for a few moments before setting him down on the ground. He had been what he would consider to be a degenerate living paycheque to paycheque for as long as he could remember. He had joked with his friends about how if any of them had ever struck it rich, that they would buy a Ferrari, park it somewhere downtown, then come back and destroy it with baseball bats until they got arrested (knowing the police would never believe they would do that to their own car), just to prove some point or other about the irrelevance if idiotic material possessions. "How rich?" he asked.

Cory Hope is the author of The Crystal Dragon, *and has been publishing the monthly* Snail Mail Photo Blog *since January 2011. He is an Interdisciplinary student at Thompson Rivers University, where he is combining creative writing, photography, and the outdoor adventure program in the hopes to avoid ever having to wear a suit and tie to work. Cory lives and works in Kamloops, British Columbia with his wife and two cats.*

CPSIA information can be obtained at www.ICGtesting.com
Printed in the USA
LVOW080142150312

273115LV00001B/13/P

9 780981 232966